MW01138358

# When Are You Leaving

by Melissa Powell Gay

*To the Sweetest "B" I know —*

*Melissa Powell Gay*

This book is dedicated to the memory of Iris Thurman Powell.

Author Note

When 17th century Virginia colonialist and explorer Robert Fallam forged through southwest Virginia, he wrote about the pleasant views of the distant Blue Ridge Mountains seen from the Piedmont's hilltops. Fallam County and its town of Mt Pleasant are imaginary places, and all the characters in this book are fictional.

*The Crooked Road, Virginia's Heritage Music Trail* is an actual chain of venues which has its gateway in Franklin County, Virginia, and winds through most of the Commonwealth's western counties all the way to the Kentucky border.

Many people contributed their time and talent in getting this story written. Agile Writers and Greg Smith helped with the first draft. Thanks to my first reader Deborah Powell Miller and the lovely ladies of Anonymous Readers book club who showed much polite interest in a very early version. Special thanks go to editors Marilyn J. Shaw and Erica Orloff and to James River Writers for all the writerly support and encouragement.

Melissa Powell Gay

January 2016

# Chapter 1

*Is that man actually wearing a wig?* Iris Lee marveled to herself. Standing in a fishbowl conference room, she stared through the glass wall into a hallway at an intense man who appeared to be reaming out an associate. The young woman was crying.

Iris walked over to the windows to survey the Manhattan skyline. Glancing at her phone for the thousandth time, she saw Jonnie Bailey's name appear.

"Got time to talk?" Iris's friend and family lawyer from back home asked.

"Apparently all the time in the world. I've been kept waiting for at least half an hour. I have an interview with Nexdorf's COO. I think they're going to make me an offer." She watched the tiny pedestrians below.

"The police are considering charges against your father for manufacturing and distributing illegal substances in one of his rental units. Thought you'd want to know."

"Mt Pleasant Police? Charge Mr. Henry? An eighty-two year-old man, with selling drugs? Sure, and they're arresting Mom for prostitution. This is a joke, right?" Iris turned from the window and discovered bad-toupee guy sitting at the conference table. "Let me, uh, call you back." She disconnected the call and smiled at the man at the table.

"Ms. Lee. I'm Stan Tenney. My staff tells me that we have to talk." Instead of offering his hand in greeting, he pressed it over his tie. "Take a seat." Avoiding eye contact, he scrolled through messages on his own phone.

Stunned, Iris froze where she stood. She wondered if he'd heard the desperation in her voice when she mentioned the job offer.

"Ah, my father's lawyer. Some mix-up about a tenant."

"Can we jump right into this?" He finally gave up a first glance. "Take a seat," he repeated.

"Do you want to reschedule?" She sat across from him, hustling over her blunder.

"No. Let's get stated." He flicked with a two-finger wave toward his starched white shirt.

*They've tapped someone else.* "Thank you for inviting me to come in. My fourth interview. I feel like a member of the team already." Iris smiled. What else could she do?

The staff had sold the meeting to her as an informal session to get to know the man in charge. He was supposed to say things like "My team has said great things about you" and "Looking forward to working with you."

"Hold on a second. I need to respond to this." Tenney's fingers flew across his phone with impressive speed. For the next minute or so, the only sounds were the clicks of his Blackberry. He came up for air. "Look, something's come up with the SEC. I've got to get some data back to the board by close of—"

"I'm happy to reschedule for another time." Iris knew all about the Securities and Exchange Commission and their timelines. After the 2008 financial crisis, she and her entire group at Bank US were sacked. Well, the group was laid-off with tidy severance packages; she had seen to that. Afterward, the CEO himself had personally traveled from New York to Richmond to fire her.

"Look. Ms. Lee."

"Please, call me Iris."

"Look. You seem very capable, but we're not sure that your skills are what we need for this position." Tenney squinted as if in pain.

"I'm not sure I understand what you mean. I thought we were negotiating another meeting time for this interview. Are we

2

going in another direction?" The interview was over; it never started.

Repressing a burp, Tenney squinted again. "We've decided to pursue other resources to address our needs at this time."

"Stan. May I call you Stan?" He gave a sideways half nod. "Yesterday, your staff contacted me and asked me to come in for an interview with you. What's happened between yesterday and this morning?"

"We've decided to go in another direction." Tenney folded his hands on the conference table and for the first time looked Iris in the eyes.

"Another direction? What does that mean?" She knew what it meant, she wasn't getting the job. After all the time and effort spent, she was furious with herself for being caught off guard. To keep her temper in check, she copied his move by folding her hands. What she really wanted was to reach across the conference table and yank the stupid wig off this guy's head and stuff it in his mouth.

"Look. HR has forbidden me to discuss this issue with you. All I can tell you is that we're going in another direction."

*Keep your cool, Iris. Think like a lawyer. What would Jonnie do?* "Stan, help me out here, I'm confused. After six months of negotiations and back-to-back interviews, then a request to meet with you, Nexdorf has decided to go with another candidate?" Iris baited him to see if he would give up his reason for not making her an offer. Now was the only opportunity she had to find out why she wasn't going to become the youngest senior executive at the world's largest financial asset management company.

"You know I can't discuss another candidate with you."

She had her answer, whether he realized it or not, Tenney just admitted that he had another, preferred, candidate. One who, Iris surmised, he forgot to mention to HR and his own staff.

Abruptly, Iris stood, took a deep breath and extended her hand. "Stan, lovely to meet you. And thank your staff for being so accommodating. I can find my way out." Hiding her humiliation by squaring her shoulders, she marched out of the conference room without looking back.

To calm her frustrations, she counted the tile squares in the ceiling grid of the elevator. As she pushed her way out of the skyscraper's revolving doors and onto the street, she mimicked her almost-future boss, "…decided to pursue other recourses to address our needs at this time. What the hell does that even mean? I'm sending a gift card from Manhattan Barber Shop with my thank-you letter so he can get that thing glued on his head shaved off."

Standing on the sidewalk she ordered a Town Car. The next LaGuardia shuttle to Richmond, Virginia was hours away, but she was afraid of the trouble she would get into if she stayed in Manhattan, like stalking a banker with bad hair, throwing her nail-clippers from her purse at him. She'd been out-maneuvered, and she didn't know by whom. Why had her expensive headhunter, Lace Barbour, insisted she take this interview? She wanted Lace's head, on a stick.

## Chapter 2

As the Town Car left the curb Iris dialed her headhunter's private line. Getting his voice mail, she delivered her message with twisted sarcasm, "Lace, you said this interview was just a formality, that I had the job. That's not what Stan Tenney thinks."

Lace Barbour was Barbour Career Management Consultants. Iris befriended Lace when he had won a contract to supply her former employer with premier executive talent. Shortly after she left the bank, the place she called work for twenty-plus years, she hired him to find her a job to replace the one she had lost. Although his fee was stiff, he was her Wall Street insider, and for that, she thought he was worth every dollar, not that she would admit this to him. When he tried to develop an intimate relationship with her, Iris reminded him of his marital status. In spite of his faults, she liked the guy.

What just happened back there? She and Lace had to figure out why the sudden left turn at Nexdorf. She needed to figure out her next move.

The crawling ride in the soundproof car soothed the sting of the COO's rejection. Unlike her colleagues, who had families and hated traveling, Iris had always volunteered for trips to New York from Bank US's regional headquarters in Richmond. She loved both cities, New York with its chaotic vitality and Richmond as familiar as a favorite winter blanket.

Iris jumped when her phone started vibrating.

Lace skipped over the hello's and protested, "That bastard Tenney. Did he offer you the manager's job instead of the VP spot?"

"No, guess again. I got the 'we've decided to go in another direction' spiel thrown at me."

"Ah, no, he didn't. The dog. Tell me what happened. I swear to you, Iris, yesterday morning they called and said the search committee liked you. They wanted you for the SVP chair. What happened?"

The car ride had calmed Iris, allowing her to clear her mind of the image of Lace's tie getting caught in a paper shredder while he was wearing it. "My guess? Tenney's got somebody in the wings but forgot to tell HR. Why didn't you know about this? Isn't this what I pay you for? I felt like a fool in there."

"Iris, let me call my contact. This is not over. Stay calm." Lace was not.

"I'm not holding my breath. We should probably move on. I'm not sure I could work for Tenney. Somebody needs to teach that drone some manners." She recalled the face of the young woman Tenney had reprimanded.

"But you've got so much time invested in this one, baby." Lace pleaded.

"First, Lace, I'm not your baby. Second, find out what's going on. And clue me in on what happened. You owe me that." The muscles at the back of her neck ached.

"Where are you? Want to meet up for lunch? Or early dinner?" Lace tried.

"No, thanks. I'm on my way to the airport."

"Iris, stay over and have dinner with me tonight. You can stay at my sister's place," he tried again.

"Nope. Find out what really happened over there today." Iris pressed the end-call button.

Instantly a text message from Lace appeared on the screen.

I'm sorry. Will make it up to you soon☺

*A smiley face? Who does he think I am, his ten-year-old daughter?* The phone's battery icon flashed yellow.

After paying the limo driver, she gathered her raincoat, suit jacket, and tote bag and slid across the slicked-leather backseat and out onto the sidewalk. As she straightened the skirt of last year's suit, she thought of her mother's fashion mantra. Always dress better than is required, Iris, and the world will take notice. She cringed as she pulled at the bright red basting thread left by her seamstress's alterations of her suit jacket. Had anyone noticed the stitching down the sides? It didn't matter, this job offer was a bust. Nexdorf was her latest hope of getting to the other side of the glass ceiling.

Losing the extra pounds gained over the years of too many expensive restaurant dinners and bad airport food was the only advantage she saw with her personal economic downturn. Her five-six frame was slender again, and her fair skin actually glowed now that she had stopped smoking.

Like her mom, Iris was a natural beauty. For make-up she only messed with a touch of lipstick and a quick swipe of the mascara wand over her dark brown eyes. The ladies back at her Richmond hair salon cooed over her thick, coffee-colored hair, which was starting to show a few streaks of grey. Her forty-seventh birthday behind her, she tried not to think about the inevitable fading of her looks and arrogant self-confidence. The Nexdorf job represented all she had craved, the prestige and power of the corner office.

Like most East Coast business day-trippers, Iris knew every grill, lounge, and electrical power outlet in La Guardia's domestic terminals. She plugged her phone into her favorite power outlet at Gate 25A; the display showed missed calls from Jonnie and Lace. All around her the noise of the other passengers, a screaming baby, a business type yakking about nothing into a cell phone, and a gaggle of girls returning from their first Broadway show, added fuel to the oncoming headache. Rubbing her temples, she decided to check in with Jonnie.

"Bailey, Bailey, Bailey, and Bailey," Jonnie's receptionist announced.

"Hi, Claire. Your boss is nagging me."

"Hi, Miss Lee. She's on the phone with another client. Can you hold please?"

Jonnie and Iris became best friends in elementary school in the small southwest Virginia town of Mt Pleasant when Jonnie tried to rescue a classmate and his show-and-tell rabbit from Iris, who had insisted that the rabbit was hers. Ever since that day, Jonnie had been giving Iris big-sister advice about boys and about life.

"Where are you?"

"La Guardia. I could spit nails. I was lead to believe that the job was mine, but this joker, Jonnie you wouldn't believe this guy's hair—"

"Iris, did what I told you earlier not sink in?" Jonnie interrupted.

"Oh, you just misunderstood. Mr. Henry gets all kinds of creeps renting houses from him on Eastend Street. Probably—"

"You remember Joe Turner, the B&B owner down the street from your parents' house?" Jonnie interrupted again.

"Yeah, I think I met him last Christmas."

"You weren't here last Christmas, but that's beside the point. He just called me. Apparently, your mother was soliciting him for SPCA donations this morning."

"So? She wants to help out with kittens and puppies."

"She was in her nightgown, and it was seven o'clock in the morning!"

"Why did she do that? Elizabeth Lee wouldn't be caught dead outside of the house in her nightclothes."

Nervously, Iris tried to make light of the conversation. She had convinced herself that not thinking about her mother's condition would mean it wasn't happening.

"Iris, come home and look after your parents," Jonnie ordered.

Iris ignored the command and asked, "Where's Miss Bert?"

A family fixture since Iris was in the first grade, Bert Tyler Swanson ran the household at 1 North Grove Street, the home of Henry L. and Elizabeth Carter Lee. Miss Bert was a paragon for the institution of housekeeping.

"Iris, they're not Bert Swanson's parents—they're yours. It's time for you to come home and take care of things."

"Me? Take care of things? Where's Mr. Henry?" At a young age Iris learned from Bert that her father's name was Mr. Henry, and throughout her life, he had done little to encourage any conventional terms of endearment like Dad or Daddy. "Jonnie, they're calling me to board the plane. I'll call when I get in." Her phone's battery icon flashed red. The cord had wiggled free from the phone.

"Call me as soon as you land. We need to talk strategy about the drug bust."

"Come again?" Iris asked as she bowed her head and pressed three fingers between her eyebrows. Her shoulder-length hair covering her face.

"You aren't listening to me. It's been on TV and in the paper. The feds arrested a band of drug dealers working out of the Shops—"

The phone double-beeped and emitted the dying gasp of a dead battery. Iris threw the useless device into her leather tote bag and stomped across the boarding bridge to the plane. Buckling up in her window seat, she massaged her temples. The day was not going the way she had expected.

# Chapter 3

"Heyu, I'm home" Iris called from the tiny foyer of her condo. As she pulled the key card from the door lock, a wiry-haired beagle-schnauzer trotted over from the living room.

Soon after Iris was fired from Bank US, Manny, a good friend with military obligations, called in a ginormous favor. Heyu needed a place to stay for a while.

After Heyu moved in, she understood why Manny didn't want him "boarding" at the SPCA. A clever sort, he was her first roommate since college and much cleaner than the debutante from Atlanta. He was a quiet dog. A look up with a cocked head signaled a need to anoint a lamppost, and a single tail swipe meant he was ready for dinner.

Since Iris's fall from corporate grace, Heyu was her officemate, her drinking buddy, and a listening friend when she felt like moping about her situation. "I'm glad you moved in," she admitted to him one day when they were coming back from the park. Heyu seemed as surprised as she at the confession.

Iris and Heyu lived downtown at Riverside on the James condominiums on the north side of the river. With access to the Haxall Canal Walk and river island parks, they spent a lot of time outdoors while everyone else was on their day jobs.

"Let's get a walk in. What do you say?" Iris said as she dropped her tote bag on the receiving table next to the door. An elevator ride and a two-minute walk got them to the canal walkway.

"Which way? Up or down river?" Iris tugged at the seat of her running tights then scooped her hair into a short ponytail with a scrunchie.

Heyu lifted his head. Sniffing the air, his nose pointed east. He picked up the pace prompting Iris to jog down the broad sidewalk beside the waterway. With their backs to the setting sun, a long-shadowed view of the James River with its mighty rapids and a labyrinth of bridges and ramps lay before them. While the rush hour on the interstate highways crisscrossing the river was coming to an end, the pedestrian traffic on the canal walk underneath was getting congested with runners and bikers. This place was Iris's home.

Back inside her condo, Iris treated herself to a beer and poured Heyu a bowl of fresh water. Speaking in her best southern hostess voice, she said, "Let's take our drinks out to the veranda, shall we?" For what it lacked in size, the closet-sized balcony offered an artistically asymmetrical view of downtown Richmond. The north side presented a skyline of high-rise buildings of all shapes and sizes. West and southern views featured a landscape of the low and wide, rocky river with its rapids and islands. Iris and Heyu sat quietly and paid tribute to another day ending.

"What's up?" Iris answered her ringing phone.

"About Mr. Henry—" Jonnie started.

"Is he really dealing drugs?" Iris took a sip of her beer.

"Iris, your dad is eighty-two years old. He's *not* a drug dealer. Can the snarky comments."

"If you say so," she responded with fake disinterest.

"Did you ever meet the current Shops at Mt Pleasant tenant? A second-hand store called New To You," Jonnie asked. Aside from the Bailey Law Offices and a handful of other law firms, the county courthouse and town hall, Mr. Henry's Lee Properties owned most of the real estate in the few blocks of rundown uptown Mt Pleasant.

"I never had the pleasure. What did she do? Set up a hookah stand in the store?" Iris laughed.

"Not funny, Iris. You need to pay attention. This is serious."

"OK, OK. What did the tenant do?"

"She and her ex-con out-on-parole-for-drug-distribution, slash, husband were arrested two nights ago. They were using the store to sell drugs to the locals. According to the police report, they had quite the retail operation going. Lots of variety: methamphetamines, cocaine, marijuana cigarettes. Lucky for Mr. Henry, they weren't manufacturing it there."

"Wow! Do you suppose Mr. Henry ever tried pot?" Iris mused.

"Iris! Listen! You're not hearing me" Jonnie scolded. "This is serious. He could go to jail, lose his business license and the property!"

Iris picked at the beer bottle label.

"The chief of police called me this morning to say that he's getting pressure from the DEA. And he's angry because the town hasn't kept him in the loop."

"So why are you calling me?"

"I can't believe I'm hearing this from you! Because he's your father? And, if that doesn't stir you, it's your legacy. Do you want the town to condemn the place? "

"Jonnie, you know where Mr. Henry stands on me helping him with Lee Properties. He doesn't think women are smart enough to run a business. Why would he want my help?"

"God, you're as stubborn as he is!"

"Remember the Wal-Mart fight? I offered to help, and he told me to stay out of it. So that's what I'm doing." The familiar lump rose in her throat, the one she felt every time she talked about Mr. Henry and their relationship. He had ignored Iris for the first eighteen years of her life, and she planned to disregard him for the rest of his.

"That's not fair. That was ten years ago. He didn't want to bother you with something that the town was going to lose anyway." She paused then continued in a softer tone. "This time I think he could really use your help."

"So, Jonnie, wise counsel, riddle me this. Why hasn't the old man picked up the phone and called *me*? He knows my number!" She shouted into the phone as the day's frustrations finally exploded. Heyu paced the patio perimeter.

"I'm not going there with you, Iris. Not tonight."

"I don't mean to take this out on you. I've had a day where I stepped in it with both shoes. What do you want me to do?" Iris asked softly.

"It's not about what I want Iris. I am calling to say that your mom and dad are at a stage in their lives where they could use a little help."

"Jonnie, I can't come right now. I didn't get the Nexdorf job. The guy who had the final word—let's just say we didn't bond. If I don't find something soon, I'll have to sell the condo, and you know what the real estate market is like." Iris tried to negotiate, "I might be able to get up there this weekend."

"I give up. I'm still at the office. I'm ending this conversation and going home." Jonnie had chosen her family's law practice and farming over a life as the Mrs. to a college boyfriend, William. When Iris ran into him from time to time at Richmond social gatherings, he cried a river over how he had let her go. Iris was glad they broke up, Jonnie was too good for the sappy drunk. "Do you want me to keep you posted on Mr. Henry?"

"Sure. Whatever. I'll call Grove House to check on Mom. You know his lordship; he won't answer the phone. And if Miss Bert or Mom aren't there, it just rings."

14

"I'll touch base with you again tomorrow afternoon. Night."

"Jonnie? Thanks for looking after the family." She ended the call. "Heyu, can you believe it? My old man is suspected of drug dealing. What a hoot." She reached over and scratched behind his ear while they both watched the emerging nightlife down below.

# Chapter 4

As the weak light of early morning filtered through the bedroom shades, Iris debated the merits of staying in bed for a daytime TV marathon. With six months gone since her last consulting gig, she had run out of things to do to avoid trolling for work. She'd painted her entire apartment, caught up on all the mystery novels on her nightstand, and reorganized her closets, twice. Plus, Junior Achievement was beginning to depend upon her time and talent a little too much for her liking.

She crawled out of bed and slipped on the previous night's running gear. Scratching at her bed head, she escorted Heyu to the nearest grassy knoll, then they made a quick trot up the canal walkway and back. After a shower and breakfast, she scrolled the TV channels for Heyu's favorite show and headed to her corner office, the condo's second bedroom.

Like the other areas in the apartment, the room hosted a living pastoral of the James River. Home to hobos and herons, eagles and islands, it had two moods, calm and muddy. River scenes played through Iris's telescope revealing close-ups of rapid riding kayakers and swimming rats. Yes, her life had come to that, watching rodents scurry among the rocks and small waterfalls.

Sitting at her computer, she clicked on her calendar. It reminded her to meet the air conditioner dude at Manny's Virginia Beach cottage the next day.

"Heyu," she called out to him as she dialed her parents' home number, one she would never forget, "want to go chase birds on the beach?"

"Hello? Lee residence."

"Hey!" No response from Bert prompted Iris to add "Miss Bert, it's Iris."

"Oh! Well, my word, it is. I didn't recognize your voice there for a minute, sweet pea."

Iris heard the faint click-clack of the housekeeper's ill-fitting dentures.

"How are things at Grove House?" Iris asked.

"How is Grove House, you say?" Bert's response was why Iris dreaded phone calls to her parents' house. For the next five minutes she would play Abbott and Costello with the family housekeeper. Iris loved Bert, like the second mother she was, but the woman had no aptitude for the art of social conversation.

"Is everything OK at the house? Is Mom there?" Iris tried another direction.

"Why wouldn't everything be all right? The house is fine." Bert sounded confused.

"How are you doing?" Iris asked.

"What do you mean how am I doing? I'm fine."

"Is Uncle Donnie doing OK?" Iris asked Bert about the housekeeper's uncle and a Lee family friend.

"How's Uncle Donnie doing? I don't know, haven't seen him since yesterday." Bert's appreciation of time was worlds' apart from everyone else's. Iris hadn't seen Donnie Tyler in a blue moon of Sundays, as Bert was fond of saying. She felt Heyu brush up against her leg under the desk, emitting a quiet snarl as the doorbell rang.

"Hold on a second. Someone's at my door." Iris tiptoed toward the apartment door, Heyu silently following at her heels.

"Someone's at your door, you say? Do you want me to hang up?"

Iris whispered, "Let me check to see who it is. Wait a second." She spied through the peephole at the floor captain of the homeowner's association Sarah Ward in a powder blue warm-up suit, her bony arms crossed.

"What does she want?" Iris complained.

"What does who want?" Bert puzzled.

"Nobody." Iris's right eyed squinted for a better view. Mrs. Ward's magnified lashless eye stared back causing Iris to jump.

The doorbell rang again.

"You better get that. Your daddy ain't here, and he didn't say when he'd be back. When I see him, I'll tell him you called. Bye, sweet pea."

The door chime screamed longer the third time. Iris dared to look through the peephole again. Standing away from the door, the scrawny Mrs. Ward was tapping her boat-sized sneaker. Then she bent over and slid a piece of paper under Iris's door.

"Emergency homeowners' meeting," Iris read to Heyu as she ambled to the kitchen. "Tonight at 7:30. Topic of discussion: AXE Management Company wants to raise our homeowner fees again." Groaning, she folded the paper in half and stuffed it into the kitchen trash bin. She loathed neighborhood politics.

Iris got a fast busy when she dialed her parents' number again. She wanted to find out why her mom was parading down Grove Street in her nightclothes. Elizabeth Lee was Mt Pleasant's fashion muse, its very own Audrey Hepburn. The very notion of being seen in public without bra or lipstick was something a sane Elizabeth could neither comprehend nor tolerate. Maybe she should drive up for a visit to check on Elizabeth, but first, she needed to see a man about an air conditioner.

"Heyu," Iris exclaimed, "let's pack up and go tonight. I can sit on the beach while you do your *Chariots of Fire* routine with the birds."

Iris reasoned that a couple of days in Virginia Beach at Manny's cottage was just what she needed to get away from rejection letters, stooges like Tenney, and nosy neighbors. And whatever was going on with her father's business, she decided, Jonnie could resolve it.

Packed and ready for a road trip, she made one last stop. The phone rattled across the bathroom counter. "Cheese and crackers! Nobody calls all day and then I try to use—" Jonnie's number appeared on the display. The call went to voice mail. Instantly, the phone started vibrating again; Lace was calling. *Good, I'll get his lame excuses on why he screwed up my Nexdorf position recorded on voice mail. Play them back to him when I fire him.*

With Heyu riding shotgun, the pair headed in the opposite direction of Mt Pleasant and onto the Interstate 64 east entrance ramp. Jonnie's name lit up the phone's display again.

"What?" Iris answered irritably.

"Where've you been? Why didn't you answer earlier? "

"I was busy. What's up?"

"Did you talk to your dad? What did he say?"

"I called and he wasn't home and surprise, surprise, he hasn't called me back." Iris glanced over her left shoulder to make the entrance ramp.

"Just get up here. We'll deal with it when you get in."

"*You* deal with it. You're the lawyer. That's what he needs right now. I'm on my way to Virginia Beach for a day or so."

"Hello," Iris heard Jonnie bang her phone receiver on her desktop, "did you just completely forget the conversation we had last night?"

"What can I do, Jonnie? I called, and he won't call me back."

"I thought you were smart, do I have to spell it out? Turn the car around and head home. Right. Now!"

"Jonnie, once, when I was eighteen, you know what my father asked me?" Iris felt her heart rate stepping up. "He asked me what my birth date was. The man who claims to be my father didn't even know his own daughter's birthday! And I'm an only child! It wasn't like he had too many to remember!" The anger rushed at her so quickly she started to hyperventilate. "If he needs my help, he can call me and ask for it. Besides, I promised Manny I'd check in on his cottage while he was gone."

"Your mom's dementia is getting worse. She's not looking after herself, and Miss Bert is worried about her."

"I talked to Miss Bert this morning. She didn't say anything about Mom."

"That's because she doesn't want to bother you, oh seed of the evil Mr. Henry. Why do you think she calls me instead of you?" Jonnie had to get a jab in. It infuriated Iris when she was compared to her father, and Jonnie knew this. "When was the last time you actually saw your mom, Iris?"

"Christmas, you know that day when families come together to eat insane amounts of spinach dip and endure each other's company for a whole twenty-four hours?"

"Cute. But excuse me? You were in Vail with Manny last Christmas."

"I *did* spend Christmas with—look I try to talk to Mom on the phone every few weeks or so," Iris rationalized. Now was not the time to talk with Jonnie about her phone conversations with Elizabeth. The calls were getting loopy.

"When was the last time you spoke to *her*, not Miss Bert, but your mother?" Jonnie kept pushing.

"Jonnie, I don't keep a phone log of calls to my mother for crying out loud."

"Come home, Iris. Your family needs you."

After a long silence, Iris said, "I'll try to get up there next week," then threw the phone at the dashboard.

Jonnie was wrong about Iris not recalling the last time she had seen or spoken to her mother. The fear in Elizabeth's face was imprinted on Iris's brain, a memory she'd carry for the rest of her days.

Just three months ago, as always, Iris rolled in late Christmas Eve to spend the next day with her folks after a week of Colorado skiing with Manny. Iris went to Elizabeth's bedroom to say "good night" and as she bent over to remove the sleeping woman's glasses, Elizabeth drew her clenched fists to her chest and cried out, "Who are you? Get away from me." Thinking her mother was dreaming, Iris reached out to touch her hand, but a panicked Elizabeth struck at her, harshly insisting that Iris leave the room. The next day Elizabeth was her old self, struggling to prepare the all-important Christmas Day dinner without the aid of her trusted helper, Bert, who was with her own family.

Mentioning the episode to Mr. Henry, the two discussed plans for a doctor's checkup after the holidays. A call home in late January revealed that the doctor said Elizabeth was fine and perhaps the stress of Christmas had caused a panic attack. Remembering the terror in her mother's eyes, Iris argued with her father over the diagnosis and insisted he take her to another doctor. Not hearing from him, Iris had planned to call the second doctor herself after the Nexdorf position was secured.

And now, driving down Interstate 64 in the opposite direction of home, her reflection stared back at her from the rear-view mirror. Tears streamed down her face. She despaired going back to watch someone she loved fading away before her eyes.

Chapter 5

What was that foul smell, and why couldn't she breathe? Her eyes still closed, Iris reached for her phone in its usual spot, the bedside table, except the table wasn't there. For a quick fight-or-flight second, she bolted upright and Heyu crashed to the floor beside the bed. In the next second she realized she was in the master bedroom of Manny's beach bungalow. Up on all fours, Heyu yipped out a single bark of pain but shook it off.

"Dude. We have *got* to get you a toothbrush!" She staggered out of the bedroom and toward the oceanfront sliding-glass doors. "You know your way around. Be back in five." Heyu cruised out onto the deck and toward the private fenced-in beach. On her way to the kitchen for coffee, Iris turned on the TV and found the local news channel.

"Yes, Gene, the fair-weather forecast for this weekend's March for the Cure10K on Saturday is not looking too bright. Runners should dress for heavy rains. And the wet stuff will continue into the middle of next week. Looks like those April showers are coming a little early this year," the weatherman droned on, but Iris tuned him out while listening to Jonnie's newest plea on her voice mail.

"Iris, Mr. Henry called me last night. He seems genuinely scared. I know that's hard to believe but it's true. He said Chief Quinn wants to meet him here in my office. He wants you to be here." And after a pause, she continued, "I set it up for six o'clock tonight to give you time to get here. You know he could be indicted on criminal charges if they believe he had anything to do with this drug gang. I hope you come." Iris sat in a kitchen chair and stared unfocused at the worn floor.

Now and again Iris thought about the day she would have to make arrangements for the care of her parents in their final years. Sitting alone in the cottage kitchen with the windows rattling from the nor'easter, the future smacked her like an out-of-control car crashing into a highway Jersey wall. All at once she understood that neither Jonnie or Bert, nor anyone else for that matter, owned the responsibility of caring for her parents. That duty was hers and hers alone.

She felt Heyu's wet body brush against her leg. "Buddy, we've got a rain storm in Virginia Beach and a shit storm in Mt Pleasant. Which do we choose? I don't believe you've had the pleasure of meeting my old man, have you?"

A six-hour drive due west from Virginia Beach, Mt Pleasant was the county seat of Fallam County and due south of Roanoke off state Route 220. After rescheduling Manny's air conditioning maintenance and stopping at her condo for some extra clothes, Iris estimated that she would just make the six o'clock showdown.

On the outskirts of Mt Pleasant, Iris stopped at Louie's Gas-N-Go East to use the restroom. Pausing at the cashier's counter, she asked for a pack of cigarettes.

"What brand?" the clerk asked.

"Whatever. Give me the foulest-tasting ones you have." Iris had given up smoking on her fortieth birthday, seven years ago.

"Trying to quit?" He smiled, revealing a row of gangsta gold-and-diamond teeth.

"Just give me the cigarettes," she snapped. "Goat-brained idiot," she added under her breath. Stepping outside, she lit one and threw the remaining pack at the overflowing trashcan propped against the building. A man walking by picked up the fresh pack and shoved it in his pocket, gawking at Iris. She ignored him. The cigarette tasted and smelled like kerosene. Gagging, she went back into the store and bought a pack of gum.

Tired from the long drive, she longed to be in Richmond on her balcony watching the river. She parked her SUV in the deck that connected to the Bailey Building on Court Street which sat across from the county courthouse.

Success came easily for the fifth-generation Bailey barristers, Jonnie and her younger brother Wyatt. Offspring to Judge John Bailey, they practiced civil and criminal law in the recently renovated but still creaky building.

"Heyu, when we get inside, you sit by Claire. There's a park behind the building. Great place, lots of squirrels. And it's named after my grandmother Matilda. Use your charm, and maybe Claire will take in a walk with you."

As she entered the firm's reception area, Iris saw her father. His back was turned to her, but she'd recognize those considerable ears anywhere. Folks around town referred to them as dumbos, umbrellas, and wind flaps.

The old man was ordering Claire Brown to summon his lawyer. The distraction of his high-handed voice kept her from noticing right away that he was leaning on a cane. Despite the cool March air, Iris lifted her shoulder-length hair away from her sweating neck. The noise of the closing glass doors caused Mr. Henry to turn. He spotted Heyu first.

"This is a place of business. No dogs are allowed. Take that stinking mutt outside!" Expected insults aside, Iris was jarred by the changes in her father since she saw him at Christmas. The skin of his face and neck were as colorless as Bert's frozen chicken parts stored in Grove House's basement deep freezer.

But the way he dressed hadn't changed. Underneath his worn, leather car coat, his suit and tie were neat and tucked, as always. Well-groomed like the Lee gentlemen before him, his wing-tips were polished, his white hair and his face were freshly barbered and his fingernails manicured and polished. Back in the day, the older neighborhood kids called him Eliot Ness behind his back because he dressed like a character on some TV show they called *The Untouchables*.

Recovering from the shock of his pallid face, Iris said, "Relax, he got a bath yesterday."

He glared at her as if she were a stranger then the recall of who she was lit up his mink eyes.

"You decided to show up," he jabbed.

"Yeah, I'm here as a character reference. Jonnie called and told me that the police want to interview you and that you wanted me here." Again, she lifted her hair with one hand and fanned her neck with the other.

"Ethan Quinn thinks he's smart like his daddy, but he's a fool," the old man quipped.

"I'm sure Jonnie will set things straight, directly," Iris responded. *Directly?* In town fifteen minutes and she was talking in full Fallam County Southern.

The elevator beside the reception desk pinged and out stepped Jonnie Bailey. Just turning fifty, Jonnie wore her age and size well. As with any woman, her extra weight was unwanted, but she hid it well with her dark blue trouser-suit. Jonnie looked like the judge's people, fair-skinned and freckled. Framing her face, her thick hair was as white as Crisco. Her eye color, like most of the Scots-Irish descendants in the county, was the same as green-gold beryl gemstones and her loveliest asset.

"Mr. Henry, good to see you. And, how is Miss Elizabeth?" she asked with a warm southern formality, extending her hand to shake his.

"Fine," he murmured, his hands gripping the ornate cane which had belonged to his father.

Jonnie greeted Iris with only a nod.

"Why is Ethan Quinn wasting his time talking to me? I didn't do anything. He should be chasing the scoundrels who took advantage of that young shop girl," grumbled Mr. Henry as he shuffled into the claustrophobic elevator.

"Let's go up to the conference room and get comfortable, shall we?" Jonnie called over her shoulder, "Claire, send Chief Quinn up to the conference room when he arrives."

Iris asked, "Claire, can Heyu visit with you while we're in our meeting?" Heyu walked over to Claire's desk and sat beside it. "I'll take the stairs," Iris said to Jonnie as the elevator door closed.

Mt Pleasant Chief of Police Ethan Quinn removed a plastic coffee straw from his mouth and asked Mr. Henry, "How did you come to know Amber Caravetti?"

Along with Iris and Jonnie, Mr. Henry and Chief Quinn were sitting around an oak ball-in-claw footed table in the conference room overlooking Matilda Park, a single-block, wooded sanctuary behind the buildings on Court Street.

"She called me last summer. Said she wanted to rent one of my vacant stores over at The Shops. I told her to call Jonnie if she was interested. Is this really necessary, Ethan? I didn't have anything to do with this outfit!"

Like other locally owned retailers about town, Lee Properties and its renters had fallen on hard times since the stuff-marts and national hardware stores opened on the outskirts of town near interstate highways and sprawling housing developments.

"Mr. Lee, I understand your anxiety. But in a situation like this, we have to follow a protocol," Quinn said in an even tone.

"Mr. Henry," Jonnie joined in, "let's just keep your answers short. In the end, Chief Quinn will have his answers and know you're a victim and not an accomplice."

"When was the last time you spoke with her, Mr. Lee?"

"Who?" The old man looked confused. His head slightly bobbled side to side. As he hesitated, Iris saw, for the first time in her life, a vulnerable Mr. Henry.

"Amber Caravetti," Quinn replied.

"I don't recall the last time I had a conversation with the young woman." Mr. Henry's voice regained its vigor. "And I don't know why you are harassing me. I've done nothing wrong."

"Do you know a person by the name of Mo Caravetti?" Quinn tried another direction.

"Mo Caravetti? Never met the man." He stamped his cane on the floor.

"He and Amber Caravetti are being charged with possession of illegal drugs with the intent to distribute them on the premises of New To You Secondhand Store at the Shops at Mt Pleasant which you own, Mr. Lee." Quinn sat back in his chair, waiting for an answer.

"Drugs? They're selling drugs on my property?" An agitated Mr. Henry responded as if this was the first time he had heard about the much publicized arrests.

"Yes, they were. And the DEA thinks you may be involved." Quinn pressed on with a raised voice.

"DEA! Federal agents think that I'm dealing drugs? This is preposterous! This is harassment!" Mr. Henry's head started shaking again.

"Chief Quinn, we can prove that Lee Properties was in the process of evicting the tenant due to non-payment of rent prior to the arrests. If Mr. Lee *was* involved, what would he gain by evicting his alleged partners?" Jonnie asked.

"Perhaps the DEA would see it as Lee Properties wanting to push out the competition," Quinn speculated.

"Ethan Quinn, you have crossed the line! You know I have been a part of this community for over eighty years." Mr. Henry stood, his entire body shaking with anger and color finally coming to his face. "Miss Bailey, I'm leaving. It appears that all the government has time for these days is to threaten law-abiding citizens with speculations of unspeakable misconduct. What's a man to do when his word is not accepted as truth?"

This was the Mr. Henry Iris knew. The old man and his cane huffed out of the conference room. The three left at the table stared at the empty fourth chair.

"Moves fast when he's mad," Iris smirked.

"Iris—err—Miss Lee, for what it's worth, I agree with your father. The DEA has a new agent for this region, and he wants to make a big splash with his first bust. He's not from around here so he doesn't know who the old man is. I tried to tell him that there's no way Mr. Henry Lee would be involved in something like this. I'll say something to the judge." Quinn stuck the coffee straw back in his mouth.

"At some point, Quinn, Mr. Henry will expect an apology from you. You know that, right?" Iris asked. He winced a nod. Friends by proxy, Iris and Quinn's fathers had been drinking buddies back when the romantic sport was running moonshine from the next county over to Roanoke. The irony of the situation hadn't escaped her.

"Yeah, that's why I was dreading this meeting. Jonnie, can you ask Mr. Lee to sign an affidavit swearing he had no knowledge of the Caravetti's illegal activities?"

"We've already written it up. We'll get it to you when he agrees to sign it," she said as she escorted Iris and Quinn to the elevator. When the door closed on Quinn, she turned to Iris and said, "Meet the new chief of police."

"When did he blow back into town?" Iris asked.

"Last year. He retired from the military. Lived in Texas, married a woman from Mexico."

"So what happened to his backbone? He can't just tell DEA to take a hike?"

"I'm not sure what's going on over at town hall. It's obvious he didn't think this was necessary. I think he was ordered to do it." Then she added as they descended the building's back stairs, "Now do you see why you needed to come home? Your dad is not taking this well. Plus, I smell a dead rat in the silo. Something's not right about this whole thing. I just hope Quinn can figure it out before your dad's property is confiscated—or worse, a criminal indictment is handed down."

"Criminal indictment? But he's not—"

"If your dad had knowledge of illegal activities, they could take possession of the entire building and charge him as an accomplice," Jonnie's voice echoed in the stairway.

"From the way he reacted, I'd say he wouldn't remember if he *did* have knowledge." Iris realized what was at stake, not the loss of property or possible criminal indictment, but her father's dignity and self-respect.

"Bingo, kiddo," Jonnie said.

"Jonnie, make this go away. He would see this as a personal humiliation. It would kill him," Iris whispered with real worry in her voice.

"I'll try my best to keep him out of court. But what he needs now is family support. He needs you. That's why I told that little fib in my message to you this morning. It was the only way to get you up here," Jonnie replied back in a hushed voice.

"What are you talking about?"

"He didn't ask me to tell you to come home. But you need to be here, Iris. And you two need to work things out."

"Stay out of it Jonnie," Iris whispered loudly. "You don't understand."

Jonnie grabbed Iris by her upper arms, gently shaking her, "Listen to me. I know you two have your differences, but you've got to let him know that you're going to be around for him. Give me your word that you will."

As usual, her best friend was right. Seeing her father's pasty pallor and the way he reacted to Quinn's questions, Iris knew the time had come to think about where she was going to park his butt when he could no longer wipe it himself.

"I'll try," Iris said. "But don't expect me to be happy doing it."

"Iris, you're missing the point—yikes! What's that?"

Heyu had found his way down the dimly lit hallway and was pressing against Jonnie's leg with his wet nose.

Iris laughed. "He's Manny's pal and my current roommate. Heyu, meet my hometown hero, Jonnie Bailey."

# Chapter 6

Iris drove east down Court Street past the law offices and the town library, which was once home to the Bailey clan, then north on Grove Street hoping to see her father on his walk home. Henry Lee was nowhere in sight.

Grove Street was named for the line of American Chestnuts planted on both sides of the street when most of the large, early twentieth-century homes were built. Only one of the trees survived the disease that had destroyed most of the East Coast's chestnut population, and it stood in front of the Lee's roomy two-story American craftsman-styled house. Iris pulled into the long driveway and stopped just before the towering carport. Mr. Henry's Buick, which qualified for antique status at the DMV, was parked underneath it.

Stalling to face what awaited her, Iris reached into her tote bag for her phone. Finding no new messages, she dialed Lace's personal number. The call went straight to voice mail. "Where are you? Call me. I need to know what you found out about Nexdorf." The slacker hadn't left a message when he called the day before.

Gathering her things, she turned to Heyu and said, "Whatever you do, don't use Mr. Henry's library for a bathroom—or we'll both have to spend the night on the porch."

Heyu folded his ears back and pushed his body against the passenger door.

The chilly breeze nipped at her as she passed the fading crocus bordering the stone walkway. Darkness hooded the house, but the light from the windows exposed the rusting gutters and paint-chipped window frames. As she approached the carved oak front door, it opened and warm light spilled from the inside onto the slate porch.

"Sweet pea," cried Bert, "I didn't know who was coming up the drive at this hour."

"Miss Bert, I'm home." Iris hugged her big, soft Miss Bert whose plain broad face was a dark honey color. Her wiry, bouncy locks were turning a lighter shade of heather grey, almost white. Mr. Henry lurked behind her. *When did Mr. Henry and Miss Bert get so old?*

"Did you have supper yet?" Bert asked. "I just finished puttin' the kitchen in order."

"I'm not hungry right now, thanks," Iris replied, "Where's Mom? In her sitting room?"

"Naw, sweet pea. She's done gone to bed. I know that if she knew you were comin', she'd of stayed up. And who do we have here?"

Heyu sat quietly beside Iris in the wood-paneled foyer. He glanced up at Bert then at Iris, waiting for an introduction.

"Miss Bert, meet Heyu. He's my new roommate. I decided to bring him down to meet the family and—"

"A dog's place is on the porch!" ordered Mr. Henry.

Bert jumped. She turned to him and said, a little too loudly, "Mr. Henry, you scared me. Dog or not, he seems better behaved than most men I know around here. Come on, sugar. Let's get you some water and something to eat." Heyu followed Bert across the wide foyer and through the door leading to the back of the house.

"Feels like it's going to get cold tonight. Are you going to have a fire?" Iris followed her father into the great room to the right of the foyer.

Mr. Henry's library and sitting room ran the entire length of the side of the house and had a sandstone mantel and fireplace centered on its far wall. The inner wall facing the fireplace hosted built-in shelves with troves of books from Latin primers to modern spy novels. Like bookends, two of Elizabeth's pastoral paintings of Fallam County landscape hung on either side of the shelves. A painted portrait of Allen Lee, Iris's grandfather, and his young family dominated the oak panel over the fireplace.

The room was sparsely furnished. A long, leather and carved-oak framed sofa lounged under the front arched windows. In the back of the great room several plant stands cradled shedding ferns and dying spider plants. An old arts-and-crafts floor lamp illuminated a pair of Morris chairs facing the fireplace. The leather cushions in one sagging more than the other.

Ignoring her question about the fire, Mr. Henry said, "I'm sorry that you were not able to have supper with your mother. You should have called to let us know you were coming."

"I was in Virginia Beach when I got the call from Jonnie about your meeting. I just got in the car and drove up. Besides, if Miss Bert's not here, no one answers the phone anyway."

"These days Bert is spending more time here. Your mother needs help with personal things now," he said as he eased himself into his chair.

"What did the other doctor say?" Iris asked about the second doctor's opinion on her mother's condition. She surveyed the dimly lit room.

"He suspects Alzheimer's."

Iris folded her arms, tucking her hands in her armpits. She swallowed hard.

"He says we should keep her in familiar surroundings and try not to expect her to remember things." He opened up his day-old *Wall Street Journal* resting on an ottoman. "I've asked Bert to stay through the dinner hour and help with getting her to bed each night. And neither one is happy about that arrangement."

"Hmm." The flashback of Elizabeth's Christmas outburst flashed in Iris's mind. *Oh, Mom.*

"Bert is asking for help. You're here now. You can help tend to your mother. Now, either sit down or move away from the lamp, you're standing in my light." Mr. Henry fished his bifocals from his sweater pocket, dismissing his daughter.

In anger over the news of Elizabeth's condition, Iris punched at the cushion on the other chair and sat. Her mother's brain was rotting away and he acted like having Bert at the house an extra hour each night was going to fix it. She had to talk about something else before the Lee household had a patricide on its hands.

"Ethan Quinn told us after you left that he doesn't believe you had any involvement in the drug scam." Iris balanced on the edge the chair.

"Ethan Quinn did what he was ordered to do. The mayor and his cronies have me in their crosshairs." Mr. Henry said as he scanned the columns of the paper.

"What do you mean?"

"Bobby Kaluchi wants the land under my Shops. He wants to build a music center or some such nonsense. I told him I wasn't interested in selling."

"But if the buildings are vacant, why wouldn't you want to negotiate—"

"I'm not selling the land," Mr. Henry said sternly as he looked up from his paper. "I've told that clown a dozen times. It's not for sale. None of it. It belongs to the Lee family. Besides, I don't trust a fool who calls himself a lawyer and has no clients. Or none that I can see."

"Shouldn't you have a counter offer? I mean with all the eminent domain cases cities are winning these days, the town could take this to court and argue a need for public use. You could end up with nothing." Iris spoke to the side of the old man's face.

"What's it to you, missy?" Mr. Henry looked up from the paper. His opaque eyes stared into hers, conveying malcontent of which she was all too familiar.

"I'm a Lee," she forced herself to hold her eyes to his. "It's in my interest to see that the family is treated fairly. I'm stating the obvious here, but I'm not having children. Other than me, which Lee do you see passing the property to? Cousin Bennie? His daughters? I hear he's got a couple of grandsons."

"I have no intention of turning this over to Bennie. Thinks the world owes him the moon and the stars, just like his father. He'd sell it all off for a quick profit and never look back." Mr. Henry went back to his paper. Iris never got the whole story about the rift between brothers—Robert and Henry.

"Then who else is there?"

He looked at her again and said, "I had hoped you would have settled down by now, given your mother a couple of grandchildren."

Thinking of Manny squatting in some dirt-floored hovel, she said, "Still waiting for Mr. Right to ask to meet the family."

A low grunt seeped from her father.

Rushing to change the subject, she offered, "Let me help with this. I've got a lot of experience with real estate negotiations. Companies pay me a lot of money to negotiate deals. I'm good at it." She waited for a response but heard only stomach growls. She slapped her hands on her thighs and stood. "Well, all right then."

Walking toward the kitchen, she paused when she heard him say, "I'll look at what you'd propose as a counter to the mayor's offer to buy the property."

She suspected that was the closest she'd ever get to a "thank you" from the old man.

"And the dog sleeps outside."

Iris's shoulder pushed into the butler's door which separated the library from Bert's kitchen, the heart and soul of Grove House. A room of doors, the kitchen serviced Mr. Henry's library, the foyer and dining room. A glass-paned door opened into Elizabeth's sun porch behind the library. On the other end of the room, another doorway led to the basement stairs and the mudroom leading to the carport. Stairs, encased in wainscoting, led to the second floor and reminded her of the nights she sat at the top listening to the quiet, angry whispers between Mr. Henry and her mother about his frequent and extended absences.

The kitchen's high, tinned ceiling amplified even the tiniest of sounds—the tinkle of a spoon falling into the enameled sink or a newspaper page turning on the kitchen table. In the center stood an old butcher's block with a slab of white marble on top. On one side of the butcher's block was the cooking galley and on the other a dining nook. Here the family took their morning and noonday meals. However, at the Lee house, dinner was always served in the dining room.

On a small narrow wall between the mudroom door and the back-yard picture window hung the black rotary-dial wall phone. The receiver was connected to the plastic beast by a strand of entrails, gnarled and sagging to the floor, which were so long, that when stretched, the cord circled the butcher's block one and a half times. Iris had tested its limits each time she talked to her friends about homework and boys. Now she smiled at the sad old phone, a faithful sentry, which had stood by and waited for her to return from the world outside and away from Mt Pleasant.

# Chapter 7

"Time to rise and shine," Bert called from the bottom of the kitchen staircase, the top of which was next to Iris's bedroom. "Pancakes are gettin' cold."

"We'll be down in a minute," Iris called from her bedroom, a shrine to her high school youth which, judging from the dust, no one ever visited.

As Iris stood at the door of Elizabeth's boudoir, she spied her mother preening in front of her dressing mirror. A straw handbag with tortoise shell handles swung from the slight woman's forearm as she tucked her elbow into her waist. Her charm bracelet, crowded with charms Iris had sent to her from all over the country and half the world, jangled as her fingers combed through her hair, as if she were being admired by a handsome, interested man. Elizabeth's self-admiration reminded Iris of the elegant sense of style her mother had once possessed. A painter and seamstress, Elizabeth celebrated each new season of the year by foraging fashion magazines for inspiration then created her own haute couture for her and her daughter. Iris was voted best-dressed her senior year, a proud accomplishment for Elizabeth. But the fashionista gene had not been passed on to Iris. Beyond the boundaries of smart pumps and stylish banker's suits, Iris didn't give two figs for frilly dresses and accessories. Her idea of informal cocktail wear was blue jeans and a silk blouse.

Gazing in the mirror, Elizabeth noticed the reflection of Heyu and Iris standing in the doorway. She frowned in confusion then pushed her heavy glasses up her nose and asked, "Iris what's happened to your hair?"

"Do you like it? I stopped dying it." Iris inhaled the scent of her mother's "old lady perfume." Elizabeth stiffened her frail limbs as Iris reached to hug her.

"It makes you look so old," Elizabeth said with her Carter candor.

"Where are you going this morning?" Iris pointed at the straw purse. Elizabeth glared at the pocketbook as if she was seeing if for the first time.

"I'm not going anywhere," she pouted as she dropped the purse.

Startled by Elizabeth's child-like behavior, Iris noticed that the dementia appeared to be advancing more rapidly then she had previously suspected. An old-fashioned epistler of the most formal order, Elizabeth Carter had written letters about Mt Pleasant, complete with newspaper clippings, to Iris when she moved away from home. The decline and eventual cessation of these letters had caused Iris to suspect that the light in Elizabeth's memory was growing dimmer, however, she was not prepared for the lost soul standing before her. Her mother, the lady known for working crossword puzzles in ink every day, was almost gone.

Iris took in a shaky breath and said, "Let's go down and have some breakfast. I've come for a visit." She took Elizabeth by the elbow and guided her toward the hallway. A sneezing Heyu followed.

"When are you leaving?" Elizabeth asked as they took the wide front stairs.

Every time she came home to visit the folks, the first question they asked was "when are you leaving," never "good to see you" or "how are you doing" but "why are you here" or "when are you leaving." Perhaps she was partly to blame for the odd reaction. Becoming more immersed in her career, day trips were rare, and only a funeral or Christmas rated an overnight trip. When asked if she ever planned to return to Mt Pleasant for good, she resounded abhorrent objections to small town living, never answering the question directly.

In the kitchen nook Bert had set out breakfast for three.

"Those black knee socks are right smart with your summer sandals, Miss Elizabeth," Bert sang as her dentures clicked. "Today, we're having pancakes because Iris is visiting. When are you leaving, sweet pea?" Clickity-clack. "Mr. Henry's already up and gone down to the farm this mornin'. He said he won't be back before suppertime gets here. So it's just us hens today."

Bert helped Elizabeth into her chair and unfolded the breakfast napkin over her lap. "After breakfast I need to tell you something, Iris." Bert's eyes rolled toward Elizabeth.

"Like you said, it's just us chickens. What's on your mind?" Iris whispered while leaning over the narrow table.

Elizabeth speared a square of syrupy pancake and shoved it in her small mouth with fork and fingers.

"Tonight, I'm giving Mr. Henry my two-week notice. By the end of the month, I plan to be o-'ficially retired from my job as domestic housekeeper." She beamed with pride. Whenever Bert needed to brag or was nervous, she cupped each elbow with her muscular hands and breathed deeply to expand her bosom.

"But, Miss Bert—" Iris blurted, then changed gears. "That's wonderful. We'll celebrate. Have a party." She measured out each word. "But we'll have to ask you to make the cake." *Crap in a cup.* She gulped her hot coffee from Elizabeth's morning china.

"I've always wanted to go visit all my cousins in Ohio. So I'm driving Uncle Donnie and me up there in May. We're gonna spend the whole month driving around and visiting," Bert said.

When she was living at home, Iris thought, except for the occasional trips to Roanoke each year, Bert rarely traveled outside of Fallam County.

"What are your plans after Ohio?" Iris tried to recover from the trauma of the news and her scalded tongue.

"Nothing. Absolutely nothing," Bert whooped as she opened up her arms and looked up at the dusty tin ceiling. "I've polished my last door knob, Iris," she added.

Elizabeth and Bert had been inseparable for as long as Iris could remember. She couldn't imagine one without the other. Without Bert, Iris was pretty sure her mother would have burned the house down several times in attempts to cook a meal. And Bert leaned on Elizabeth for affirmation of her taste and social graces.

"What do you think about Miss Bert retiring, Mom?" Iris searched for any signs of surprise or sadness on her mother's face.

"Well, I don't know much about that," she answered and continued eating her pancakes.

"You're leaving? Where are you going?" Mr. Henry asked Bert when she delivered the news of her pending departure at dinner that evening.

"I'm going to take Uncle Donnie and me up to Ohio to visit my cousin." Then she asked, "You remember my cousin, Silas Jones?"

"I don't know why you want to drive halfway to Canada to see that egg-head, it's not my business to know. Donnie Tyler sure doesn't have a high regard for the man." Henry Lee and Donnie Tyler were members of the way-back club, their boyhood friendship sparked over a shared pack of Lucky Strikes in a roadhouse speakeasy or so that's what Bert told Iris. "Why do you want to quit the family?" Mr. Henry asked.

After her husband Otha died in a traffic accident just three years into their marriage, a childless Bert had become a Lee family member by default. Iris secretly agreed with Mr. Henry. How *does* one retire from their own family?

"Mr. Henry, I'm tired. I can't be doin' all the things you want me to do no more. My doctor says I need to stay off my feet 'cause of my gout and my blood pressure," Bert explained as she cut up Elizabeth's chicken. "Besides, I ain't trained to give Elizabeth the type of care she needs."

"I have no complaints with how you've been handling things," Mr. Henry said as he looked to his wife for confirmation. "Elizabeth?—"

"You're right," Iris interrupted, "you deserve a break. When was the last time you took a vacation?"

"Sweet pea, the last time I went anywhere was back in 1990 when I rode up to Richmond with Uncle Donnie to see his army buddies. Or was it 1980? See there, I can't remember the last time I had a vacation."

"Who's stopping you from visiting?" Mr. Henry grumbled. "I still don't know what that's got to do with you leaving the family?"

Judging from the agitated look on the old man's face, Iris guessed that he had given little thought to Bert's future other than her obligations to him and his wife.

"Why don't you take some time off," Iris said. "I'll hire someone to help out while you're away. And when you come back, we can see about getting you some help."

The sharp clash of Mr. Henry's silverware landing on his plate caused Heyu to dash from underneath the table. "We are *not* having strangers in this house, missy," he lectured as he pointed a crooked finger at Iris.

"What do you propose we do?" Iris argued back.

"Now that you're here, you can take over," Mr. Henry puffed as bits of half-chewed chicken and biscuit propelled from his lipless mouth. "It's high time you started taking on some responsibilities instead of traipsing around God knows where, doing God knows what."

Everyone except Elizabeth stopped eating.

After the soft tinkling of silverware on china began again, Iris responded, "I'm not sure if you've noticed, Mr. Henry, but housekeeping and caregiving are not my best skills. Excuse me." Throwing her napkin at a half-eaten dinner, she got up from the table and banished herself to her childhood room.

"I don't believe this. He expects me, someone who has run divisions for a multi-billion dollar company, to do the dusting and cooking," she muttered to herself as she blew out puffs of air. "Quit it, Iris, why do you let him get to you like this? Stop acting like you're his ten-year-old daughter." To calm her heart rate, she took in a deep breath and pulled her hair on top of her head, fanning her face. Opening the window to cool the room, she paced from the window to the Virginia Woolf poster then back again. Heyu shifted from paw to paw at the bedroom door.

"Heyu, I'm not going to do this. I *won't* do this," she exclaimed. "If he thinks that I'm going to stay in this flea-trap town—darning socks—and—and—driving to doctors' appointments—and—well—I'll fix his little red wagon and have him committed to the old folks' home." Grabbing all the pillows from the bed, she threw them across the room, one at a time.

Things were getting out of hand. The events of the last two days had jumped onto the pile that was already smothering her old life; the life of going anywhere she wanted whenever she pleased. That life, Iris was afraid to admit, was leaving her behind.

Chapter 8

The few blocks that residents referred to as uptown rested atop a small plateau. English explorer Robert Fallam called the place Mt Pleasant for its panoramic views of the rolling green hills and the Blue Ridge Mountains to the west. Lately the smoothness of the hills had become scarred with Southern suburban encroachment of crowded housing developments and ubiquitous, flat-topped warehouses touting bargains Fallam County folks never knew they needed.

As the county seat for Fallam County, Mt Pleasant hosted the courthouse square. The courthouse and town municipal buildings fronted the southeast side of Court Street while the Bailey Building and the town library bookended a string of single-story law offices on the north side. Court Street terminated in front of the courthouse square at Main Street. Across Main Street and due west were The Early Riser Café, Fallam Community Bank, Fallam County Hospital, and The Shops at Mt Pleasant. With bright yellow crime scene tape crisscrossed over the doors of the New To You shop for all of Fallam County to see, the Shops was now tenantless.

As in many small Southern towns, a lone stone soldier stood high on a pedestal in front of the towering granite courthouse, memorializing the veterans of the War of Northern Aggression. At the age of ten, Iris had learned from Judge Bailey, Jonnie's dad, that a local hero Confederate General Jubal A. Early had donated the funds for the statue. As she waited for the light to change at Court and Main Streets, Iris peered up at the sentry, recalling a few years back when she had seen the exact same statue while vacationing in Vermont. However, the Vermont version bestowed praises to the bravery of the soldiers who fought during The Great Rebellion of 1861.

Catty-corner to the lone soldier was uptown's only surviving eatery, The Early Riser, established in the 1920s and named for the general. By day the café catered to lawyers and their clients, court clerks, reporters, municipal office workers, and law enforcement types. When court was in session, it was packed wall-to-wall with defendants and their families waiting for the hour they would walk across Main Street to recite their excuses in front of a judge.

Lee Properties owned the building, but the café was owned and operated by Chunky Brown, who lived on the second floor with his black labs Homer and King. Inside, the place looked like a time capsule representing each decade of the building's existence. The 1920s style high ceilings, covered in years of cooking oil mist and dust, caused the patrons' chatter to rattle and bounce off the walls. The worn-down Formica bar and swivel stools were from the 1950s. Hanging from the tin ceiling were various cardboard cut-outs of life-sized NASCAR drivers and football helmets. Over the bar hovered Chunky's prized possession, the bar's talisman and symbol of what was all good in America, a neon Budweiser sign.

By night the place became Chunky's, a virtual coliseum where locals from all parts of town and county came to sip the golden nectar and watch sports gladiators on the surround sound, satellite-fed monster TV in the back. While worshiping at the altar of cable TV and drinking from the communal tap, patrons turned their backs to the courthouse sentry and all it represented and pretended for a while that the vestiges of the Confederate heritage of slavery and lost causes were finally forgiven and forgotten.

"Look what the cat done drug in. Hey Iris!" Wearing a grease-stained cook's apron over his Dallas Cowboys jersey, Chunky fanned at grill smoke behind the bar.

"Chunky, good to see ya. My friend here would like water, straight up, and I'll have a cup of the high-test."

"That's a good lookin' seein'-eye dog you got there Iris," he laughed and motioned both of them over to a tiny table tucked next to the end of the bar and under the café's front window. Standing at the end of the counter and serving Iris a cup of coffee, Chunky asked, "How long y'all in town for?"

"Few days. Guess you heard about the drug scandal," she remarked as her nose acclimated to the hints of sour beer and bleach.

"What? Do I look like I live under a rock?" Chunky grinned big, his eyes disappearing. "That's all anybody's talking about."

While sipping her coffee, a Manhattan number lit up the display on her phone. Confirming it wasn't Lace, she let it go to voice mail and laid the phone back on the table. She watched Jonnie cross Main Street and enter the café.

"Over here." Iris waved to Jonnie.

"Good morning. What? Chunky's greasy eggs over Miss Bert's breakfast buffet?" Jonnie joked as she looked down at Iris and Heyu.

"I'm giving Heyu the walking tour of big uptown Mt Pleasant. Tomorrow we'll do downtown." She motioned for Jonnie to sit.

"Can't. I'm meeting a client," Jonnie said over the restaurant noise. She waved at two banker types across the room.

As Iris leaned sideways to look around Jonnie for a peek at the clients, she said, "Miss Bert has announced that she's retiring and running away to Ohio with her uncle."

Looking up at Jonnie, she said, "Can you see Miss Bert driving through West Virginia?" Iris imitated a surprised Bert griping a steering wheel on a sharp, downhill grade. "Maybe we could ask Morgan Freeman to drive her up there."

"Iris, they're waiting for me. I'll talk to you later."

Did Jonnie just blow her off? With envy, she watched as Jonnie extended her hand to the first gentleman. Iris missed the corporate camaraderie, late-night preparations, and the rush of early-morning pitches, the business of haggling, then winning. She hoped that those days were not over for her. She checked her voice mail; the mystery Manhattan caller hadn't left a message.

Glancing out the window, her eyes briefly met with those of another Early Riser patron as he reached for the café door. Somehow he seemed familiar to her but she wasn't sure why.

"Great balls of Bacchus, Heyu. Who is that?" She breathed in softly. She knew the type. This guy was unaware of the affect his presence had on others. He caused women to daydream and men to pine for their youth. Dark curly locks framed his tan and smooth Romanesque face. His illuminating blue-green eyes were trusting, the kind of eyes that gaze at a woman and appreciate not just the beauty of her naked glory but her secret self, the one hidden and rarely revealed. Those eyes caused Iris to shiver.

His workman's coveralls, zipped down to his narrow waist, exposed a clean, white T-shirt. Iris noticed that the tee was stretched tight across the young man's chest. Like most Fallam County laborers, his boots were caked with mud. The mud was hard and dense, like a potter's clay, and dark red as in the passions of the heart; passions this man could instill in any woman if ever he had a need for it.

A long stride got him to the counter in two steps. Iris heard him order breakfast to go. While he waited for his egg biscuits, he sipped coffee and watched the morning news on the TV over the bar. As she took in his regal profile, Iris's notion of fair play caught up with her lusty yearnings. *Get a grip, Mrs. Robinson. He's waaaay too young for you.*

As if hearing her thoughts, the young man turned to face her; he smiled shyly and self-consciously tugged at the soul patch below his chapped lower lip. Iris slowly savored the last few drops of her cold, bitter coffee.

# Chapter 9

"We're having company for dinner tonight," Iris announced as Mr. Henry entered through the mudroom door, returning from his usual Saturday visit to Elder Home where most of his poker buddies now resided. "Jonnie Bailey is bringing over someone for us to meet."

Earlier in the day, Jonnie called to say she'd found someone interested in the housekeeper's position. Ethan Quinn's son Vinnie and daughter-in-law Ludie had left Santa Fe in a hurry and landed on his doorstep. Quinn had managed to get Vinnie on as a carpenter's helper at Smith Mountain Lake but Ludie was still looking for work. Iris was surprised when Jonnie conveyed that the new chief of police had married, fathered a son then divorced before moving back to Mt Pleasant to care for his parents. The thought that others went on to lead their own lives in spite of no longer being involved in hers rarely occurred to Iris.

"She's my replacement," Bert added as she wiped her flour-covered hands on her apron.

"I told you all that I will not allow strangers in my house," Mr. Henry snapped. He shuffled over to the kitchen table where Iris had been trolling the Internet on her laptop. "Elevator broke down at Elder Home again. Had to take the stairs." After he tossed the day's mail on the table, he draped his leather car coat, a gift from Elizabeth on the occasion of his fortieth birthday, over a kitchen chair, then eased himself into it.

Leaning over the butcher's block, Bert narrowed her eyes and asked, "You feeling OK, Mr. Henry?"

"I expect I ought to eat something. I'll have a cup of coffee and a piece of last night's cornbread to tide me over 'til the dinner hour." He rubbed the knotty joints in his sallow hands then sorted the day's mail on the table.

"Don't you want to know who the person is?" Iris asked as she slammed her laptop shut. She was determined to get her way in the matter of hiring someone to help Bert.

"No, because they're not working in this house. People will rob you blind if you give them room to do so," Mr. Henry said.

"Look, I'm not going to argue with you about this," she said. "It's already settled. I'm hiring Ludie Quinn, Chief Quinn's daughter-in-law, to help us out." Sliding her pen behind her ear, she collected her laptop and sauntered past him and up the back stairs, leaving Bert on her own to prepare for the evening's guests.

Standing in the foyer, Jonnie introduced a gaunt young woman. "Iris, Mr. Henry, this is Ludie Quinn. She's interested in helping you with the housekeeping."

"Nice to meet you, Ludie." Iris reached for the woman's hand; what she got felt like the phalanges on the high school biology skeleton. Iris watched as Mr. Henry sized up the woman's Goodwill couture of a too large dress-suit with jumbo shoulder pads and three-inch heels. Not extending his hand, he merely offered a sharp nod and grunt.

"Mr. Henry, Ludie and Vinnie moved to Mt Pleasant a year ago. Did I get that right, Ludie?" Jonnie encouraged Ludie to offer information about herself.

"Yes ma'am. We got married in New Mexico and decided to move back east to be with Vinnie's dad," Ludie rasped with her smoker's voice. She raked her stringy brown hair behind her right ear and paused as she bought her jittery hand to her mouth as if to take a hit on a cigarette.

"Welcome to Grove House, Ludie. Please join us for dinner." Iris swept her arm with a grand gesture toward the dining room where Bert was helping Elizabeth into her

49

chair. "I'm glad you could come for dinner. Having company is the only way I can get Miss Bert to make chicken pot pie," Iris said, hiding her sarcasm. Since Iris's return home, Bert had managed to serve chicken "something" every single night.

During an hour of courteous interrogation, Iris and Bert pulled from Ludie that she was born in Ohio, which scored high marks with Bert, and that her extensive resume in domestic labor included: barista, motel maid, diner waitress, and trail cook.

"Wow," Iris exclaimed, "with all that experience I'd say you're well qualified to run our household." Not wanting Mr. Henry to contradict her assessments of Ludie's skills, Iris quickly offered, "We'd love for you to join us. Can you start on Monday?"

"Hold on, missy," Mr. Henry objected. "What about a background check? Didn't this whole mess at The Shops teach you anything?" Iris noticed that his head started bobbing side-to-side like it did the day of Chief Quinn's interview.

Iris lifted her water glass and nodded at Jonnie. The entire dinner party eyeballed the attorney, patiently waiting for her to say something profound, something that would satisfy all parties, injured or otherwise.

"Mr. Henry," Jonnie spoke for the first time since dinner began. "I can vouch for Ludie. She and her husband are living at Ethan Quinn's farm. Consider me as a reference."

Looking directly at Ludie, Mr. Henry pounded his fist on the table and barked, "Do you do drugs, young lady?" Every woman at the table jumped.

Elizabeth emitted a quivering "Oh my." Then the room fell silent.

"No, sir," Ludie peeped. She looked at Jonnie for affirmation then stared at her untouched chicken dinner.

"Don't yell at our dinner guest like that! It's rude," Iris interjected angrily. The room was silent for the second time. "Besides, isn't Jonnie's word good enough for you?"

His voice rose to match hers. "She could be Quinn's or Bobby Kaluchi's spy for all I know. Let this woman, a total stranger, come in this house and—"

"Now you're just being paranoid. Why do you always expect the worst from people?" Iris interrupted him. More silence. "This is really about not letting your daughter run things, isn't it? Why can't you trust me to help out? Is it because I'm not a son? I'm just a stupid girl—"

"Perhaps it's time for us to go, Ludie," Jonnie quietly suggested. And as she and Ludie stood, she said, "Miss Bert, thank you for the lovely dinner. Mr. and Mrs. Lee, nice to see you again. Iris could you see us to the door, please?"

"But Jonnie, ya'll ain't staying for dessert? I made your favorite. Banana pudding with marshmallows," Bert pleaded. As Iris got up from the table, she patted a worried Bert on the back and followed the departing guests into the foyer.

"That blew up in our faces," Iris admitted. "Don't take what he says personally; he does it to everybody. When can you start?"

"I don't know, Miss Lee. I'll have to think about it," Ludie mewled.

"Ludie, can you wait in the car for me?" Jonnie asked then she turned on her friend. "Iris, it is amazing to me that you got as far as you did in this world. Did you hear yourself in there?" Jonnie was pointing toward the dining room. Iris had never seen Jonnie this angry.

"But he was bullying her—" Iris sounded like a teenager negotiating a lighter punishment.

"He's an old man who doesn't know what he's saying half the time. What's your excuse?"

"I'm tired of listening to his pettiness. All my life he berated and belittled me just like he was trying to do to Ludie. It's why I stayed away," Iris said.

"When are you going to move on? You think your daddy never loved you. Boo-hoo. Get over it!" Jonnie excitedly whispered. "It's time for you to grow up and treat your father with the dignity and respect you seem to think he never gave you." Jonnie hurriedly put on her jacket. "I'll see if I can work a miracle and convince Ludie to come work for you. Good night." For the first time in a long time, Jonnie racked up the last word, leaving Iris staring at a closed door.

Later that night on the back porch off the kitchen, Iris scrolled through a sea of junk email on her phone. She fished out a letter from Nexdorf Group. Six months of her life wasted, and all she got was a lousy machine-generated rejection letter.

Calling Lace again for what seemed to her the hundredth time, she jabbed at her phone harder than was necessary, only to receive a message telling her that the mailbox she was trying to reach was full.

That night, to the bedroom ceiling, she tallied up all of her miseries. One, like a cheating husband, the life she had built over the last twenty years had dumped her and showed no signs of ever having known her. Two, she was being forced to administer CPR to a relationship with her crabby, loveless father. Three, the one that hurt her most, she had disappointed her big sister Jonnie, the one person in Mt Pleasant who might still believe in her. She felt trapped with no options for escape.

Chapter 10

Before Manny left for his overseas assignment, Iris
agreed, at his request, to attend Sunday Mass with him.
Later at brunch she cracked that the place where she grew
up probably had more Protestant churches per square mile
than any other county in the state.

As the oldest church in town, Mt Pleasant Methodist
Church held bragging rights to having the largest
congregation in the county. Built with timber and tobacco
money, the striking two-story brick and stone building and
bell tower greeted every traveler who entered the town.

Sunday morning church was for finding out who drank
too much on Saturday night, Mr. Henry always said. While
her fraternal grandparents, and later her mother, had
claimed their allegiance to the Methodists' lot and donated
much time and money to the church's causes, Mr. Henry
had reserved his adult church-going to his own wedding
and family funerals.

On their morning trek Iris and Heyu waded through
unmowed weeds and trash at the backside of Matilda Park.
As they crested the small hill which hosted the church and
the town's final resting place, Mt Pleasant Cemetery, they
heard the church's electronic bells calling the eight o'clock
worshippers to service. Merging onto the sidewalk with the
late arrivals sprinting for the sanctuary, Iris heard someone
call her name.

"Iris Lee? Is that you?" A voice from behind her called.
She turned around while Heyu kept walking. With the sun
in her eyes, a large silhouette towered over her. The hem of
a shower curtain-sized choir robe whipped in the light
breeze kicked up by passing cars.

"Got to keep moving," Iris said, walking backwards.
She pointed at Heyu who was getting rock star attention

from a crew of pre-teens. "I have to keep him out of trouble. He might mistake a Methodist for a tree." She turned back around and picked up her pace.

"A bunch of us always meet for brunch after service. You remember Barbara Roberts, our homecoming queen? She's back in town. She married some guy from Wisconsin; she's Barbara Carson now. Besides, I need to talk to you about your dad's property."

Hearing the last comment, Iris instantly matched the voice to its owner, the town's mayor Robert Lorenzo "Kooch" Kaluchi, Fallam County High School's Class President of 1982.

Back in the 1960s Mayor Kaluchi's mother, nee Dalphine Hodges, married a guy who moved to Fallam County from New Jersey. Other than the Methodist ministers who rotated every few years, Kooch's dad was one of very few persons to immigrate into the county.

While in the public school system, Kooch's insecurities from being born a Virginian without the benediction of a Virginia name escalated. The other kids teased him unmercifully, calling him Hoochie-Koochie or Koochie-Koochie or Kootie Bug. By the time he reached college, he had settled on "Kooch" Kaluchi and felt that the name would serve him in business and in politics.

Once at a mutual friend's wedding, Kooch confided in Iris his life's goals: state senator, governor then U.S. senator. Apparently his political career was off to a slow start as he was currently mayor of a small town, an appointed, part-time position.

"Well?" Kooch called after her. "When can we talk?"

With her back to him, she shouted, "Call me," then picked up the pace.

Iris and Heyu followed the Main Street sidewalk south and found their way to the lone soldier in the town square.

She noticed Jonnie's car parked in front of the Bailey Building.

"Good," she said to Heyu, "I can pop in and apologize again about last night. Ask her if she knows who that hunky guy is I saw at The Early Riser the other day." She dialed Jonnie's office number on her phone. "Hi, I'm at the front door. Can you let me in?"

"I'm working on a case. I have to be in court in Roanoke first thing tomorrow morning. I don't have much time to spare." A buzzing sound came from the front glass doors. "Come on up, I'm in the apartment."

When Jonnie and Wyatt renovated their father's law offices, they built a small efficiency on the third floor, jokingly referring to it as the penthouse. And, because both lived in remote parts of the county, it came in handy for all-night trial preparations, which were common.

"I promise I won't take long," Iris called out as she took the stairs in twos. She pulled up a chair at the kitchenette table as Heyu searched for a water bowl. "I'm sorry about how I handled things last night."

"I talked with Ludie in the car when I drove her home. She'll work at Grove House under two conditions. One, it's a trial for two weeks. And, two, she doesn't take orders from Mr. Henry." Jonnie shoved her reading glasses on top of her head and rubbed her eyes.

"Done!" Iris exclaimed. Her excitement caused Heyu to swing his hips side to side, nearly lifting his hind legs off the floor. "Can she start tomorrow?"

"Here's her phone number. And Iris, I don't think it's Mr. Henry she's afraid of. Take it down about three notches when you talk to her."

"I'll try. Can we talk about Lee Properties for a minute?" Iris asked.

"You've got ten minutes then I'm kicking you out, kiddo." Still in her PJ's, Jonnie went into the bathroom to change.

"I ran into Kooch Kaluchi on the way over here. What happened to him? He blew up like a Thanksgiving Day balloon. I didn't recognize him."

"Is there a question about Lee Properties in there somewhere?" Jonnie called from the bathroom.

"He said he wanted to talk to me about dad's property. What's their plan?"

"After losing the bid for the Crooked Road Music Trail's eastern entrance to Franklin County, our mayor and the county supervisors are trying to figure out how to ride their coattails," Jonnie said. "Your pop owns a lot of what the mayor calls undeveloped potential and he wants it so he can build a performing arts and culture center."

"A performing arts center," Iris snorted, "in Mt Pleasant? That's entertaining."

"Don't be so condescending. Besides, selling The Shops could help Mr. Henry with his cash flow challenges."

"He told me he doesn't want to sell. Does Lee Properties have a cash flow problem?" Iris asked.

"Haven't you been reading the financial reports I've been sending?" Jonnie emerged from the bathroom dressed for Sunday desk time.

"I've been kind of busy with my own cash flow problems. I haven't had a real job in two years."

"*If* you had taken the thirty minutes it takes to review them—and you have less than six minutes left by the way—you would have discovered that last year was not kind to Lee Properties. It's barely breaking even. Owes Uncle Sam, Cousin Virginia, and Mt Pleasant back taxes." Jonnie scooped up her laptop from the table.

"Taxes! Mr. Henry isn't paying his taxes?" Iris screeched. Heyu barked. And they both tumbled down the stairs behind Jonnie.

"Refuses," Jonnie said. "Claims they're all leeches who want to steal his hard-earned money to buy cell phones for lazy people who don't want to work. You didn't see the note in my last report?"

"Come on. He's got to pay his taxes."

"Yes, he does. And, as his attorney and business manager, I've advised him on several occasions that if he doesn't, he's subject to fines, penalties and jail time."

"That's all we need, an IRS audit. What did he say when you told him to pay his taxes?"

"'They can throw my bony white hind-parts in jail for all I care.' That's a direct quote. Oh, and he's refusing to pay his attorney. I haven't been paid for twelve months. There's a nice young man next door who just started practicing. Perhaps he can take Mr. Henry on as a client."

Standing at the front doors of the firm, Jonnie added "Your ten minutes are up. Time for you to go." Jonnie raised her hand and made a shooing motion toward Iris.

"Get serious. How are we going to solve this?" Iris asked anxiously.

"I am serious. I have obligations to my business and my partners. Until Lee Properties pays its past due bills, I can't work for it. I have paying clients who require my attention."

"But Jonnie, can't you just take care of it?" Iris pleaded. Once her fingerprints found their way on a paper copy of the reports, she'd own the problem of what to do with Lee Properties, which translated into getting stuck in Mt Pleasant for all eternity.

Jonnie's laugh echoed in the empty reception area. "No, I can't just take care of it, I'd be disbarred. Get Mr. Henry

to give you power of attorney and pay us. Now get out of
here. And let me know how things go with Ludie," Jonnie
said before she closed and locked the front doors.

Iris didn't appreciate Jonnie's laughter, it sounded like
she was enjoying Iris's predicament a little too much.
Getting the keys to Buckingham Palace would be easier
than convincing Mr. Henry to give her power of attorney.

As she turned on to Grove and started for the house, she
snapped her fingers. "Dag it, Heyu, why didn't you remind
me to ask Jonnie if she knows that hunky Mr. Early Riser?"

The next morning the Grove House doorbell chimed
exactly at nine a.m. Immediately afterward, the door was
assaulted with heavy pounding.

"Hold your water," Iris shouted. When she opened the
door, she found Ludie Quinn, gnawing at her fingernails.

"I didn't hear the doorbell. Wasn't sure it was
working." Ludie stooped to pick up her maid's bucket.
Squaring her shoulders, she stood tall in her new blinding-
white sneakers, reporting for her first day of work.

"We're up in Mom's room sorting through some old
clothes. Leave that stuff here and follow me," Iris said.

"'Mornin'!" Bert greeted Ludie as she and Iris entered
Elizabeth's bedroom. Iris turned to Elizabeth, who was
clutching the bed's footboard to keep her balance, "Mom
do you remember Ludie from dinner the other night? She's
come to help us." Iris cringed as she realized she'd just
asked her mother to remember something.

"She's come to help us? Help us do what?" a confused
Elizabeth whimpered.

"Today she's going to be our fashion consultant and
help us decide which of these forty-five black skirts should
go to the dress consignment store downtown." Iris pointed
to the black mountain of fabric on the high bed. Ludie's
buggy eyes followed the pile toward the ceiling.

"Mom, I bet every piece of clothing you ever made or bought is in that closet."

"What do you want me to do?" asked Ludie.

Thus, Elizabeth watched with uncertainty while the other three women gutted the sizable closet of its shoes, clothes, hats, pocketbooks, coats—one mink, a tattered lampshade, department store boxes filled with received Christmas cards and letters from friends and family, several bags of half-finished knitting and crochet projects, and a rattan bird cage.

"You probably want to go through all the pockets and handbags before you take them away," Ludie suggested. "A friend of mine found five hundred dollars in a handbag she bought at a Goodwill store."

Following Ludie's advice, the women found cash, crumpled handkerchiefs, folded church bulletins and playbills, lipstick tubes, and long-forgotten lost mates to earrings. The last article of clothing to be checked for pocket bootie was Elizabeth's full-length mink coat.

Iris slipped it on and said to her mom, "How do I look?" She went to Elizabeth's dressing mirror and turned the coat's collar up. Standing on her tiptoes, she turned from side to side pretending she was at the end of a Paris fashion runway.

"It fits you real nice," Bert offered. "Might want to shorten the sleeves." She stood behind Iris, looking in the mirror with her. Ludie and Elizabeth rubbed the arms of the coat, feeling its plush velvety texture.

"Mom, remember when you used to wear this to PTA meetings. I think the other ladies were a bit jealous." Iris stuffed her hands into the pockets and turned to go the other direction on the imaginary runway. "Wait a sec," she said staring at the ceiling. "What have we here?" In contrast to the smooth satin lining, she felt a coarse fabric

59

in the right pocket wrapped around something hard like a block of wood. She pulled it from the pocket. "What's this?" They all stared down at a stiff, discolored linen handkerchief. One corner of the hemmed fabric had the embroidered letters "JAE."

"Mom, who is JAE?"

Elizabeth looked as clueless and as curious as Bert and Ludie. Still wearing the mink coat, Iris forged a path through piles of clothes to the windows. The others followed behind anxious that they might miss out on important developments.

In the afternoon light Iris unbundled the swatch while the other detectives looked on. Nestled in the cloth was a faded burgundy velvet-covered box, the type used for fine jewelry such as a pearl necklace.

Iris handed the handkerchief to Bert. She examined all four sides of the case for clues as to its origins—nothing. The tiny rusted hinges gave up a hoarse groan as she opened the box. For a long quiet moment, her eyes saw the content, but her brain wasn't entirely sure of what it was seeing. Somehow the thing inside just didn't look like it belonged with the box, a mismatched set.

# Chapter 11

With Bert and Ludie hovering around her, Iris marveled at what lay inside the jeweler's box. She lifted the glittering ornament by its wide blue and red grosgrain ribbon, stained with watermarks and unraveling in places. As it unfolded, the ribbon gave up the faintest scents of mold and sweat. In contrast to the frayed ribbon, the oversized pendant winked and sparkled from its clusters of jewels or rhinestones, Iris couldn't tell which. The square and round cut stones were framed in heavy gold-pronged settings and together the mounts formed the shape of an eight-point Maltese-styled cross. To Iris only its creator could have loved the thing, it was gaudy. But, at the same time, as she held it in her palm, she felt dominance and power in its weight. She dangled it higher and the sun shone through the large crimson center. A garnet? The smaller clear stones cast prisms of light around the room. Iris counted twenty-nine stones in all.

"Glory day," Ludie whispered.

"Christ on a stick," Iris swore softly.

Elizabeth wandered over to Iris's side to get a closer look at the dancing lights.

"That's the necklace Mr. Henry gave Elizabeth for their wedding anniversary one year," Bert volunteered. "She never wore it though. She thought it was ugly."

"I told Henry I wasn't going to wear that thing because it looks like something a man would wear." Elizabeth surprised everybody. When they turned to face her, she rubbed her hands together as if she was washing them. "That's how I feel about that."

"She's right," Ludie said. "I wouldn't wear it to the Christmas dance."

Twirling it in the sunlight again, Iris mused in a hypnotic trance. "It looks like some type of medallion."

She pointed at the linen swath, which Bert had folded and held in her hand, and asked her mother again, "And who is J A E?"

"Who?" Elizabeth asked. Iris looked into her mother's eyes and saw her slipping away again. She put the medallion back in the box and hugged her mother. To her surprise, her mother wrapped her skinny arms around Iris's waist. Iris buried her face in the hair atop her mother's head to hide her tears and to catch her breath. "I love you," she said for the first time since she was a little girl. She tried to remember why it had always been so hard to say those words.

Later that day, after all the closet donations had been packed into Iris's car for a Goodwill delivery, the four women convened around the jewelry case on top of the butcher's block.

"If these stones are real, this thing is worth a lot of money. Until I can figure out what it is and where it came from, let's just keep it to ourselves," Iris commanded. Ludie and Bert nodded vigorously. "Miss Bert do you know if anybody else knows about it?"

"No, I don't, not living anyway." Bert straightened the collar on her dress. "Elizabeth told me it belonged to one of your Granddaddy Allen's law clients, and they never came back to get it. You might want to ask Mr. Henry."

"Where is he?" Iris asked reaching for another homemade sugar cookie.

"Sweet pea, it's Monday. Your daddy goes over to the farm on Monday afternoons. He'll be home in an hour or so." Bert brushed crumbs from the counter into her hand.

"Do you need me for anything else today?" Ludie backed into a kitchen chair and it crashed onto the floor.

"Nope, we'll see you tomorrow," Iris said. "What do you say, Miss Bert? Tomorrow we take on the dining room?"

"Whatever you say, sweet pea, you're the boss now." Bert's dentures clicked.


After dinner and dish drying, Iris stepped lightly into the library. "What are you reading?" she asked as she sat down in the chair next to Mr. Henry's.

"A story about a man who survived the Japanese POW camps." He lifted a book from his lap to show her the cover. "When I was in California in 1950, I read about this man in their local papers."

Iris noticed her father's hands trembling. "I didn't know you were ever in California. How long were you there?"

"About a year.    They were about to ship me out to Ko-rea, but I got called home. Your Aunt M. Ellen had died. I had to come home to look after your grandmother."

"I didn't know the military granted discharges for the death of a sibling." Iris challenged his comment.

"My father had a lot of pull with a certain congressman." He stared into the empty fireplace. Then he said, "I was the only person who could console my mother. So, I was sent for. She was never the same after we lost M. Ellen."

As he continued to stare at the cold and dusty fireplace bricks, Iris noticed an unfamiliar expression on Mr. Henry's pale face. She wondered if he regretted leaving a life in California or still mourned the loss of a beloved sister. In all the years they had shared, he never once confided in her on such matters. In a tender voice, she said, "You must have loved your sister very much."

He raised his eyes to the portrait over the fireplace but said nothing.

"Miss Bert, Ludie and I cleaned out Mom's closet today." Iris changed the subject.

"I'm telling you hiring that girl is a mistake. You'll regret it. She'll rob us blind."

"I'll keep an eye on her. We found this." Iris extended the jewel case for Mr. Henry to examine. "Miss Bert says you gave it to Mom for an anniversary gift and that it belonged to a client of Granddaddy Allen's."

Henry did not take the offered case.

"Bert Taylor should stick to housekeeping instead of gossiping about things she knows nothing about," Mr. Henry grumbled.

"Is she right? Did this belong to a client?"

"Before my father died, he gave it to me. He said that he wanted me to have it. A client of his gave it to him for payment of services," Mr. Henry said.

"Can you prove that it was given to him?" Iris asked.

"What is it with you people? A man's word isn't good enough? I said that Allen Lee gave it to me. He said it was given to him for payment of legal fees. End of discussion."

After a long pause and much staring into the empty fireplace by both, Iris said, "Speaking of legal fees, do you plan to pay Jonnie Bailey for the work her firm's doing for Lee Properties?"

"She's billing me for bad advice. I don't pay for bad advice," Mr. Henry reasoned.

"What part of 'pay your taxes or you'll go to jail' do you consider bad advice?" Iris felt her temper stir.

"She wants me to sell The Shops to pay taxes. What's happening to this country? Selling capital assets to pay taxes." Mr. Henry mounted his high horse. "I refuse to participate in a system that encourages laziness. And, frankly, I pay her to represent my interests, not to side with the other man. That's a conflict of interest."

"That's rich, Mr. Henry. Jonnie colluding with the evil taxman."

"You think you know everything, don't you, missy? You think you're smarter than your old man. She represents the town in half a dozen projects. It only takes a short hop to see where she's going with this notion of telling me to sell my property. She gets a kickback from the town for convincing me to sell."

"Kickback!" Iris raised her voice as she stood and faced her old man, "How dare you question Jonnie Bailey's integrity! She's the most ethical person I know. She'd never do anything illegal for financial gain. She told me that if you don't pay your bill, you're going to have to take your business to another firm. Is that what you want?"

Mr. Henry thought about Iris's question. "She can't fire me," he continued. "I'm the client. I'll take her to court for breach of contract."

Iris exploded. "OK, Clarence Darrow, you think that any court of law would agree with you? To withhold payment from a business that's provided you services?" She paused to check his reaction. "Mr. Henry, you've got to pay your taxes or we'll lose everything, not just The Shops but the farm, this house, all the other properties. You want to put Mom and Miss Bert out in the street? Is that what you want?"

A loud rush of silence filled Iris's ears as she placed one hand on the mantle and the other on her hip. Neither she nor Mr. Henry spoke for what seemed to her an eternity. At first she felt guilty for yelling at a helpless old man. But then she realized that he was staring at her with that all too familiar expression of disdain.

"Do what you want," she said. "But if you don't pay Jonnie, you're a fool and you'll lose the only advocate you have in this town. One with any brains." Climbing the front steps to her bedroom she felt a sudden liberation from her father's judgments. *I can't believe I just called my father a fool. What's he going to do? Send me to my room?*

The next morning, after giving Ludie her cleaning instructions, Iris convinced Bert to take Elizabeth to Elmer's, the beauty parlor downtown.

Sitting at the beat-up study desk her parents had purchased from a school board property sale, she laughed and said to Heyu, "I've come a long way, baby." The desk's surface was barely wide enough for her laptop and a cup of coffee. She decided that it was time to rethink her job search campaign. Lace had to go. She dialed his private number at his downtown office.

"Barbour Career Management Consultants," a woman answered.

"Lace Barbour, please." Iris thought it odd that someone else was answering Lace's private office number.

After what seemed like enough time to find Lace and get him to the phone, a man answered, "I'm sorry but Mr. Barbour isn't in right now. May I ask who's calling?"

"This is Iris Lee. I'm returning *his* call from last week."

"May I ask why he was calling you?" the man asked.

"You may, but I'm sure he knows why he called me. Who are you?" Iris hated nosy assistants.

"I'm Mr. Barbour's brother-in-law, Marvin Sheppard." The man offered nothing else.

"Why are you screening Lace's business calls?" First Lace was ignoring her calls to his cell phone, and now he wasn't answering his office phone. Was he avoiding her? Did he play a part in her not getting selected for the Nexdorf gig?

"When was the last time you spoke with him?" the man asked.

"He and I spoke about a week ago. Lace was supposed to get back to me on something. He left a message on my phone, and I haven't heard hide nor hair of him since."
*Hide nor hair, Iris? Really? I've got to get out of this place.*

"Did he say anything else? Like where he was? What he was doing?"

"No, just 'hey babe'—I hate that by the way—and 'call me back.' What's this all about? Where's Lace? The guy owes me" Iris demanded.

"Ms. Lee, all I can tell you is that Lace is not here. He's disappeared. His family is worried." The man's voice almost cracked.

"Holy sky fairy," Iris responded. "Have you notified the police?"

"Yes, they're investigating. I'm sorry to be so vague, I know he thought a lot of you, but the police have told us not to give out any information." And after a pause, he said, "Look if he contacts you again, tell him to call his wife. She's really worried about him." He gave Iris a phone number and hung up.

Iris sat at the small school desk thinking about what she just heard. She dialed another number.

"Trust Department, Betty Kitter," answered a self-assured voice.

"Betty, I need a favor."

"Iris! How are you?" Betty seemed sincerely happy to hear from her old boss. They had started at the bank the same year, the same day they later discovered. While Iris rose into the senior management ranks, Betty had preferred to stay on the front line in first-level management, allowing her more time for her family and home life.

"Listen, I know you're busy, so I'll keep this short. Have you heard any gossip on Nexdorf or Lace Barbour and Nexdorf?" Iris and Betty had dubbed the whispers among the rank and file "The Vine." It anteed up the best intelligence on who was getting dropped, who was moving up, and who was misbehaving with whom. Iris was fishing to see if Lace's disappearance had hit The Vine yet.

"I heard last week that your old boss, Sandy Summers is leaving to go over there. The Vine says he's being forced out here. Everybody's still wondering why the board allowed him to fire you. What's going on?" Betty asked.

"Don't know. Have you heard from Lace lately?" Without Lace calling her back, something felt hinky about the Nexdorf fiasco.

"I haven't heard anything. Why?"

"No reason. I'm trying to reach him, and he's not at his office," Iris responded.

"Anything you want to share?"

"Keep it off The Vine, OK?" Iris entrusted Betty with all of her corporate secrets. "Nexdorf has been courting me for the last six months for a senior VP slot. Everybody wanted to take me home to meet the folks. Last week Lace set up an interview for me with their COO who does a one-eighty on me, and now I can't find Lace."

"Goodness. Sounds like the COO brought in Summers and didn't tell his HR about it."

"That's what it's looking like to me too. Hey! Change of subject. Is Fred still at Sotheby's?"

"Yes, he's now in charge of early-twentieth-century paintings." Betty bragged.

"Wow! Can you give me his number? I might have some business for his firm."

Hanging up the phone, Iris scratched behind Heyu's ear. His back paw thumped on the floor.

"Buddy, I think Betty's on to something. Where in the blazes is Lace?"

# Chapter 12

"Heyu, let's go get a bowl of Chunky's chili for lunch. Maybe we'll run into The Early Riser man again." Iris pressed the send button on the last email for the day. Her new job search strategy was to bludgeon her business associates with "top-five" business tips.

Her other task for the day was to send Fred Kitter at Sotheby's a picture of the mysterious medallion. He said he'd forward her request to their jewelry and artifacts department.

In times like these Iris wished that Mr. Henry and Elizabeth came from larger families. Everyone else in Fallam County seemed to have no shortage of aunts, uncles, and cousins to draw upon when it came to questions about family history and heirlooms. Finding this medallion or broach or whatever the hell the thing was had prompted Iris to think about her parents' past. Until yesterday she didn't know Mr. Henry had been stationed in California or that his Army tour had been cut short. As far as she knew, aside from the four years at The University in Charlottesville and his Army tour, he had spent his entire life right here in Fallam County. And her mother never talked about her family except for her distant cousin Junie Marks, who owned a jewelry store in Roanoke.

Suddenly, a noisy crash rose from the first floor. Racing down the stairs, Iris and Heyu heard a string of foul utterances conjoined with the names of the Lord and the Virgin Mary, the likes of which should never be heard again by another living soul. The sounds were so guttural that Heyu turned tail and hiked back up the stairs. Ignoring Heyu's retreat, Iris rushed into the dining room to discover Ludie on the floor with a brass chandelier clutched in her fists and a ladder tangled in her legs. Her face was turning purple.

"Ludie!" Iris called. "Are you OK?"

"I think so," Ludie said as she lay stiffly on the floor, not moving and hanging on to the light fixture as if she was taking a left turn on a race track.

"You can let go of the light now." Iris pried it from her hands. "You feel any pain anywhere?"

With his head slunk low, Heyu peered around the corner of the dining room entranceway. He stood shaking and ready for another retreat if necessary.

Iris said to Ludie, "Should we call an ambulance?"

"No! No ambulances," Ludie objected. "We don't have in-surance. Can't afford a ride in an ambulance."

"Don't worry about that right now," Iris assured her. She looked up at the dangling electrical cables. "Can you feel your toes?"

"Of course I can feel them." A second string of words Iris didn't even know existed foamed from Ludie's mouth, then, silence and the tic-tic-tic of paw nails. Heyu was running up the stairs again.

"If you feel that way about it, I'd say you're OK," Iris laughed. "What happened?"

"I was trying to dust around the top of the big candle-lier and I lost my balance and the ladder fell over and I tried to hang on to the candle-lier." Ludie started to cry. "Oh, Miss Lee, are you going to fire me?"

"Ludie, I'll make a deal with you. I won't fire you if you promise not to sue me."

Ludie started crying again. "But what about Mr. Henry? He's going to be mad, and he'll want you to fire me." By this time she was wailing. "I need this job, Miss Lee."

"It'll be our secret. Mr. Henry doesn't need to know all the details," Iris said as she placed the tarnished brass fixture on the table and righted the ladder. "Just, please, stop crying," Iris pleaded. A headache the likes of the one she had last week on her flight back from New York was warming up. "Now show me that you can stand. Can you walk into the kitchen?"

After a few minutes of sitting at the kitchen table and sipping hot tea, Ludie seemed to have recovered. However, the fall had managed to rattle something loose inside of the new housekeeper's noggin. She wouldn't stop talking, rambling on and on about nothing.

"Let me drive you to the hospital to get you checked out," Iris urged. She was worried that Ludie had suffered a concussion.

"I'll be OK if I could just have a cigarette. Can I smoke out there on your back porch? Most times when I feel bad, I just light up and it makes me feel better."

"No, I insist. Let's get you checked out. We'll figure out a way to cover the emergency room expenses later." After finding Heyu cowering underneath her bed, Iris persuaded him to join her and, together, they escorted the yakking Ludie to Fallam County Hospital's Emergency Room.

By this time, Iris's plans for lunch and a chance to see The Early Riser man had been thwarted. But she consoled herself by knowing that Ludie's husband, the poor bastard, and not she, would have to listen to her the rest of the day.

As a nurse assisted Ludie into a wheelchair, Iris said, "Ludie, give me your cell phone and I'll call your husband to let him know where you are."

Ludie replied with a monolog on the beauty of camping in the New Mexico desert and nocturnal nudity. Annoyed, Iris retrieved Ludie's phone from the bottom of her faded

backpack. What to say to the poor devil? *Hi, my parents'
light fixture just fell on your wife and now she has
Tourette's.*

"Yeah?" answered a distracted voice on the other end
of Ludie's phone.

"Hello, this is Iris Lee, is this Vinnie Quinn?"

"Yeah, that's me. Where's Ludie?" Vinnie seemed
more anxious than Iris was expecting.

"She was cleaning in the dining room, and somehow
she and the light fixture ended up on the floor. She didn't
break any bones, but I brought her to the hospital just to be
safe—" The call dropped. She tried the number again.

"I'm on my way," Vinnie said. The connection dropped
again.

The whooshing sounds of the automatic hospital
exterior doors distracted Iris from the castaway *Fallam
County Citizen* she was reading on a bench outside of the
visitors' lounge. The Early Riser man was galloping past at
full speed. "What's he doing here?" Iris asked Heyu.

The young man rushed to the ER admissions desk and
shouted to anyone who would listen, "Which room is Ludie
Quinn in?" As he searched for Ludie, the double doors
from the emergency suite swung open and out poured the
same spew of mangled curses Iris and Heyu had heard
earlier. Heyu hid behind Iris as she stood at the entrance
doors.

"Ludie!" shouted Vinnie as he dashed past a stunned
admissions clerk and toward the ER. Iris couldn't believe
it. Vinnie Quinn was The Early Riser man?

A nurse in green scrubs folded her muscled arms and
stood in Vinnie's path. "Sir, we need you to stay out here,
please. Are you a relative?" she asked. In the background,
Ludie was doing a number on the Pope and all the apostles.

"She's my wife. Ludie! " He called to her while trying to see past the nurse who was a head taller.

"Sir, she seems fine. No broken bones. We're checking for concussion. Please wait in the visitors' lounge." The nurse disappeared through the swinging doors.

"Hi, Vinnie, I'm Iris Lee," she called out. "We're waiting out here." She pointed at the bench. As Vinnie approached, she said, "Ludie gave us a scare." She tried to read the worried look on Vinnie's face. She sensed that somehow his worries extended beyond the concern for Ludie's current condition.

"Hello," he said. Iris noticed a slight Spanish accent. Pacing up and down the walkway, Vinnie pushed away his free-flying hair, then rested his hands on the top of his head.

"I'm not sure where she learned it," Iris tried to relax the tension, "but Ludie has an impressive urban vocabulary." She motioned Vinnie toward the steel bench. As he sat, he kept his hands on top of his head and blew out a long breath.

"Yes, she uses bad language when she hurts herself," Vinnie said. "Mostly at the Pope. She's Catholic."

"This is normal for her?"

"Oh, yes. Hearing her now lets me know that she will be OK." He tried to smile. "You are Jonnie Bailey's friend, the one who hired my wife?"

Why did he have to remind her that he had a wife? "That's me," she said. She couldn't pull her eyes away from his handsome face and dreamy eyes with their short, brindle eyelashes. The lashes, they were defiantly Ethan's.

"Tell me what happened." Vinnie begged.

"Like I said on the phone, she was on the ladder dusting the dining room light fixture and she fell. Pulled it right out of the ceiling. The girl's got some grip."

Vinnie chuckled, "Ludie and ladders, they don't get along."

Heyu slunk over to Vinnie and was rewarded with a scratch behind one ear.

"Nice pup. I'll repair the chandelier for you, Miss Lee."

"That's Heyu," she said. Heyu sat up taller and leaned all his weight against Vinnie's leg. "You can call me Iris," she blushed. "That would be nice of you. To fix the light."

Watching Vinnie vigorously rub Heyu's back with both of his hands, she imagined the firm sensitive grip on her own backside. She couldn't believe that this, this boy was arousing such randy feelings inside of her.

"You can go now. I'll take Ludie home," Vinnie insisted. "Thank you for all you have done."

"No, I'll—I'll stay. Want to make sure she's not hurt," Iris replied. Her headache was gone, but she wasn't going anywhere.

"This has happened before. It may take awhile," he said as he scratched Heyu's ear again. "I can call you later and let you know what the doctors say."

"I don't mind watch—er—waiting," Iris said as she watched The Early Riser man's hands give Heyu the massage of his life.

# Chapter 13

"Iris, this is Jonnie." Iris listened to her voice mail messages. "Thank you. Mr. Henry came by and paid his bill. Now work on getting him to pay his tax debt."

The next message replayed a confused Bert. "Iris, pick up the phone. Are you there? Hello? Pick up your phone, sweet pea. What did that girl do to Elizabeth's chandelier?"

Iris prepared for the accounting of the carnage in the dining room. Once she made it home and explained to everyone that the chandelier somehow dropped from the ceiling and that Ludie had fallen off the ladder, the predicted responses commenced. Mr. Henry blustered on about Ludie leading a conspiracy to steal everything, even the things that were nailed down. Bert nervously inquired whether the junior housekeeper was still on track to replace her because she and Uncle Donnie were leaving for Ohio in a few weeks.

"Don't you guys care about Ludie?" Iris protested. Tiring of the complaints, she retired to her room to review Jonnie's reports on Lee Properties. She had put it off long enough. She needed to understand how bad it really was.

Two centuries ago, all of uptown Mt Pleasant was owned by the Lee family. Then Iris's great-grandfather sold land to the county for the courthouse and her grandfather sold land for the town hall and the hospital. Both men were lawyers and by the standards of the times, sagacious businessmen.

Sifting through the mountains of data Jonnie had sent, she found two realities. First, for the last five years, the business was lucky to break even and Jonnie's cash flow projections for the current year were as red as Miss Bert's pickled beets. Second, to pay off his tax debt and to make improvements to stave off code violations, Lee Properties, for the first time in its history, would have to borrow money. The Shops needed a major facelift if they were to compete with the retail big boys out near the interstate east of town. The vacant movie theater, across the street from Mt Pleasant Methodist Church, was a safety hazard and needed to be torn down. The Early Riser's roof leaked and the repair estimates for the HVAC system were greater than the assessed value of the building. Jonnie had forwarded several church and community organization proposals on stewardship ideas for the boarded up Farmer's Mercantile and Exchange, all suggesting that the property be donated. On top of the commercial property headaches, an infinite number of requests from residential tenants on Eastend Street, just a few blocks from Grove Street, demanded the attentions of the landlord.

After four generations, Lee Properties was worn out. One option, the one Iris liked best, was to sell all of the assets, except Grove House. But, in the middle of the biggest economic slump since Jimmy Carter was in the White House, Mr. Henry would be lucky to get fifty cents on the dollar. Iris outlined a plan to dissolve the company.

Too tired to get undressed or crawl under the bed covers, Iris curled into a ball on top of the mountain of pillows on her bed and fell asleep. She dreamed of Mrs. Ward, her next-door neighbor in Richmond, pecking on her arm with her twiggy finger and shrieking "Missy, you're in charge now. Do something!"

"Wake up, sweet pea. Iris. Iris," Bert was poking a sleeping Iris with the business end of a pancake spatula. "Did you sleep like that all night? That's how you get arthur-ritis."

"Hmm. What? What time is it?" Iris unfolded and stretched her arms up into the air; she locked both knees and flexed her heels.

"It's time for you to get up. There's someone on the phone for you."

"Who is it?" Iris yawned.

"I don't know. Some woman. Said she was calling from your condo. Said it was an emergency." Bert pointed her kitchen scepter in the direction of the wall phone downstairs.

"Something's wrong at my condo?" Iris tripped out of the room and took the back stairs two at a time. "Hello?"

"Iris, this is Sarah Ward," a shaky voice came down the ancient phone line. When Iris heard Mrs. Ward speak, a creepy déjà vu sensation rippled through her.

"What's wrong? Why are you calling from my place?" Iris asked.

"From your place? I'm calling from my living room," the old bird squawked.

Iris softly banged the phone receiver on her forehead "You called about an emergency?"

"I'm sorry to call you at this number. I got it from the management office. I tried to reach you on your personal number, but the call wouldn't go through. You know the phone company thinks they can pick and choose which calls go through and which one's don't—"

"What's the emergency, Mrs. Ward?" Iris interrupted.

"It's not a real important emergency, but I thought you'd want to know. I saw a strange man with the security guard at your door. Did the guard call you?"

"No. Did they enter the apartment?" Iris asked. *Manny?*

"I don't know. My pot of potatoes was boiling over, and by the time I looked again, they were gone. I called the manager to tell them you were out of town. He told me to mind my own business. I told him it was my business to keep an eye out for my neighbors."

"Thank you, Mrs. Ward. I'll give the security office a shout," Iris said. "What did the guy with the guard look like?"

"All's I could see was his backside. Tall, broad-shouldered. He was peeking in the keyhole. Why do people do that?" she asked.

"Do what?" Iris rubbed her puffy eyes then finger-combed her hair with one hand.

"Look through the wrong side of a keyhole? They can't see anything."

Iris recalled the last time she saw Mrs. Ward. The woman was staring through Iris's keyhole with her raptor-like eye.

"Was there anything else?" Iris asked.

"No, I just thought you'd want to know. When are you coming back? We need you to help us on this maintenance fee increase."

Iris didn't know where to start so she decided not to try. "Mrs. Ward, I'm going to hang up now. I'll call security. Thanks for the head's up." As she hung up and thought about what her neighbor had said about the visitor, she frowned and said softly, "Manny's not due back for two months. Why doesn't he just call or email me?" The night before he left for his tour of duty he'd explained that she wouldn't be able to reach him and he'd call once he was back in the states. As she turned away from the phone, she bumped into a grinning Elizabeth. Iris hugged her, and it made the anxiety in her melt a little. Slowly, she thumped back upstairs to shower and get ready to slog through another day.

"Jonnie, what happened to all of it?" Iris sipped a beer in the Bailey Building penthouse that evening. Frustrated from the day's job hunt and the runaround she got from the condominium's security office, she had invited herself over for beer and pizza. Earlier she had left a third message on the security captain's voice mail, saying that she was on her way to see her lawyer.

"What? All the money Allen Lee made? For one thing by the time your grandfather died, your Uncle Ben had managed to burn through most of it. I remember my dad telling me that Mr. Lee had his heart broken twice, once when he realized that Ben wouldn't go into practice with him and the second time when your grandmother Matilda died. Ben practiced law for a few years in Roanoke but was disbarred for lying to a judge. It was scandalous." Jonnie arched her eyebrows twice and took a sip of her own beer.

"Mr. Henry never told me Uncle Ben was disbarred. Is that why he and Aunt Sarah and Benny moved to California?" Iris felt like a kid, being schooled by her big sister.

"Daddy said that the reason your uncle went out West was to get away from the bootleggers and racketeers he stole money from," Jonnie said. "I guess he got desperate when Mr. Lee finally cut him off financially."

"I remember when they would come to visit us. Benny always stole my Archie comic books. He called me a fag because I went to Fallam County High School. Wonder what he's doing these days?"

"Selling real estate," Jonnie said. "He called me about a year ago looking for some information about Allen Lee. Claimed he was working on a family tree for his grandsons. The questions were more about Lee Properties than family."

"That doesn't smell right." Iris wrinkled her nose. "What do you suppose he's up to?"

"Don't know. But if I were you, I'd keep my eyes open," Jonnie advised. "He's a bad penny. He could turn up when you least expect it."

"Did Grandpa Allen include Ben's family in his will?" Iris chewed on her thumbnail.

"Nope. Left it all to Mr. Henry and his heirs. That would be you." Jonnie pushed the button on the phone to let the pizza guy in.

A few long-necks and a couple of slices of Chunky's pork barbecue pizza loosened up what seemed, at the time, to be ridiculously grand ideas for restructuring Lee Properties. However they both knew that by the next morning, like the empty beer bottles, the ideas would end up in the recycle bin out back.

"There's just no way Lee Properties can keep going. I've got to liquidate most of the assets. I've got an appointment with Junie Marks over at Links Jewelry tomorrow to have that broach I told you about appraised. Maybe it'll cover the taxes. I'd like to keep Grove House and maybe the farm, but the rest has to go," Iris said.

"There *is* one other solution. It's so obvious, I can't believe you haven't considered it," Jonnie said.

Iris tilted her head to one side, her floppy bangs resting on her eyelashes. She blinked a drunkard's blink. "Not gonna happen. No way, Jose," she slurred. "Don't even go there in your dreams." She swayed while hanging onto the kitchen counter. "As soon as I get this tax thing cleared up and Ludie running Grove House, color me on a pony so I can ride out of this no-horse town. Is there any beer left? Let's go to Chunky's for a nightcap."

# Chapter 14

In Iris's dream this time Mrs. Ward had a crow's beak. She cawed, "Do something, do something!"

Iris fell off the bed with a loud thump. Heart pounding, she sucked in the musty odors of the bedroom carpet and rolled onto her back, taking inventory. Her lips were cracked, and the inside of her mouth was as gritty as her river sneakers. Behind her eyelids an aurora borealis exploded. Her bladder screamed for relief. When she stood, her head felt like a giant, overripe watermelon tittering side-to-side on her neck. Still drunk from the night's festivities, she vaguely remembered walking home and crawling through a sun porch window like she used to do after staying out all night with her delinquent buddy Ernie Bangar from Eastend Street.

"Iris? Sweet pea?" Bert shook Iris with both of her hands. "Are you going to sleep the day away? It's going on eight o'clock." She drew open the curtains and exclaimed, "What's that terrible smell? Did your dog do his business in here?"

As Bert pushed up the wooden-framed window, the sash weights bumped along inside the frame. Iris smothered her face with her pillow.

"Close that window. You're letting in cold air." She grabbed for Heyu for warmth, but he wasn't around.

"Lord forgive me for blaming that poor dog for making a mess." Bert placed her hands on her hips. "It's you! What kind of trouble did you get into last night? You smell like rotten damsons." She tugged at the bed-sheets. "I'm gonna have to wash your bedclothes."

"Let me sleep," Iris squeaked out. She pulled the sheets over her head.

"Did you forget that we was going to Roanoke this morning to see Mr. Marks about the broach? He called yesterday after you left to make sure you was still comin' by his store today." Bert ripped the sheets from the bed causing Iris to curl into a ball to keep warm.

"I'm not going anywhere today. Call and tell him I'll talk to him tomorrow."

"What do you want me to tell him?" Bert's dentures started clacking. "That you were too hung-over to come see him? I'd be ashamed to tell him that Iris."

Iris heard the loud tapping of a size-eleven sneaker.

"Fine!" Iris pulled herself out of the bed, staggered down the hall and slammed the bathroom door. A Goth-like creature clad only in underwear and socks stared back at her from the floor mirror that stood beside the claw-footed bathtub. In the reflection she spied remnants of the gawky eighteen year old who had left Mt Pleasant for college with the foolish adolescent vow to never return. Husky laughter erupted from the back of her sore throat—the result of yelling over the ear-splitting classic rock at Chunky's the night before. Miss Bert had just played that girl, played her like a worn-out fiddle.

Because Ludie was still on the mend from her solo trapeze act and Mr. Henry had already left for his daily rounds, Iris had a logistics problem. Secretly she wanted to see if Bert's driving skills were up to par for her pending trip.

"Miss Bert, we have to take Mom with us. Can you drive? My head is killing me."

"OK, but I ain't driving that monster car of yours. We'll take my car."

With Iris and Heyu crammed in the back and Elizabeth planted up front in Bert's faded school-bus-yellow Pacer, they headed north on Route 220 for Roanoke, the Star City, once known as Big Lick. Just as the car began vibrating from acceleration in the slow lane, Elizabeth said to no one in particular, "I have to go to the bathroom."

"Oh Lord," Bert said. "Miss Elizabeth can you hold it until we get to Boones Mill? There's no place to stop between here and there. Unless you want to do it behind a tree," Bert giggled.

"Do what?" Elizabeth asked.

"Go to the bathroom. Behind a tree on the side of the highway," Bert offered.

"Why would I want to do that?" Elizabeth asked.

A few miles later they pulled into the rest stop at Boones Mill. Bert walked around to the passenger side and opened the door for Elizabeth.

"I thought we were going to Roanoke. Why are we stopping here?" Elizabeth looked up at Bert.

"You said you had to go to the bathroom," a very patient Bert reminded Elizabeth.

"Go to the bathroom? In that place?" Her shaking hand pointed at the colonial brick public outhouse where people were hurrying in and strolling out.

Iris got out on the driver's side and walked around to help Bert, followed by Heyu. "Mom, you said you had to go to the bathroom," she said with not quite the finesse Bert used.

"I don't have to go to the bathroom." Elizabeth was adamant. "Why did we stop here? I thought we were going to Roanoke."

"OK," Bert said. "But you'll let me know if you have to go. Right?"

"Well, of course I will. You don't think I would pee all over this charming car seat do you?" Elizabeth said with enough bite to surprise both Bert and Iris. Iris held her breath to keep from laughing as she pointed toward the restrooms, signaling to Bert that she was taking advantage of the pit stop.

What Iris saw as she walked out of the building made her think of Annie Leibovitz and her quirky street-life photographs. An elfin-like man, with his Harlequin Great Dane, was conversing with Bert and Heyu as Elizabeth waved her tissue from the faded yellow clown car.

"When did my life get so surreal?" Iris placed an icy hand on her burning forehead.

Back on the road, Iris watched the farming landscape tumble by from the Pacer's wide-back window as the comical little car snaked its way through the Blue Ridge hills and over into the big valley of Roanoke. To her critical eye, the only things that seemed to have grown and expanded were the dull gray dormant kudzu vines engulfing the trees and hillsides.

"I have a little trouble when I get to the county line," Bert announced from the driver's seat as they approached the city limits. "That Greenville Pass is a little tricky. 'Specially in January when it's icy."

As the little car took the hairpin curves, car sickness and carbon monoxide seeping through the rusted-out floor joined the alcohol poison in Iris's brain. Through the green haze of her thoughts, Iris realized that Bert was a pretty good driver. Her driving wouldn't kill her and Uncle Donnie on their drive to Ohio, the car's fumes would do them in.

Valley View Mall played host to all of the former downtown shops that had followed everybody out to the suburbs. While Bert parked, Iris, Elizabeth and Heyu waited at the mall's main entrance.

"Where are we going?" Elizabeth asked. Her small, white hands clutched Iris's forearm like steel clamps. Fear lit her mother's eyes. Iris spoke softly to assure her that she was safe.

"We're going to see Mr. Marks about the broach we found," Iris answered.

"Who's Mr. Marks?" Elizabeth sounded lost.

"You know, Mr. Junie Marks at Links," Iris tried to keep an upbeat tone despite her hangover.

"Where's Bert?" Elizabeth wondered.

"She's parking the car. We're waiting for her," Iris replied.

"Where are we going?" Elizabeth asked.

"We're going into the mall to see Mr. Marks at Links," Iris said.

"Who's Mr. Marks?" Elizabeth asked again.

"Mr. Marks owns Links," Iris answered.

"Where's Bert?" Elizabeth asked.

"Mom? Who's on first?" She asked as she fished for her sunglasses and a bottle of aspirin in her tote bag.

"Who is. What's on second, I don't know's on third," Elizabeth answered.

Iris turned away, holding her breath to stifle her laugher.

"Iris, good to see you, young lady," said Junie Marks, owner of the oldest jewelry and collectibles store in the Roanoke Valley. He took Iris's hand in both of his. Mr. Marks and Elizabeth were distantly related somehow, Iris never got it straight. Before she married Mr. Henry, Elizabeth worked as a clerk at the downtown location of Links Jewelers, before there was a mall. "And, Elizabeth Carter, what a wonderful surprise," Mr. Marks said as he reached out to embrace her.

"Who are you?" Elizabeth raised her voice and pushed him away.

"Elizabeth, it's Junie Marks," he said with a jovial laugh. "I know it's been a few years, but don't you recognize me?" His fingers twisted at a diamond pinky ring as sadness rippled over his face.

"Mr. Marks, you remember Bert Tyler Swanson," Iris stepped in quickly. "Miss Bert, maybe Mom wants to look at the watches while Mr. Marks and I talk."

Bert took Iris's cue and led the skinny little woman toward the other side of the store.

"I have to pee," Elizabeth announced loudly enough for the entire store to hear.

The dapper jeweler extended his arm toward the cashier's station, signaling Iris to follow. "Iris, I had no idea," an embarrassed Mr. Marks started. "I apologize—"

"No, Mr. Marks," Iris said. "I'm the one who should apologize. This morning I thought this was a good idea. Get her out of the house. See some old friends." Iris recalled what her father had said the day she'd arrived about keeping Elizabeth at home and in familiar surroundings. As much as she hated to admit it, he was right.

"Did you get my email with the picture?" Iris turned to business.

"Yes, yes we did," Mr. Marks jumped in. "It's a lovely piece. Where did you say you got it?"

"I didn't." She fished out a lint-covered breath mint from the bottom of her tote bag and popped it in her dry mouth. "I was hoping you could give me your opinion about the piece without having any background." Again she dove into her bag and pulled out the jeweler's box and handed it to Mr. Marks. He accepted the case with the reverence of a Sunday morning tithe offering.

"We used cases like this years ago," he said holding it close to his eyes. When he opened the box, he gazed down at the medallion. "This way, please." She followed him back to his jeweler's bench and watched as he examined it. After a few minutes, he lifted his head and smiled his happy smile again. "Young lady, you have a very interesting work of art here. I'm not sure I can place a value on it without further study."

"What can you tell me about the stones? Are they real?" Another wave of the previous evening's tequila rhapsody rolled up from her chest, she lifted her hair off her neck and used her hand to fan herself.

"Well, it has a total of, let me see, twenty-nine precious stones. The one in the center is a ruby, the blue ones are sapphires and the white and yellow ones are diamonds. They're surrounded by gold mounts that look to be handmade. And see the small pearls; I haven't seen pearls like that in years."

"I get it. It's old. But what else can you tell me?" she asked impatiently.

"This case was not designed for this piece. It shows wear in places where the ruby medallion doesn't touch it. See?" He pointed with a wooden pointer.

"So you called it a medallion. Why?" Iris drilled him.

"When you sent me the picture, I started looking through some of our catalogs." He smiled.

Iris suppressed a wave of nausea. Her memory caught a whiff of Chunky's private stock of homemade tequila.

"This piece looks very much like a lot of the military medallions worn by eighteenth- and nineteenth-century European officers—and royalty." Mr. Marks' eyes actually twinkled.

"You mean I'm in possession of some dead white guy's crown jewels?" she asked in mock surprise. She refrained from doing the golfer's fist pump right there on the spot for fear of restarting the head pounding and the colored lights.

"I don't know about that," Mr. Marks chuckled. "If you were to appraise the value of the individual components of—let's call it a medallion—you have at least a million dollars' worth of stones here. Probably more." He qualified, "Retail that is."

"You're saying—that combined—the stones are worth what?" Iris blinked her dry eyes.

"If you can find the original owner and show provenance, the medallion could be worth much, much more than the sum of its parts." Mr. Marks answered excitedly.

"By provenance you mean proving that it once belonged to the dead white guy and it now belongs to me?" She pointed to her chest.

"Basically. You must be able to show the history of ownership, and I assume you would want that history to include how you came by it, which gets me back to my earlier question. Where did you get this?" Mr. Marks turned serious.

"Mr. Marks, I learned a long time ago not to divulge any more information than necessary when negotiating. I can tell you that it was given to my mother. Thank you for doing this for us."

"Iris, we're family," Mr. Marks brightened. "I do it for Elizabeth. At no cost."

Warning bells shot off in Iris's swollen head.

"Thank you. And Mr. Marks? Can you not share this with anyone else?" She leaned in close to his face.

"Of course, discretion is why my customers come to me," he smiled again as he discretely shifted away from her. "Don't worry. Your secret's safe with me."

"I want to buy Miss Bert a nice watch. She's retiring. What do you have that she might like?" She shoved the medallion and its case back into her bag, and they strolled to the front of the store.

On the way home, Iris instructed Bert to drive through downtown Roanoke and park the car in front of the local Bank US office. Praying that she wouldn't run into anyone she knew, Iris rented a safe deposit box and planted the medallion and its box inside. She put the key on her key ring.

As she climbed into the back seat of the smelly Pacer, she said, "I'm hungry. Anybody else hungry? How about I treat all of us to a burger and milkshake at The Roanoker?"

"I was going to fix us chicken salad from last night's leftovers," Bert offered.

"Miss Bert, don't get me wrong, I love your cooking, but we've had chicken every single day since I've been here," Iris complained. "Let's leave the poor bird alone for today and have a nice hamburger."

"Whatever you say, you're the boss now," Bert laughed as she peeled her yellow taxi away from the curb and into the busy downtown traffic.

# Chapter 15

After dinner that night, Iris found Mr. Henry sitting in his usual spot in front of the unlit fireplace. He was reading the local paper, which was published on Mondays and Fridays. She sat on the edge of the twin chair and spoke to the cold hearth.

"You were right about keeping Mom at home and surrounded by familiar things. She was really scared today when we went to the mall."

"From what I've read, the disease makes the person paranoid and untrusting of people. Even the ones they knew but have forgotten," Mr. Henry said behind the newspaper. Folding the paper and dropping it to the floor, he said, "I know you want to be coming and going all the time, but it's best to keep her here."

"OK," she said quietly. "I took the broach, ah, medallion to Links to have it appraised. Mr. Marks says the stones are real and their value is around a million."

"I'd get a second opinion. If Junie Marks says something is worth a million dollars, it's probably worth three." He took a single cigarillo out of his breast pocket and started chewing on its tip. He had given gave up drinking and smoking several years back, but he carried the cigarillo around and occasionally chewed on it. "You know he's your mother's cousin on her mother's side. But I wouldn't trust him if I were you."

"I don't. I put the medallion in a safe deposit box at the bank," she said. "I'm getting another opinion from a friend at Sotheby's." She paused as she made a mental note to call Betty's husband the next day. "He also said that because it appeared to be some type of old medallion, it would be worth a lot more if we could prove its provenance. Where did you get it?"

"My father gave it to me before he died. He wanted Elizabeth to have it, so I gave it to her." Mr. Henry used his fingertips to remove tobacco bits from the tip of his tongue.

"The other day she said she thought it was ugly." Iris smiled. "It's the first coherent thing I've heard her say since I've been back."

"No, she didn't like it. I was just doing what I was told to do," Mr. Henry said quietly. "That's what I always did, do what the important Mr. Lee ordered me to do." Iris caught the resentment in his comment and wanted to pursue it. But she was on another mission at the moment and didn't want him to stray from the topic of the medallion.

"Did he say where it came from? Where he got it?" Iris asked.

"He said that he had a client who had asked him to hold it for her and if anything happened to her, it was his to keep." Mr. Henry closed his eyes and winced.

"Did he tell you her name?"

"If he did, I don't remember." Mr. Henry stood. "I'm tired." And with that he walked out of the library and climbed the front stairs to his bedroom.

"Good night to you too, dear old Dad," Iris scoffed at the empty room. As she puzzled over how she could identify Grandpa Allen's mystery woman, Heyu crept into the room and leaned against her leg. "Heyu, stop ignoring Mr. Henry. Try to get to know him. I bet deep down he really likes you." She fluffed the fur on his head.

Iris tried to think of other relations or acquaintances who might know something about her grandfather and his clients. Aside from her Cousin Bennie in California there were no close relatives. They were all gone. And she, an only child born after several miscarriages, had no siblings to rely upon. She'd have to quiz Bert again in the morning. Heyu looked up at her and wagged his tail.

"OK, once around the backyard, let's go."

The clanging of old metal garbage cans woke Iris the next morning. Unable to go back to sleep, she found Mr. Henry in the kitchen.

"Who picks up garbage at six o'clock in the morning?" she complained as she filled a coffee cup. "And why is the town still using metal cans? Don't you guys use the big plastic bins?" Iris sat down across from Mr. Henry at the breakfast nook. He was reading his day-old *Wall Street Journal*. "You know if you had a computer, you could read the current edition online?" Several times she had tried to automate Mr. Henry but each time he insisted that computers and the Internet were set on this earth for no good purpose.

"Computers have ruined our financial system. Nowadays, anybody with a hundred dollar bank account can trade stocks. Computers make it easier for the banks to steal your money."

To the newspaper, Iris mouthed the words verbatim as she had heard the old man's diatribe on banking too many times before.

After a moment of silence, he said, "Bella Sorin."

"Come again?" Iris asked.

"Bella Sorin was the client who gave my father the medallion." Mr. Henry laid his paper aside and began cutting into his ham and eggs, which were sunny side up just as they had been served to him for the last seventy years.

"Who was she?" Iris palmed her coffee cup and leaned over the table on both elbows so she wouldn't miss a single word, knowing he most likely wouldn't repeat them.

"She was from somewhere up north. Came into town with a tall tale about her mother and the general. Nobody believed her except my father. He was a sucker for lost causes." He turned to Bert as she walked into the kitchen with an armload of dirty laundry. "Bert, my coffee needs warming up. What time should I expect dinner this evening?" Sticking out her tongue to his back while shuffling all the laundry under one arm, Bert poured his coffee and headed down to the basement laundry room.

Not wanting to get him off track from the Bella story, she asked, "The general? Which general?"

"Old Jube Early."

"You mean Jubal Early, the confederate general from Franklin County?"

"My father said that Miss Sorin's mother had died. She claimed her mother was from Fallam County and she bought her home to bury her in the family graveyard, over near the county line next to Boones Mill."

"What was her mother's maiden name?" Iris asked.

"Don't recall if Father ever said. He did tell me that Miss Sorin said her mother's dying wish was for her to know her real father. Apparently the mother was living with another man when she died," Mr. Henry answered.

"So what happened to Bella?" Iris asked. She was convinced that he was taking his own sweet time in telling the story just to irritate her.

"I suppose the general sent her packing. Father said that he escorted her over to Lynchburg to see the general several times. But he was not privy to their conversations."

"Did she stay in the area? Is her family still living here?"

"I do not know. My father told me that she gave him the medallion for safekeeping. She claimed that the general had given it to her mother before he left Canada to come back to Virginia. I don't know a judge in this commonwealth who would see such a claim as proof of paternity, do you?"

"What incentive would Bella's mother have to lie?" Iris tried to reason with Mr. Henry. "Anyway that doesn't matter. So she never came back to claim the medallion? Grandpa Allen never heard from her?"

"When my father was on his death bed, he told me to give it to Elizabeth. He said Miss Sorin told him to keep it. She didn't want it. She said consider it payment for all the legal work he had done for her. Then he said she left and he never saw her again." Mr. Henry looked as if he had more to say but only offered, "That's all I know."

"Legal work? What sort of legal work? If he did legal work for her, chances are we can find a trail in the court records." Iris's mind was racing ahead. How could she prove that the Lees owned the medallion? If it had belonged to Franklin County's favorite son, General Early, the historians would be crawling all over Grove House to have a look at it and to claim it.

The sale of the medallion could put Lee Properties back in the black. And maybe there would be enough left over to pay a full-time health care provider for Mr. Henry and her mom. Now she was extremely motivated to find the rightful owner of the odd ornament. She hoped it was Elizabeth Lee. The sooner she figured it out, the sooner she could hightail it back to Richmond and to her own life.

"Whew!" Bert exclaimed as she topped the stairs from the basement and put her hands on her ample hips. "Either those stairs are getting steeper or I'm getting older. Mr. Henry I talked to Uncle Donnie last night, and he wanted me to tell you that the game starts today at eleven instead of twelve and to make sure you ain't late."

"What game?" Iris asked.

"None of your business," the old man groused. Rising from the table, he energetically swept biscuit crumbs from his front and rolled his shirt sleeves down and began to button them. "Bert, I'll be home at the usual time. Go easy on the starch this week. My legs and hind parts are chapped from the starch you put in my skivvies." He tugged at his trousers then reached for his everyday fedora and faithful car coat from their hangers in the long mudroom behind the kitchen and left through the back door.

Iris questioned Bert with a wrinkled brow. "What are you grinning about?"

Bert rolled her big brown eyes and cupped her elbows in her hands. She hunched her shoulders which triggered a giggle. "Sometimes when I'm pouring in the starch," she demonstrated, "my hand starts shaking, and I just can't stop." Between the women, the laugher started as a low, plucky chuckle. Then their full cackles conjoined and filled the kitchen, that rare combustible kind of laughter that reignited every few seconds and caused tears to flow.

With her bosom bouncing up and down, Bert showed Iris again how she accidentally poured too much Stay-Flo into the wash and another bout of laughter broke out.

"I. Guess," Iris tried to calm herself with deep heaving breaths, "Mr. Henry. Won't have to. Worry about. Getting. His," she stopped to wipe the tears from her eyes, "his shorts. In a knot."

They both leaned on the old butcher's block, howling like backyard dogs. The laugher felt sweet like the endorphin rush after an early morning run and as glorious as hearing someone read the Declaration of Independence on the Fourth of July. Not wanting to be left out, Heyu joined in with a harmonizing howl of his own.

## Chapter 16

Someone rang the doorbell just as the chimes from the clock in the foyer struck seven.

"Who could that be this early in the morning?" Iris asked Bert as she wiped her tear-stained face with a smelly dish towel.

"Didn't expect to see you so soon" Iris said as she ushered Ludie and Vinnie into the house, Ludie with her maid's bucket and Vinnie with his carpenter's box. Like a pair of swans they appeared utterly devoted to each other. One complemented the other; he was beauty and she was plain and truth. She was quick and nervous; he patiently waited for her to lead the way.

"I'm feeling much better now," Ludie said. "And Vinnie wants to fix the candle-lier. Are you all right, Miss Lee? What's wrong with your eyes?"

"I'm fine. Miss Bert was telling me a funny story."

"It shouldn't take long," Vinnie interrupted as he looked around for the scene of the accident.

"Let me show you the dining room" Iris mumbled as she watched Vinnie tug on his soul patch. Catching her breath, she continued, "Ludie, you can help Miss Bert with the laundry."

For the next hour Iris and Heyu watched Vinnie as he reattached the rickety old light fixture. Cradling it in one strong, brown hand while reconnecting it to the ceiling, his forearm tensed, exposing muscle and sinew. Iris sighed out loud. Vinnie looked down from the ladder and shyly smiled at her. He seemed embarrassed to have an audience watch him at work.

"Be careful on that ladder. We don't want you to fall like Ludie." *Yes, Ludie, the guy's wife.*

The door chimes rang again. At the same time, Iris's cell phone vibrated in her pocket. Glancing at the phone, she recognized the 212 area code exchange for Manhattan, the mystery caller again. Another round of door chimes distracted her from taking the call. The phone stopped vibrating.

With Heyu at her feet, she squinted through the door's peephole and saw Mt Pleasant's mayor, Kooch Kaluchi. His back toward the door, he was glancing around the front yard as if assessing the property's value. One hand hidden in his Big and Tall trouser pocket, the other held a thin leather business folder which he nervously tapped against his leg. He toggled his wrist to check for the time on a gigantic wrist watch.

Unlike most of his high school peers who attended Virginia Tech with him, Kooch had opted to return to the small pond of Mt Pleasant after completing law school in Richmond. Iris suspected his return was a self-preservation tactic, a way of hiding from the urban, man-eating sharks, rather than the chivalrous proclamations of giving back to his hometown that he frequently orated to anyone fool enough to listen. To her, his ambitions and ineptitude were as large as his girth and his moral intentions disingenuous.

"Larry!" Iris greeted as she opened the door with her favorite nickname for him. Heyu trotted out onto the expansive porch, sniffed the air and sat like a sentry by the stairs.

"Don't call me that, you know I hate it." Kooch pointed his chubby finger at Heyu. "Does he bite?"

"Only people who point at him," Iris deadpanned.

"Really!" Kooch quickly dropped his hand by his side and two-stepped toward Iris and the front door.

"What's up?" Iris stood in the doorway blocking the chairman of the local Democratic Party from entering her father's house.

"I tried calling you on the phone for an appointment, but there's never an answer," Kooch protested. Although it was technically still winter and a cool, breezy fifty-five degrees on the porch, miniature sweat beads gathered on the mayor's massive forehead and above his upper lip.

"The phone works fine. I used it the other day. Mr. Henry's not home anyway."

"I'm not here to see your father. In fact, I just saw him at Bubba's Barber Shop downtown, and I know he's on his way to Elder Home. I'm here to talk to you," he said with a lopsided laugh. "May I come in?"

"What's this about?" Iris knew what Kooch wanted. He wanted her to persuade Mr. Henry to sell The Shops. She'd rather be watching Adonis in the dining room.

From behind her, Vinnie spoke softly "Excuse me, Miss Lee. It's fixed. Again, we're sorry this happened."

"Hey, no problem, Vinnie. Thanks for doing this for Mr. Henry." Iris moved just enough for Vinnie to slip past her. She gazed on his exit a little too long.

"Earth to Iris." Kooch snapped his fingers in front of her face. "Are you going to invite me in?"

Iris led the mayor into the dining room to the faded arm chairs in front of the arched dining room windows which looked out on the front lawn. She sat and offered Kooch the other chair. He dropped his leather folder onto the small table between the chairs, looking around as he sat.

"I have to get to the office, so I'll keep this short and sweet." Kooch used his hand to mop his forehead. "Have you heard about the proposals the town has made to Lee Properties?"

"Mr. Henry told me there were offers. He told me he wasn't interested in selling and the leasing options you proposed were unacceptable. That's all I know." Iris put on her poker face.

"We've made him a fair offer. Several, in fact. Frankly, I question his ability to make sound decisions" He let this implication trail off.

"If you're referring to the drug bust, Chief Quinn interviewed him and found no cause to suspect Mr. Henry was involved." Iris willed herself to stay calm.

"Iris, does your father have a transition plan?"

"What do you mean?" she asked, a little too defensively.

"You know my management company helps with maintenance calls and such, but eventually somebody will need to make some long-term decisions. I'm not sure he's thought about the day when he'll be unable to make those decisions. What're his plans when that day comes?" Kooch carefully watched Iris's face for her reaction.

"You'll have to ask him that question. I don't have any legal status with his business." Iris was tap dancing. "Your guess is as good as anybody's. He could be planning to leave it all to the Sierra Club or the Nature Conservancy for all I know." Iris laced her fingers together to keep them still.

"Right, you're joking again," Kooch said looking around for Heyu.

"I've had some discussions with him about it, but my hands are tied. I legally can't make him *do* anything. He's going to do what he wants." Iris shrugged her shoulder and opened up her hands. "So you're wasting your time by talking to me." She stood to show him the way out.

"'ang on. 'ang on. I think we got started off on the wrong foot. Let's start over." Kooch mopped his brow again. "Sit down and give me a chance. Why don't you come over to Town Hall and see what we're trying to do here. I've developed a ten-year plan to get Fallam County recognized as a place people'll want to visit. Make a home for their families." He counted out Mt Pleasant's attributes on his linked sausage fingers. "We've got good schools, no crime to speak of. With the advent of buying from local farms, our agribusiness is finally growing again, pun intended."

"What's that got to do with me, Kooch?" Iris asked as she sat back down. "I'm here to help my parents through a rough patch and then I'm going back to Richmond."

"Well, it's obvious, Iris. You'll inherit your father's business. And with your background and Lee Properties' holdings, we could have a winning team," he pitched.

"Winning team, huh? What's your bottom line?"

"I'm glad you asked." He opened up his business folder and extracted his proposal for the town's future. "Here's your copy. Take a look at it and tell me what you think."

"Give me the summary." Iris folded her arms across her chest.

"Sure. Do you know anything about the Crooked Road?" he asked.

"Very little. From what I've read, it's some marketing scheme somebody in Richmond cooked up to get people to drive down dangerous roads spending their vacation money in backwoods country stores listening to any fool who thinks he can play a banjo." As she said this, Iris realized she sounded just like her father.

"We like to say we're supporting economic development by promoting heritage tourism and the Blue Ridge way of life, running from Fallam County all the way out to Kentucky." Kooch put his hand on his heart. "And there are hundreds of thousands of dollars in tax revenue at stake here."

"Does Mt Pleasant have money problems?" Iris asked.

"With this economy? Every town and county is looking for new revenue streams to sustain their programs. As my hero Bill Clinton once said, 'I haven't ever met a tax I didn't like,'" he teased.

"Oh, brother," Iris responded.

"Anyway, a lot of folks around here think your father was the main reason why we lost the bid to Franklin County as the entry point to the Crooked Road. We wanted him to come into the deal." As he leaned over the small table, she felt his body heat and smelled his strong, sticky deodorant-or-cologne-or-whatever.

"So, the town would buy the property outright and own it? What do they plan to do with it? More government offices? Resell it for retail?"

"Heck Iris, our chamber of commerce can't compete with the big boxes out in the county. That ship left for China twenty years ago. In fact, we don't want to. They can have it. The beauty of the proposal is that we're creating something unique. Something everybody would drive into town for. Like the movie says: If you build it, they will come." The mayor's head jittered up and down like a bobble-head doll's.

"And what is 'it'?" she asked making quotation marks with her fingers.

"We plan to tear down that whole block, including The Early Riser, and build a Culture and Performing Arts Center." Kooch was so excited about the prospect he stood to shake off energy, and in the process his hand flung sweat onto Iris's face. Kooch and Iris both froze. Using her shirtsleeve, she slowly wiped it from her cheek.

"What's in it for you?" Iris quietly asked.

"What do you mean what's in it for me? I told you. We'll build the Center to get people back into uptown. Give people of Mt Pleasant a sense of community. We ain't Dee-triot, but we have our problems. And the Center would mean so much to the children."

"You didn't answer my question. What's in it for you, personally?" She stared into his sweaty face.

"Iris, I can't believe you would ask a question like that. That's just rude. I'm a servant of the town and the county, and it's my job to see this thing through."

"Kooch, that works with Mr. and Mrs. Wingfield down the street, but I know horse manure when I smell it. It's me, Iris! I grew up with you, remember?"

"First of all, Mr. Wingfield passed last fall. God rest his soul. And second, there's no need for ugly talk. I have nothing to hide." A bead of sweat slid down his red face. He was mad. "Just read the darn thing and call me. My number's on the front page." He dropped the proposal on the table and lumbered out of the house and toward the driveway.

"Yes sir-ree, Heyu," Iris said as they watched Kooch stuff himself into his expensive, oversized SUV. "Something's in it for Robert Lorenzo Kaluchi. Figure out what it is, and we'll be able to get a fair price for the property." Iris felt a little like her old self and invited Heyu to go for a run.

That evening Iris entered the library. "Got a minute?"

Mr. Henry ignored her as she sat down beside him. Heyu watched from the butler's door.

"Kooch Kaluchi came by today," Iris said. She waited for a response.

"What did he want?" Mr. Henry said behind his newspaper.

She waited until he put the paper in his lap before she answered. "He gave me a copy of a plan for economic development for the town. It includes buying the entire western side of Main Street, The Shops, Chunky's, the movie theater."

"They're not for sale." The old man raised the paper again.

"Tell me, Mr. Henry, what are your plans for Lee Properties?" Kooch's question was a fair one, and she wanted to hear Mr. Henry's answer. In response to his silence, she continued, "I mean, at some point you're going to have to give up the business and retire."

"When I was living in California, everybody called me Hank," Mr. Henry said as he thrust the paper aside and reached for his cigarillo. "They didn't know who the hell Allen Lee was. I was nobody's boy. I was just Hank Lee. I had planned to stay out there after I got out of the Army. There was nothing in Fallam County for me. I didn't want to come back. Ben was supposed to take over the business." He paused and gazed into the cold fireplace. "Then, they made me come home. Had the Army kick me out so I could come home to take care of my mother. Imagine that, a twenty-year-old man. Asking him to do woman's work." The room was quiet. Iris studied her hands.

"A lifetime is an awfully long time to carry a grudge," Iris muttered. "What does that have to do with not selling property to the town?"

"I promised my father that I would not sell any more property. He regretted selling the plots for the park. Said they mismanaged the land. That's neither here nor there. I trust Robert Kaluchi about as far as I can throw him." His voice started shaking with anger.

"I agree with you on that score. He's up to something." Iris kept her voice low and calm. "So what do you want to do with the property? People keep asking me."

"What do you mean 'what do I want to do with the property?'" he asked. Iris noticed he was bobbing his head again the way he did when Chief Quinn asked him about his renters that day.

"According to Jonnie's reports, Lee Properties is a new roof or heat pump away from being insolvent. Plus you owe the government a fair amount in back taxes. You've got to either sell off some of the property or go to the bank to borrow." Iris knew that he wouldn't like either option.

"Borrow money to pay taxes?" The confusion abandoned his face as he switched into auto-pilot on the arguments of tax obligation. "There is no way on God's green earth that I am going to borrow money from Artie English," he said as he pointed toward the front windows and beyond to the center of town, "to pay the federal government so that all those fools down at the Elder Home can have more money to gamble away every afternoon."

Arthur "Artie" English was the one-time general manager of the local Fallam County Community Bank. Dead five years, Artie had been one of Mr. Henry's poker buddies and business partners.

"So," she tried to reason with him, "if you're not going to borrow money from the bank, your only choice to cover your bills this year will be to sell property or get some new renters. Do you have any prospects to rent out the space at the shops?"

"I'm working on it," he said. "Stumpy Quinn's boy says as soon as the grand jury votes to go to trial, I can have my building back." He was referencing the New To You Shop.

"Mr. Henry, that's too little too late. You'll still have to borrow money to cover your expenses this year. Why don't we go over to Town Hall and just listen to what they have to say. Who knows? Maybe they'll sweeten the pot. I sense that Kooch really wants this deal to go through."

"If you want to go, be my guest. I'll not waste my time."

*Right, you've got better things to do, like playing poker and whittling sticks on the front porch at the farm.*

Changing the subject she offered, "Like I told you at dinner tonight, Ethan Quinn's boy fixed the dining room light today. Do you think he would make a good replacement for Mr. Layman?" Connor Layman, now retired, had worked for Mr. Henry as his maintenance supervisor and single employee. On her daily walks with Heyu, Iris had surveyed many of the properties. With Mr. Layman gone and Kooch's management company responding to service calls, the repairs were falling behind. Iris was thinking about offering Vinnie Quinn a job.

Chapter 17

Iris gave Bert a ride to Elder Home to visit her uncle, Donnie Tyler. Technically, Donnie was not a resident. He had started working at Elder Home as their daytime janitor back in the '70s. One day three springs ago he just didn't go home after his shift. His bed was a cot in the janitor's closet. His living room was the activity room where the men came each day to watch TV and play gin rummy. He took his meals with the residents and helped with the dishes.

Donnie was as slight as a fifth-grader. His too-short polyester pants were last in style when Gerald Ford was president. And his no-iron shirts were always short-sleeved no matter the season. The amazing thing about Donnie was his memory. The skinny Elder Home denizen was everybody's go-to man when it came to the private histories, and gossip, of Fallam County families. He kept tally of events like who was feuding with whom and who fathered children with women other than their own wives. Iris hoped he might know something about her grandfather's relationship with Bella Sorin.

"As I live and breathe." Donnie stood up from a game of checkers with another resident to greet Iris. "Sweet pea, ain't you a sight for these tired old eyes." He wrapped his stringy arms around Iris and hugged her. "Hey, Sissy." He saluted in Bert's direction as she beamed at her uncle.

"Sissy told me you was in town. How long y'all in for?" Pointing to the other checker player, Donnie added, "Iris, this here's Eddie Moran. He's from Eastend Street."

"I'm here for a few days. Will you excuse us, Mr. Moran?" Iris nodded toward a pair of worn cargo sofas. She and Bert sat facing Donnie. "I'm sure Mr. Henry's told you all about the trouble at The Shops." She leaned into him as she spoke softly.

"Yeah, that's some bad news there. Y'all want Co-cola, coffee?" Donnie straightened his leg and reached into his trouser pocket for his roll of antacid tablets. Offering one to Iris, he popped two in his mouth.

"No thanks." Iris shook her head. "Donnie, Granddaddy Allen had a client by the name of Bella Sorin. Do you ever remember him talking about her? Or who she was?"

"Mr. Lee never talked to me about nothin'," Donnie responded.

"Rumors had it that she came from up North, and everybody gossiped that she was a client and that they had an affair."

"Who told you that?" Donnie asked quickly.

"I did." Bert asserted herself. Her dentures clacked. Donnie waited for her to explain herself.

"Like I told Iris this mornin'," Bert lowered her voice, "when I first come to work at Grove House, Elizabeth told me that Mr. Lee had an affair with one of his clients. Elizabeth didn't know the woman's name. But she said that the woman wanted Mr. Lee to move away with her, but he had just married his Matilda."

"Sissy, you know better than to go around talkin' trash about white folks. Did she have any proof?" Donnie asked.

"The two of you are the only ones I've ever repeated this to. As for proof, Donnie Tyler, if Elizabeth Lee says it's so, then it's so." Bert hitched her substantial purse up on her shoulder. "Besides it don't matter none, they all dead now," Bert lobbed back.

Iris watched the two bicker over the finer details of verifying gossip as truth. She noticed for the first time how different they looked. Donnie's skin, as dark as her morning coffee, contrasted the honey brown of Bert's. But their eyes were the same, full of life and love with an abundance of laugh lines.

"Well, I swannee, I never heard as such," Donnie scratched the back of his head. "But I was just a kid when your granddaddy practiced law. If I heard anything, it wouldn't have made sense to me, being a kid and all." Donnie seemed disappointed that he couldn't help Iris.

"It's no big deal. I hear you and Miss Bert are going to Ohio."

"Now that's Sissy's idea. I'm not too sure this place can stay afloat with me being gone for two whole weeks," Donnie said.

"Uncle Donnie, you told me you wanted to go," Bert insisted.

"I'm not so sure I want to drive all the way to Ohio in that piece of junk you call a car," Donnie reasoned. "Driving through West Virginia. Thing's liable to fall apart and us roll down the side of a mountain."

"I had my heart set on going up there Uncle D. You have to go with me." Disappointment trickled from Bert's plea.

"Who's Queen Victoria over there?" Iris nodded toward a tall, bony woman dressed head to toe in a black mourning costume, complete with bonnet and hoop skirt.

"That's Plinkus Young. She might know something about this—what was the name?"

"Bella Sorin." Iris leaned her shoulder against Bert's. "Remind me how I'm supposed to know Plinkus Young."

"She's the head cheese here at Elder Home. She's also the president of the historical society. If she don't know Bella Sorin, there ain't no such person," Donnie offered as he tugged at the few wiry white hairs on his upper lip. "You may not remember her, but I guarantee she knows who you are."

"That's a scary thought," Iris said.

"Speak of the devil." Donnie stood and welcomed the woman into their circle. Plinkus's red plastic glasses and ID card, attached to a chain of flashy beads, contradicted the mourning ensemble.

"Good morning, Donnie. Bert, how y'all doin'?" Plinkus nodded. "Y'all have to pardon my dress. I just come from leading a cemetery tour for the historical society."

"Morning," Donnie replied. "This is Iris Lee, Mr. Henry's daughter."

"I know who she is, Donnie." Plinkus reprimanded him as she faced Iris. "I'm in the same Sunday school class as her mama. Hi, Iris. How's Elizabeth doing? We never see her at church anymore." Plinkus had already started reaping grains for her gossip mill.

"She's fine, Mrs. Young. She just doesn't get out much these days," Iris replied.

"Please, call me Plinkus. Mrs. Young was my mother-in-law." Plinkus flashed a toothy smile at Iris. "You in town visiting your folks?"

"Something like that," Iris answered.

"Iris was asking me if I knew anything about one of Allen Lee's clients. Ah, Bella Sorin?"

"Have you ever heard of that name?" Iris asked Plinkus.

"No, can't say that name rings any bells for me." Plinkus picked at her lower lip. "I'll check our archives. Who was she?"

"She came from up North and had Mr. Lee do legal work for her. Apparently her mother was from here and she had business with Jubal Early while he lived in Lynchburg. So she would have visited here in the 1890s, I'm guessing." Iris left out the part about the medallion and the claims of paternity.

"She had business with the General?" Plinkus gasped. "I'll call you if I find anything." Iris gave Plinkus her cell phone number, something she suspected she would later regret.

As Donnie walked them back to the parking lot, Iris asked him "Does Mr. Henry come every week to play poker?"

"Most weeks, yeah. He shows up for a few hands. He always quits when he starts losing though. Tells us since we livin' on the government dole, we already got most of his money." Donnie laughed. "Your daddy is a mess, but I shore love 'im like a brother."

"Have you noticed if he's acting differently? Forgetting things?" she asked.

"Naw. Mr. Henry got a mind like a steel bear trap. He ain't forgot a thing. He knowed who owes him and who he owe. Your daddy's doin' OK in that department. That ain't what I hear about Miss Elizabeth though. I'm sorry about what's happening to her. And, in his own way, Mr. Henry is mournin' her loss 'fore they even put her in the ground," Donnie said quietly as he stared at his shoes.

"Thanks, Uncle Donnie. Mom always liked you. Why don't you come by and see her sometime?" Iris offered. "Seeing you might perk up some happy memories for her," she said as she got into her car.

"Ah-ite, I'll do that. Nice ride." Donnie leaned into the car window. "Now, Sissy, I could take a road trip in this here. Know what I'm sayin'?" He winked at Iris and saluted a good-bye to his favorite niece.

Before lunch, Iris called the number the Internet directory gave for Benjamin Robert Lee Jr. in Los Angeles. With a little luck, she hoped to catch her cousin before he left for work. After they moved out West, she had lost touch with Bennie, Aunt Sarah, and Uncle Ben. Until her death, Aunt Sarah and Elizabeth had traded Christmas cards every year. Aside from that, the two families rarely talked.

"Hello?" A man answered.

"Is this Bennie Lee?"

"This is Ben Lee. Who is this?"

"Hi, Bennie, ah, Ben," Iris said. All of the sudden she was a pre-teen and he was her older, smarter cousin from the big city. "This is Iris, your cousin."

"Hello," was all he said.

"It's been awhile." After all these years, he still intimidated her with his too few words.

"Yes, it has. Why are you calling? Is Uncle Henry—"

"Oh, gosh no." Iris interrupted nervously. "Mr. Henry and Mom are doing fine. Just getting older. They had a little excitement here a couple of weeks ago. Some of Mr. Henry's renters were arrested for drugs."

"Yes, I saw that online in *The Roanoke Times*," he offered. "Is this why you're calling?"

"No. I wanted to find out if you could help me with a family matter." She waited from him to prompt her, but all she got was silence. "Did Uncle Ben ever talk to you about any of Granddaddy Allen's clients?"

"No, but Iris if you knew anything about the law, you would know that lawyers don't typically talk about their clients," he responded.

*Yeah, especially when your clients were thugs and wise guys.* Biting her tongue, she asked, "Did Uncle Ben ever mention the name Bella Sorin to you?"

"Not that I recall. Why?"

Iris sensed that her cousin suspected she was hiding something. "Nothing really. Mr. Henry told me that she was Granddaddy Allen's client and had ties to Jubal Early. I'm trying to find out who she was and if she was more than a client, if you know what I mean?"

"No, I don't know what you mean," he responded. Then he was quiet.

"Well, was there a personal relationship between them, for instance?" she said. "So that name doesn't mean anything to you?" she tried again.

"No," was all she got.

"All right. If you think of anything, can you give me a call?" After repeating her cell phone number, she decided to move on to more innocuous questions. "How's your family?"

"I don't know. They don't live here anymore." Again, this was all she got.

"So the fledglings have left the nest?" Iris inquired about his daughters.

"Megan and Sarah are grown, married, and have children," he offered.

"Wow! You're a granddad. That's fantastic." She was trying to get some excitement into the conversation but talking to him was about as fun as a flat tire on Interstate 95.

"Two grandsons," he said.

"Did you ever think about doing a genealogy chart for them? Since Mr. Henry and Mom are getting older, I've been asking them all sorts of questions about our relations and the past." Iris wanted to see if Bennie would confide in her his genealogy expedition call to Jonnie.

"I'm not sure what you've been told, but we were forced to leave Virginia. My father's life was threatened. And his death—I'm not sure I want to expose my children or grandchildren to that," he added. "Before he died, my father said that Allen Lee forced him out of the law practice and the property management business. He said that Uncle Henry subsequently ran it into the ground." Many a day, Iris believed the same thing, but she wasn't going to let someone else say nasty things about her father.

"In his defense, Mr. Henry did what he could to keep the business running. He's not a lawyer, never wanted to be one, and the property management business was forced on him. In fact he told me the other night that he wanted to stay in California after he got out of the Army. Isn't that ironic? Uncle

Ben got what Mr. Henry wanted and Mr. Henry got what Uncle Ben wanted." *Zing, take that smarty pants.*

"Do you plan to take over the business?" Bennie asked.

"To be honest, there isn't much there. With all the new development out in the county, the uptown area is dying. It would take a major capital investment to get things running again."

"I see," Bennie said.

"It's been good talking to you. If you ever plan to make it back East, we'd love to see you and your family." Iris was itching to get off the phone. If he knew anything about Bella Sorin or the medallion, he wasn't sharing with her.

"Yes, good to hear from you too. I'll let you know when I make it back to Roanoke." Click. He hung up before Iris could say goodbye.

She leaned back in her desk chair. When she thought of Cousin Bennie, she fretted at trying to remember why her cousin always acted so hostile toward her. One Christmas after Bennie and his parents had departed Grove House for their home in Roanoke, eight-year-old Iris discovered that her brand-new Miss America Barbie was missing, the one in the Christmas edition of the Sears and Roebuck catalog. Miss America Barbie came with all the accessories necessary to win the pageant: evening gown, bathing costume, and travel suit. A set of luggage and a trip around the world were her rewards for taking the crown. Winning and world travel, that's what young Iris wanted when she grew up. She was going to be a world-class businesswoman who traveled to exotic places like Rome and Paris just like Barbie did.

She was positive that Bennie had stolen Miss America Barbie because she watched him, over her loud objections, take the doll from its place on her bookshelf. He ripped off the evening gown and forced carnal knowledge on Barbie with her Ken doll. Later, when she complained to her mother about the purloined doll, Elizabeth shushed her and told her that it was a sin to accuse someone of stealing if she had no proof.

"But the proof is that I can't find Barbie," she whined after Christmas dinner. For days afterward, she complained to her mom and Bert about Bennie's unforgivable act. But her lobbying had fallen on deaf ears.

After much angst and cogitation, she decided to appeal her case to Mr. Henry. She had been confident that after he heard her argument, he would call Bennie and demand he return the doll. Once she recited her rehearsed argument, Mr. Henry had asked without looking up from his newspaper, "What would a boy want with a doll?"

"But Mr. Henry, I've looked everywhere," she pleaded.

"Go look again. Now get out of here and go do your homework."

No justice, no justice at all, had been what she got.

Years later when she was in high school, she went looking for a place to hide her private stash where Bert wouldn't find it. She crawled to the farthest end of the low closet in her room. Stuffed beside a box of old books and wrapped inside one of Elizabeth's Christmas hand towels was a naked Miss America Barbie. Her raised plastic arms were bound at the tiny wrists with a dry-rotted rubber band. Dress pins had been nailed into the pert breasts where the nipples belonged and a curly triangle had been drawn in with black Magic-Marker at the doll's crotch.

Secretly, Iris had been vindicated. She had her proof. Bennie not only stole Miss America Barbie but he had violated her. But there was no way she was going to show the doll to her parents.

For reasons her parents had refused to share with her, Ben Sr. and his family had never been talked about, or referred to, after their move to California.

Even now Iris wondered why Ben Sr.'s remains were not returned to the family cemetery at the farm. She scratched a note on her phone to ask Mr. Henry about them when she caught him in a talkative mood.

*Good luck with that.*

# Chapter 18

It was the worst of times. After Wall Street and the federal government declared it was over, the Great Recession of the first decade of the twenty-first century continued to steamroll over every homeowner's property value and hard-working employee's retirement savings plan. For Iris, this meant her 401(k), which consisted mostly of bank stock, had dipped so close to zero that it was hardly worth the effort to sell the shares. But friends in the financial trading business assured her the account would bounce back.

Unlike the millions without jobs who spent their days cursing employment websites and applying for jobs online, Iris believed the activities a whopping electronic paper chase. But her new job search method of nagging her ex-business colleagues for introductions wasn't providing any results either. She wasted most of her job-hunting day noodling through online financial news sites.

Sitting at her school desk, she spotted a headline on the *Wall Street Journal* website, "Nexdorf Gets New Executive VP." Speed reading through the article, she fought the urge to throw her laptop across the room. Sandy Summers, the old toad who had fired her for his mistakes, managed to leap over her and into the arms of *her* Prince Charming. Her Nexdorf deal was officially dead. Tenney probably knew the day he met with her that they were bringing Summers into the group.

"Trust Department, Betty Kitter."

"Betty, this is Iris. What's The Vine say about Summers?"

"His assistant called me for a job last week," Betty whispered. "Did you see the story in the *Journal* this morning?"

"Yea. I bet he was fired," Iris speculated.

"That's what I thought too. The Vine says he's being investigated by the SEC."

"Is it true?" Iris asked.

"I don't know. If I find out, I'll try to give you a call. We're so busy right now. That last round of layoffs left me down two people, and we inherited another group's work," Betty said.

"Who's replacing Summers?"

"They're not saying," Betty said.

"That means there's a re-org coming. Who's approving his team's requests?"

"Jack Storm. Can you believe it? The chairman wants to review everything," Betty said.

"Has Lace surfaced over there?" Iris asked.

"I haven't heard anything. Oh, Fred told me last night that he got a response on your medallion thingy. Did he call you?"

"No, he's next on my list." The two agreed to talk again in a few days.

"Fred Kitter speaking."

"What's it worth?" Iris was excited.

"I'm well. And you?" Fred joked with her.

"Oh, sorry Fred. How are you? How are the plans for the Connecticut B&B coming along?"

"I assume Bet told you all about it. Keep it to yourself, OK?" Fred whispered.

"Fred, I'm sequestered in a town that still uses rotary dial telephones. Who am I going to tell? Louie Pyle, the guy who owns Louie's Gas N Go? What did you find?"

"We got a couple of inquiries. The last one was from your neck of the woods. From a place called Row-ah-no-key?" Fred attempted to pronounce the city's name.

"Let me guess, Links Jewelers?" Iris asked.

"Yes, do you know these people?"

"Junie Marks is related to my mother. Don't ask me how. I don't know. What did you tell him?"

Iris heard Fred's keyboard clicking away. "On the fifteenth of this month, we gave him an estimate of one dot five." Iris looked at the calendar on her laptop and noticed that the fifteenth was the day before she visited Marks. So much for family loyalty, he had low-balled her.

"Mr. Marks told me that it would be worth more if we had proof of origin or provenance."

"Yes. Any rare or unique piece like this one can always fetch more if there is a record of ownership and an interesting history. Plus, it could put it into the museum collection category," Fred said.

"If we had provenance and auctioned it, how much do you suppose it would bring?" Iris was anxious to get to the bottom line, hoping that the value of the medallion matched the tax bill and enough capital to help with the much needed property upgrades.

"I can't say until I have a jeweler and a historian take a look at it."

"Fred, I appreciate what you're saying, and I assure you Sotheby's will represent me on this thing. But friend to friend and based on your experience, what do you think it'll bring?"

"If we have documented proof of the original owner, the value could double. That's 'if,'" Fred said. "And if the original owner was someone famous like the King of England, the sky's the limit on the value. We're literally talking about crown jewels now." Fred was getting caught up in the excitement, too. "But Iris I'm not an expert in this field. Don't get your hopes up. For now I would assess the value of the medallion based upon the value of the stones."

"Fred, you said that there were two requests. Who was the other one? And what makes you think this thing belonged to the King of England?"

"Jeeze, I almost forgot the best part! I posted a request at our London office. The same day Links Jewelers sent in its request, we got a hit on our posting in Europe. Are you sitting down?"

"Go ahead. I could use some good news." Iris held her breath.

"The Louvre is interested in looking at it." There was silence for a full ten seconds. "Hello? Iris, are you still there?"

"You're joking." She was stunned by Fred's news.

"No, they want to see it! But before you meet with them, I suggest that you produce some proof of ownership." Fred's excitement had left his voice and he was speaking in a serious tone.

Iris wasn't ready to tell him the Bella Sorin story. The ramblings from an old goat, who only days earlier was suspected of dealing cocaine out of his dilapidated storefront in a small town in Southwest Virginia, was hardly a convincing testament of ownership. "I have proof that it's been in our family for three generations, if you count me," she said slowly. "But I'm not sure how my grandfather came to own it. According to my father someone gave it to him."

"That would prove that you, the current owner, didn't steal it," Fred reasoned.

"When can I meet with your historian?" A weekend excursion to New York would be a nice break from the monotony of Mt Pleasant.

"Oh, our guy will come to you. He's based in Richmond. Let me give you his number and you two can schedule a meeting. His name is Syke Darcy. Good luck with the provenance."

"Fred thanks for everything." Iris ended the call. How was she going to prove that the medallion belonged to the Lee family? She needed a history detective, preferably one who didn't live in Mt Pleasant.

"Iris?" Bert called from the foot of the kitchen stairs the next day. "You got a phone call."

"Who is it?" Iris stood at the top of the stairs.

"It's Plinkus Young," Bert answered in a loud whisper, covering the mouthpiece of the old telephone receiver.

With her face scrunched and her head tilted to one side, Iris gave Bert a questioning look. She bounced down the stairs like a teenager and mouthed to Bert "Who?"

"Mrs. Young, let me go bring her to the phone," Bert said into the receiver as she made a circle in the middle of the kitchen to untangle herself from the phone cord and laid the receiver on the butcher's block.

"Hello?" Iris said.

"Hi, Iris. This is Plinkus Young. I checked our archives and there wasn't any mention of a Stella Borin in the General's records."

"Thanks for looking Mrs. Young. But the name is Bella Sorin, b-e-l-l-a s-o-r-i-n." Iris rolled her eyes toward Bert.

"Oh! Well no wonder I couldn't find nothin'," Plinkus shouted. Iris reflexively jerked the phone receiver away from her ear. "Anyway, I was over at Wanda's yesterday and told Adie Aiken about you bein' in town and lookin' for information about your granddaddy."

"Who is Adie Aiken?" asked Iris.

"She was Adie Austin of the Franklin County Austins not the Roanoke Austins. Her father was your granddaddy's master builder. Mr. Austin and his boys built most of the houses on Eastend Street for your granddaddy."

"That's interesting but what's this got to do with Bella Sorin?" Iris interrupted. She sensed that Plinkus would go on for hours if she wasn't stopped, like Sarah Ward, her Richmond condo neighbor.

"Bless Pat! I get carried away." Plinkus took a deep breath. "Adie and your Aunt M. Ellen was best friends. That is before they both got married. But not to each other," she cackled. "Adie married Jamie Aiken and you know your Aunt M. Ellen married a Baptist preacher from Richmond."

"You think that this Mrs. Aiken might know about Bella Sorin?"

"Honey, I knowed it. She told me to tell you to come see her. She'll tell you all about it."

"About what?" Iris was confused.

"I don't have a clue what the old gal was goin' on about. She just told me to tell you to come and see her."

"Where is she now?" Iris asked.

"Like I told you, she's at Wanda's. She's livin' at Wanda's on account Jamie died and her daughters won't keep her at their houses. Can you believe that? Her own daughters won't take her in! Great day, what's the world coming to?"

"Where does this Wanda person live?"

"Wanda and Cleodis Stone live on his folk's home place over in Franklin County. After Wanda lost her job at the sweat shirt factory on account of it closing down, she started keeping ladies in her home. I don't know how she does it. She charges –

"Where in Franklin County?" Iris asked, frustrated.

"Oh, I keep forgettin' you ain't lived here for a while. Just go by Louie's Gas N Go-West and take a left. Go about three, four miles and you'll pass the English place and take a left on Posey Trail. Or is it Turkey Trail? Then—"

"I'll find it. Thanks for the tip, Mrs. Young." Iris tried to hang up the phone.

"Call me Plinkus. Mrs. Young is my mother-in-law's name, 'cept she died last winter—"

"I got to go. My other phone is ringing," Iris tried again to hang up.

"You got two phones? Bless Pat. What do you need two phones for?" Plinkus asked.

As Iris hung up the receiver, Plinkus was still talking. "Miss Bert, I think I've found someone who can fill in the blanks on the Bella Sorin mystery. How do I get to Wanda and Cleodis Stone's farm?"

Chapter 19

Early the next morning, Iris and Heyu headed to Franklin County for a visit to Miss Wanda's Home for Ladies. Located south and west of Fallam, Franklin County was full of the Blue Ridge foothills and bordered by two man-made lakes, Philpott and Smith Mountain. With the help of the lakes and the new Crooked Road attractions, Franklin County was slowly pulling itself out of a forty-year economic drought. Amid the loss of its cash king crops of tobacco and its many factories, Franklin County folks relied on their European serfdom traits to persevere. According to Plinkus Young, Wanda and Cleotis Stone were scratching out a living from the land and their wits just as their parents and grandparents before them.

Wanting to make a good impression, Iris brought some of Bert's fried chicken along with her. She stopped at Louie's Gas N Go-West to fill up and to purchase a box of The Lord's Acre chocolate-covered butter cream drops for Miss Wanda and her ladies.

Louie's Gas N Go-West and its sister store at the opposite end of the county, Louie's Gas N Go-East, were legacies of the Louie Pyle dynasty. With a lot of sweat and elbow grease, the high school dropout had managed to amass a fortune by Fallam County's measure by providing his customers with what they needed at a price Louie Pyle wanted.

At times, Iris tried to describe the retail experience at Louie's Gas N Go to her cosmopolitan friends in Richmond and New York. Per square foot, a New York bodega had nothing over Louie's. The home-grown store sold everything an addict could legally purchase—lottery tickets, coffee, cigarettes and cigars, walk-in cooler beer and wine, candy and chips, ice cream, and home-made cakes and pies. Unlike every other convenience store in the country, Iris explained to her big city friends, a customer had to ask at the counter for girlie magazines or condoms.

Iris was impressed that the town councilman, a friend to her father, had managed to stay in business in spite of the national chains. Although she had never met the man, she often viewed him as her competition for Mr. Henry's favors. At home her father spoke of Louie Pyle as if he were a younger brother or a son whom Mr. Henry helped out quite often.

After getting lost on the corkscrew roads, Iris finally found the entrance to the Stone's driveway. The smoke curling out from the two-story stone chimney reminded Iris of how far she was from her urban, high-rise apartment life. In the distant field behind the clapboard house, she saw a tractor plowing the dormant earth as a black dog followed behind, surmising that the man on the tractor was Cleodis.

"Can Heyu visit too?" Iris asked when Wanda answered her knock. With graying hair swept up in a bun, Wanda was as wide as she was tall.

"Of course," Wanda exclaimed while wrapping her faded Christmas sweater around her thick middle. "All the ladies love making friends like Heyu." She stooped down and tousled Heyu's wiry mop-top.

"Thank you for inviting us into your home," Iris said as she stepped into the simple and clean hallway. The house smelled of lemon furniture polish and breakfast bacon and coffee.

"We love getting visitors. Mrs. Aiken is all excited. Two visitors in one week. The ladies are just finishing up their morning devotionals." From the back of the house, the visitors heard music streaming from an out-of-tune piano and voices trying to harmonize "How Great Thou Art." Iris bent down and whispered to Heyu, "No howling. OK?"

Heyu shook from head to toe.

They entered a sunlit room just as the piano rested its last note. Iris hadn't given much thought about what to expect but she was startled by what she saw. Seven pairs of curious eyes stared back at her. Six of the ladies were lined up in overstuffed recliners, three against one wall and three on another. At the back of the room a bank of windows offered the view of a bare garden, waiting for spring, complete with clay gnomes and oversized wind chimes. Dressed just like their caregiver, the ladies wore blue jean skirts, blouses of every shade of the rainbow and sweaters draped over bony shoulders. Their bodies and minds appeared to be in varying stages of atrophy. The piano player was sitting in a wheelchair. She wore the same outfit but somehow seemed different from the others.

After going around the room with introductions, Wanda ended with the maestro. "Iris, our piano player is Adie Aiken."

"Hello, Mrs. Aiken. You play beautifully."

"I learned to play when I was a little girl." She extended her hand to Iris.

"I spoke with Plinkus Young and she relayed your message to me." Iris reached for Mrs. Aiken's hand and felt an energy which was lacking in her mother's small and shaky ones. "May we sit over here for a private chat?" Iris pointed to a table and chairs next to the piano.

The caregiver welcomed Heyu to follow her out of the room. Having forgotten that they had just been introduced to a visitor, the other ladies went on about their morning rituals of pulling off their socks or calling for loved ones long gone from the physical world.

Iris asked "Is it OK if I record our conversation?"

Mrs. Aiken nodded. "As you heard by my piano playing, God blessed me with a good mind. But the warranty on my legs has expired, I'm afraid." She laughed and exposed a full set of perfect white teeth. She pressed down on the armrests with her elbows to keep from sliding out of the wheelchair.

"Plinkus Young said that you knew my father's older sister M. Ellen Lee," Iris began.

123

"Oh, yes. M. Ellen and I were best friends when we were young. We had the same music teacher. Mr. Truman said we were his best students. I wanted to go to music college, but we couldn't afford it. What with the Depression and then the war—" Mrs. Aiken bowed her head and smoothed out her wadded tissue. "She was a lovely person, your aunt. M. Ellen would do anything for anybody. I guess that's why she decided to do missionary work," Mrs. Aiken reminisced as her bright eyes met Iris's.

"Did my aunt ever say anything to you about a person named Bella Sorin?" Iris asked.

"Oh, yes. Before she went away to boarding school, she talked about her all the time. You see, your aunt fancied herself as a private eye. She wanted to be just like Nancy Drew," Mrs. Aiken chuckled at the memory. "She told me she found letters written to her father, *your* granddaddy. The letters were from Bella Sorin and post marked Toronto, Ontario, she told me." Mrs. Aiken paused to rest and then pulled her slumping body back upright in the chair.

"Did she say what was in the letters?"

"You have to know that, at the time, gossip held that Mr. Lee was having an affair with a Yankee woman. Everybody just assumed that since he traveled out of town a lot, he must be steppin' out on Matilda. That's what most folks believed, including my own mother. But he never confirmed or denied it. The Allen Lee I knew was a gentleman, Iris, and I'm sure he kept his silence for a good reason. When M. Ellen told me about the letters, she said that they would prove that her father did not have an affair." Mrs. Aiken smiled at Iris who started biting her thumbnails. "You do that just like your daddy used to do."

Iris jerked her hand from her mouth. "What else did she say?"

"All she said was that they proved that Bella Sorin was a client and not a mistress," Mrs. Aiken said.

"Did you ever see the letters? Do you know what happened to them?"

"I remember the day M. Ellen confronted Mr. Lee about them. We were at his office on Court Street playing secretary in the front room. Don't you know, she got into big trouble. He made her put them back where she found them. That was the one and only time I ever heard him raise his voice. He told her never to speak of them again," Mrs. Aiken said.

"So she put them back in a file cabinet in the Court Street office?" Iris wanted to keep Mrs. Aiken focused on the letters.

"I never saw M. Ellen jump to it so fast." Mrs. Aiken giggled as if she was that little girl playing secretary in the law offices again. "Later on, after she swore me to secrecy, she told me that Bella Sorin claimed to be Jubal Early's daughter and that she had hired Mr. Lee to represent her in the matter. God forgive me, M. Ellen." Mrs. Aiken folded her hands in prayer and looked at the ceiling. "You know I've never told another soul that story. Not even Jamie, my late husband. But since you're M. Ellen's family, I figure she'd want you to know."

Mrs. Aiken and Iris looked around. The dames were napping quietly, with the exception of the occasional poot.

"Mrs. Aiken, did M. Ellen mention anything about a broach or medallion?"

Adie Aiken braided her hands together and bit on her tiny purple lips. She remained quiet for a full minute, her head twitching up and down. The old woman's face showed the internal debate of trying to decide if she should reveal all the secrets her long ago friend had entrusted with her.

"She asked. I never told a soul M. Ellen," Mrs. Aiken shouted while looking up as if Iris's long dead aunt was hanging from the ceiling fan. Mrs. Aiken lowered her voice. "M. Ellen showed it to me. She said that according to the letters, it was proof that Bella was the General's daughter. And if anything happened to her, Mr. Lee was to have it."

"Yes, but *how* was it proof? Did she say?" Iris suspected there wasn't going to be any court-worthy proof found at Miss Wanda's Home for Ladies.

"No, just that the medallion was the proof she needed. I'm not too sure M. Ellen knew what the letters meant. We were just children. We knew nothing of the adult world."

"Do you remember what it looked like?"

"Never forgot it. The thing was ostentatious, shaped like a cross. It had a ruby in the center with diamonds around it."

Iris scrolled through the medallion pictures on her phone for Mrs. Aiken.

"That's it. Do you still have the handkerchief? " the old lady asked.

Iris nodded.

"I have to use the bathroom. Would you mind rolling me down the hallway?" And to Iris's surprise, she didn't mind at all.

Before leaving, Iris leaned into Mrs. Aiken's ear and whispered, "Mrs. Aiken, can you keep M. Ellen's secret and not tell anyone about our conversation?"

"I reckon so. I kept it a secret for over eighty years. I guess I can keep it awhile longer. Besides," she said as she winked at Iris, "if Mr. Lee had wanted people to know about Bella, he would have told them."

At dinner that night Iris decided to bring up the Sorin-Lee gossip. She was angry with Mr. Henry for not sharing family history with her.

"I went over to Franklin County to see Adie Aiken today," she said as she tried to tame Bert's spaghetti with a fork and spoon.

"Who?" he asked.

"Adie Aiken, M. Ellen's friend," Iris said.

"Do you mean Adie Austin?"

"Yeah. I thought she might know something about the medallion." And with her voice raised, she asked, "How come you never told me Aunt M. Ellen was a missionary?"

"You never seemed interested in knowing. Why are you traipsing around hell's half acre talking to everybody about our private affairs?" Mr. Henry set his fork down.

"I wouldn't if you would talk to me. You know more about this than you're telling me. And if you don't tell me what I want to know, I'll keep asking other people," Iris snapped. She took in a deep breath and said, "Look, Sotheby's says that we can get a better price on the medallion if we can determine provenance. And according to you, and now Adie Aiken, this woman gave it to Granddaddy Lee. We have to show proof of ownership. That's why it's important to know who she was. I know you understand all of this. What are you holding back?"

"I've told you what I know about that damn thing. Allen Lee turned his law practice over to John Bailey. Ask his chaps about it." Mr. Henry lifted his china cup with both hands and sipped on his cooling coffee.

"But what about the rumors about the affair? Did anyone in the family ever know the truth about that?"

"There was no affair, Iris! For God's sake, you're worse than the lot of them. A bunch of nosy busybodies trying to stir things up." Mr. Henry slammed the cup in its saucer. The clanging caused Elizabeth to jump and drop her fork onto the floor. "Now look what you've done. You've upset your mother."

"Do you remember seeing any letters from Sorin?" Iris wasn't letting this go. The sale of the medallion was her ticket back to her solitary life in Richmond.

"Letters? What letters?" Mr. Henry asked.

"According to Mrs. Aiken, M. Ellen found some letters that Sorin had written to Granddaddy. The letters claimed she was

Jubal Early's daughter and she also wanted granddaddy to have the medallion," she answered.

"I never saw any letters," then lowering his voice, "and your mother cared for him in his later years, but I don't think that she would remember if he said anything about any letters." Mr. Henry stared at his wife who had given up using a fork and spoon to eat her spaghetti. Elizabeth smiled when everyone at the table looked her way. "Your mother cared for him until he died," he said while Bert wiped spaghetti sauce from Elizabeth's hands and mouth.

Iris pulled out her phone and tapped in a reminder to go through all of the old letters and Christmas cards they'd found while cleaning out Elizabeth's closet. Maybe she'd get lucky and find them there.

"Turn that thing off while you're at the dinner table," Mr. Henry barked. "And put that mangy mutt outside!"

Chapter 20

Saturday night was family night at the Bailey Farm. As there was no night life in Mt Pleasant, Iris invited herself to Jonnie's for a break from her bickering with Mr. Henry. Bailey Farm was on the far west side of the county only a few miles from Skyline Drive. Driving through an early evening mist, the curvy roads and stone pile fences reminded Iris of the Scottish country roads she had explored the summer after her college graduation.

As she drove she thought about all the places her work at Bank US had taken her. She had visited just about every state in the union. As her responsibilities at the bank increased, she was expected to consult global clients and had lived in England for a year.

"Feels like I'm back in the UK," Iris said quietly as she drove up the cherry tree lined driveway on her first visit to the farm since Jonnie had built the new house. Several vehicles, parked in the circular graveled driveway, gave the place the feel of an exclusive resort. As she parked her car, she half expected to see a white-jacketed valet pop out from the English basement.

Before knocking Iris stood on the porch lined with rocking chairs and took in the view of wavy blue mountains. Iris agreed with most everyone who had stood on the porch before her, the mountain vistas from this place, and others in Fallam County, were scenic and serene. But she never felt the tie to the land the way it held her father and Jonnie. She didn't like the mountains. She was convinced she had been a flatlander in another life.

When all the dinner guests had left for the evening, Iris helped Jonnie load the dishwasher. Against the black of night, the kitchen's picture window over the sink reflected the happy chaos of stacked dirty dishes, opened cabinets and messy counter tops generated from an evening meal with family and friends.

With her Carter candor, Iris asked, "So what's the story with you and Ethan Quinn? That was a surprise to see him here tonight."

"Like I said when you got here, we're just friends. He wants to join Wyatt and me in our wine-making venture." Jonnie folded her dishcloth. "The clean-up can wait. Let's finish our coffee in the den. Want something in it? Scotch?" She raised a perfectly tweezed eyebrow.

"Are you kidding me?" Iris joked. "After those tequila shots we had at Chunky's, I hallucinated for three days. Is wine-making profitable?" Iris asked as they drifted toward the den.

"The startup costs are steep. We'll make a decision on whether to continue at the end of this year. Wyatt wants to quit the law and be a full-time vintner. We'll see."

"So you're doing all the business law and he does the criminal work?" Iris asked.

"These days it's split pretty much that way. Of course, I have the honor of keeping Henry Lee from being indicted," she teased.

"Any word on that?" Iris hoped that the feds were backing off on the preposterous notion that Mr. Henry had knowingly rented his building to a methamphetamine dealer.

"A little bird over at the courthouse told Wyatt that the county is still pretty sore at Mr. Henry for not helping with the Crooked Road project. They're apt to leave him hanging out on his own," Jonnie said.

"They would do that?" Iris asked.

"They could. If they stayed out of it and let the feds take over, the investigation could find its way into court. Fast-forward a few months, then Lee Properties has to sell assets at auction to cover legal expenses, the town and county come in and get what they wanted all along."

"What a bunch of slimy toads."

"Iris, I'm speculating. Take it with a grain of salt. But it *could* happen. You need to prepare for it," Jonnie said as she got up from her easy chair. "I'm getting a glass of wine. Want one?"

"No, thanks, I'll stick with the coffee." Thinking about Jonnie's guesswork on someone stealing Mr. Henry's property, Iris protested, "But Jonnie that's almost as bad as eminent domain proceedings. In fact, it's sneakier."

"Don't give Robert Kaluchi that much credit," Jonnie said as she opened a bottle of Chateau Morrisette. "The drug bust fell into their laps and anybody with half a brain would use Mr. Henry's misfortune to get access to his property. Let's hope they don't seek outside counsel."

"You're saying any good lawyer could connect the dots?" Iris asked.

"Um-hmm," Jonnie affirmed.

"The sunny beaches! What can Mr. Henry do? He can't fight town hall on this?" Iris felt the coffee acid burning in her throat. She chewed on her thumbnail.

"He could make some friends there." Iris and Jonnie both knew that by "he" she meant Iris, the wanderlust daughter. "Iris, most of these guys—and by that I mean there's not a single female council member in Mt Pleasant or supervisor in Fallam County—you either beat up in grade school or dated in high school. Start a goodwill campaign. That would be a good first step. Find someone on council who isn't impressed with our mayor's performance in office so far. Believe me, that won't be difficult."

"I'm a short-timer here. I really don't want to get caught up in this." Iris hated any kind of politics: civic, corporate or personal. To her it was a form of groveling and Iris Lee did not grovel. Mr. Henry had taught his daughter at an early age that the bow and scrape method of negotiations was undignified and only served to expose weaknesses to an opponent.

"Iris, you've got to get involved. It's critical for the survival of Lee Properties. Since the drug arrests, the Lee name could use some positive publicity. Think about it," Jonnie said as she started putting the kitchen back in order.

"I don't know the first thing about small town glad-handing." Iris loudly objected from the den sofa.

"It's easy. Take a council member to lunch. Ask them how Lee Properties can help with community programs. Get Lee Properties to sponsor a little league soccer or softball team. Sign up for the United Way fundraisers." Jonnie suggested.

"Do I have to?" Iris flailed her arms across the downy sofa cushions. Publically sponsoring social or community causes in exchange for business considerations was, to the Lee sensibilities, inappropriate. Lee Properties obtained the good graces of its clients through its actions not by shamelessly telling the world about its financial contributions to those in need. This type of grandstanding was vulgar. Iris had given up on arguing with Mr. Henry about the merits of advertising and public relations while she was in college. No amount of debate about financial gain or community goodwill would change his mind. And over time she came to understand his position and had adopted it as her own. Each year she quietly donated to causes she believed where helping her local community and none were the wiser.

"Iris, this is common business practice. Supporting the community. Didn't you get involved in community projects at the bank?" Jonnie asked.

"We had a staff to do that," she said with a yawn. "I hosted clients at the PGA US Open every year. Does that count?" Iris thought about the golf tournaments and the red carpet treatment she and her clients enjoyed. She really missed her job.

"You are absolutely hopeless." Jonnie waved a dishtowel at her from the kitchen.

"I'll have a glass of your wine," Iris said as she rolled off the sofa and stepped back into the kitchen. Climbing onto a bar stool, she said, "I need to get you up to speed on my adventures over the last few days." Iris told Jonnie the story of finding the medallion, the appraisals from Junie Marks and Sotheby's. "Can you believe it?"

"Iris, that's amazing," Jonnie said. "Are you going to sell it? A windfall like that could help Lee Properties with its tax debt and improvements."

"It'll do all that. But then what?" Iris asked. "I don't think Mr. Henry will want to move into Elder Home with the common folk. I'll still have to set up Grove House for assisted living care for him and Mom and Miss Bert. And what about the rental houses?"

"What about them?" Jonnie poured herself another glass of the cabernet. "I thought you wanted to sell it all and get out?" Jonnie looked at her friend with hopeful anticipation.

"I'd like to keep the farm. Why I want to keep it, I don't know. It's where my grandfather was born, I suppose." Iris held her glass out for Jonnie to pour her another glass. She ran her fingers through her thick hair and shook out the tangles. "Criminy, I need a haircut. Maybe I'll go native and start wearing a bun." Iris had given up on dressing for success. Most days she found herself living in her workout togs. Tonight was the first time in many days she had bothered to dress in her favorite designer jeans and a silk blouse.

"And Lee Properties?" Jonnie asked again.

"I've visited most of the properties and they all need a lot of work. Kooch's management company is worthless. There's a revelation. I can't believe Mr. Henry actually hired Kooch."

"Yes, I've struggled with that one myself," Jonnie said. "He's told me not to renew when this year's contract expires."

"The wonder of small miracles," Iris shook her head then moved on, "we need cash to update the buildings. My Sotheby's friend says that if I could show the history or provenance on the medallion, we could double or triple the sale price. Yesterday I drove up to Richmond to meet their appraiser who's an expert on eighteenth- and nineteenth-century military artifacts. And get this, his name is actually Mr. Darcy. Can you believe it? I wonder if his wife's name is Elizabeth," Iris snickered. "Anyway, he thinks it's eighteenth-century goldsmith work. And was probably made for some French general."

"You *have* been busy," Jonnie said.

"But I need your help." Iris told her Mr. Henry and Adie Aiken's tales about Bella Sorin and Allen Lee and the letters. "We need the letters or some other proof like some old first family local-yokel's testimony or journal that says he saw Bella give the medallion to granddaddy. And it would be even better if we knew where she got it and who she was." Iris waved her hands in excitement as she recounted her investigation. "According to Mrs. Aiken, she saw the letters in granddaddy's office. Do you guys still have his case files?"

"Gosh, Iris, I don't know. I'd have to get Claire to crawl around in the attic."

"Who do you think would make a good manager? To run Lee Properties?" Iris changed the subject again.

"Did you get a job and not tell me about it? Why don't you hire yourself?"

"Are we going over this real estate again?" Iris leaned with her elbows on the kitchen service island and rubbed her face with both hands. "I'm getting this cluster straightened out and going back to Richmond. How many times and how many ways do I have to say it?"

"What cluster?" Jonnie asked.

"Never mind. And nooo, I am not available for the job," Iris answered.

"Well, I suppose you and Heyu have so much to do in Richmond that restoring the family business is just not a priority," Jonnie said.

Iris exploded. "Yes, Jonnie. My housemate," she looked at Heyu as he licked around the bottom of the kitchen trashcan, "is a dog. And yes, I have nothing to go back to because I've lost my freakin' livelihood. Why? Because a swarm of Wall Street poker players and navel gazers were too greedy or too scared to admit the sky was falling on the burning house." Iris took a deep breath. "Will you *please* stop guilt-tripping me into coming back to the land that time forgot?" Iris signaled to Heyu. "Excuse us. We need to take a walk."

The two of them walked out onto the kitchen patio and into the hibernating flower garden. Heyu ran ahead following the path to the tractor barn. Iris sniffed the crisp air and imagined Heyu was probably hoovering the riot of farm smells, wet earth, moldy hay, and overturned manure composts.

Her neat and perfect life was fading away. The business community she loved no longer needed or wanted her. In fact her colleagues were doing their best to forget she had ever existed. What was she doing wrong? Why couldn't she find her way back? Iris tormented herself with these thoughts while following the path. She stopped and shivered while gazing at the sea of stars in the pitch-black March sky, then silently cried for a long time in peace.

# Chapter 21

"Iris, I'm sorry about last night," Jonnie offered at breakfast the next morning.

"I'm sorry, too. I'm having trouble accepting that I'll never again have what I had," she said. "The career I mean. It's so daunting, having to start over."

"Sweetie, that bank and the people in that business could give two flips about you. Why are you spending all your emotional equity trying to rebuild a bridge of sand when there's a whole town just waiting to love you? Besides, you're missing a lifetime opportunity by not jumping in and making Lee Properties something special. It's what you've been training for all these years at the bank. Don't you see it?"

"I just can't see myself living here with my parents," Iris sighed.

"Get an apartment. Renovate one of your dad's rundown shacks on Eastend Street."

"You don't understand. Moving back means I've failed— failed at everything."

"Don't make me bring up the countless nights you called me literally screaming into the phone about how miserable you were," Jonnie warned.

"I know. I know. I'm just having trouble letting it all go," Iris said.

As Iris was driving back into Mt Pleasant, her cell phone rang.

"Iris! Where the hell are you?" An agitated Mr. Henry demanded.

"So you do know how to dial a telephone." Iris pulled into Louie's Gas N Go-West.

"Don't get smart-mouthed with me, missy. I want to know who told you to tell that jack leg real estate agent that my house is for sale." Mr. Henry was breathing heavily.

"What are you talking about?" She asked getting out of the car to pump gasoline.

"Wilmer Thompson sent two of his squirts over here this morning, snooping around saying they needed an appraisal to sell the house. I ran them off and then they came back," Mr. Henry shouted.

"I didn't tell anybody you were selling the house. They must've gotten the wrong address."

"That's what I told the boy!" Mr. Henry's anger was escalating.

"Calm down," she spoke loudly into the phone. Then she mumbled to herself, "Don't get your shorts in a knot." She chuckled nervously, thinking of Bert and the extra starch.

"What's that?"

"I said that we'll get to the bottom of this. Did they leave a business card?" she asked.

"They left nothing but tracks on the front porch right after I threatened to kick their asses off my property," the old man ranted.

Yikes, something was wrong. Mr. Henry only cursed when he was drunk or when the argument truly mattered to him. He hadn't had a drink in decades.

"Where is your revolver right now, Mr. Henry?" Iris feared the answer.

"By God, I've got it right here in case the sons-of-bitches come back," he said.

"If you made it clear to them not to come back while holding a loaded revolver, I'm pretty sure they got the message. Has Miss Bert left for the day?" Iris's heart raced, Mr. Henry didn't sound like Mr. Henry.

"She's not here. I don't know where she went off to. Maybe they took her with them."

"It's Sunday. She's probably at church," Iris tried to calm him. For the past forty years, Bert spent her Sundays at Zion

Baptist Church of The Lost Lambs. "I'm almost home. When I get there, we'll sort it out."

A trickle of sweat poured down her back. She lifted her hair off her neck and tried to slow her breathing. Sitting in the car she calculated the probability of a pistol crowding her face while entering her own home, again. Her hands trembled slightly as they tucked her credit card back into her wallet.

The flashback flew over her optic nerve. While sneaking back into the house through her mom's sun porch after an all-nighter with her Eastend rowdies, Iris came nose-to-nose with the barrel of Mr. Henry's Colt .45. In the shadows of the pre-dawn, a very drunk Mr. Henry yelled at her as if she were an intruder, swearing to haul her off to Stumpy Quinn's jailhouse. She had managed to tackle the old man and secure the gun without waking Elizabeth. She left for college the next day. And, as was the Mt Pleasant way, the light of acknowledgement or forgiveness had never washed over the incident.

"Ethan Quinn," a relaxed voice answered.

"Quinn, I need your help. Mr. Henry's acting funny." Iris tried to control her anxiety by speaking slowly. "Was on my way home from Jonnie's, and he called me with some wild story about somebody trying to get into the house and Miss Bert leaving with them. He's got his gun out. I don't want to go into the house by myself. I don't want to get shot at. Something's not right."

"I'm at the jailhouse. I'll meet you at your place." Quinn said.

Twenty minutes later, Iris met Quinn in her parents' driveway. "I'm sorry to bother you about this. He sounded— you know how he used to get when he went on his benders with your dad," she said.

"You did the right thing by calling me," he assured her.

As they stood facing each other, Iris recalled the day they climbed the stacked hay bales all the way to the top of the barn rafters at the farm. They took turns confiding to each other the nasty behavior of their alcoholic fathers. Iris cried through her accounts of Mr. Henry's emotional abuse, ignoring her when he was sober and berating her when he was drunk. Consoling Iris, Ethan had one-upped her with his tales of getting pulled from a dead sleep and beaten with the buckle side of Stumpy Quinn's belt. To lighten things, Ethan had said he got even with his daddy by trading the coveted Confederate flag buckle to a guy at school for a bag of weed. The experience had strengthen their friendship even though the confessions were never mentioned again.

"Let's just stay calm and go see what the ol' guy's up to," Quinn said.

"OK, here goes. Heyu stay in the car." Iris fumbled with her keys.

"I can't believe you named your dog Heyu," Quinn teased.

"I didn't. That was his given name when he was born."

"Fascinating." He shook his head and followed her up the stairs.

An unshaven Mr. Henry greeted them at the front door. His unbuttoned shirt and bare feet confirmed to Iris that Mr. Henry had either found Elizabeth's Tawny Port or he was suffering a dementia induced paranoiac episode.

"Where've you been? Get your ass up them steps and help your mother," Mr. Henry commanded.

Iris froze. She blinked with deliberation, trying to erase what she'd heard. *He can't hurt you anymore. Remember what Jonnie said, he's just an old man who doesn't know what he's saying half the time.* But, to Iris, it still felt like he meant every word.

"Mr. Lee." Quinn stepped from behind Iris and offered his hand. "You have a report of an attempted burglary?"

"Ethan Quinn, it's about time you showed up. Your office boy needs to be taught some manners. He was rude to me when I called," Mr. Henry said and started for his library.

"I'll go check on Mom," Iris said to Quinn. She slipped into the kitchen. And there it was, Mr. Henry's revolver, lying on the butcher's block along with the telephone receiver emitting the loud, fast busy noise. She hung up the receiver, then hurried up the back stairs two-at-a time, hearing her father and Quinn's muffled voices below.

Elizabeth was sitting on top of the made bed in her Sunday morning best.

"Mom, are you getting ready for a nap?" A strong odor rushed at her as she reached down to take the Bible from her mother. Elizabeth's skirt and the bed clothes were soaked in urine. Iris sat on the edge of the bed, hugged her mother and together they rocked gently to the soft classical music streaming from Elizabeth's beside radio.

Minutes later, Iris appeared at the butler's door leading into the library. "Quinn can you come out to the kitchen, I've got something for you." When he stepped into the room, she pointed at the gun. "This is how I found it." She wasn't sure why she thought she needed a witness.

Quinn confirmed the gun had not been fired. He emptied the rounds and handed them to Iris. She stuffed them in her pocket. He extended the butt of the gun to her. Not sure where to hide it, she pulled off her yoga hoodie and wrapped it around the gun. Iris noticed Quinn's quick glance at her lacy teddy.

"Does he keep any others in the house?" Quinn spoke softly.

"He keeps a gun safe in his bedroom." Iris stuffed the wrapped pistol under her arm.

"You'll need to talk with him about this, Iris. You know what would have happened to the person on the business end of that thing?" Quinn whispered.

"You know I do," Iris whispered back harshly. As teenagers, she and Quinn had borrowed Mr. Henry's guns to shoot at barn rats on the farm.

"He really thinks that a couple of shady characters tried to force their way in. I looked around but couldn't see any signs of forced entry. I'll ask the guys at the station if there've been any other reports. He seems to have calmed down. I'm supposed to be at Vinnie's, but I'll stay here if you—"

"Iris?" Elizabeth called from the front stairway. "Iris? Where are you?"

Iris followed the sound of Elizabeth's frail voice with Quinn at her heels. Smiling down from the top of the front stairs, Elizabeth had dressed herself in her favorite silk blouse and pearls. Unfortunately she had as yet to put on the underpants and skirt Iris had laid out for her.

"Elizabeth! For God's sake, get you some clothes on, woman. We have a guest," Mr. Henry shouted. Standing at the foot of the stairs, he gazed up at his wife's nakedness in disbelief and horror.

"Show some compassion, you idiot, she can't help it!" Iris yelled at the old man and brushed by him as she ran up the steps. "Wait right there. I'll be back in a minute," she called over her shoulder to an open-mouthed Quinn.

"Good Lord, Mom. Aren't we a pair? Me parading around in my lacy bra and you struttin' your stuff without any underpants."

Elizabeth giggled, and it broke the tension built up in Iris's shoulders.

When Iris and Elizabeth rejoined Quinn and Mr. Henry in the library, Quinn asked Iris to see him to the door. "I'm not sure if there was anybody here. I'll file a report just in case. He seems to be doing OK now. Seems coherent. I'd get him to the doctor tomorrow morning for a check-up. I take my old man to

Dr. Stone, a geriatric physician, just moved into town couple months back."

"Bert said she's tried to get him to go to the doctor, but he refuses. Does this Dr. Stone make house calls?"

"I don't need a doctor and certainly don't need one coming to my house," Mr. Henry shouted from his library.

"At least we know there's nothing wrong with his hearing," Iris called back to the old man. "Thanks for the tip about the doctor. I'll check it out." Then she whispered, "Thanks for coming."

"You've sure got your hands full." He smiled down at her.

"Miss Bert's here most days. And you know Ludie helps out."

"Really, Iris, don't try to do it all by yourself."

Iris punched his arm and asked, "And when were you going to get around to telling me that you're dating my best friend?"

"Keeping it a secret was Jonnie's idea," Quinn said.

"I knew it!"

"Oh, you got me," he acted out a shot to the chest. He smiled and added, "You call me if you need me."

As she watched Quinn lope away from the house, she smacked her forehead with the palm of her hand. Heyu, his front paws draped over the open car window, was still waiting for her next command. She signaled, and in a flash, he sailed out of the car and headed for the front porch by way of the boxwoods.

Back inside, Iris watched her parents as they sat in the matching Morris chairs, Mr. Henry reading the paper, as if this was just another Sunday, and Elizabeth rocking back and forth. Without Bert's constant chatter and hovering, Iris realized how helpless and pitiful they had both become.

That evening, after a long soak, Iris crawled out of the tub and wrapped a thread-worn towel around her body. She took inventory at the standing mirror. To Iris, her beauty had been fading for some time now. Yet today, Ethan Quinn had given her that same hang-dog, love-sick look he used to give her when they were teenagers. "A time when my breasts where high and my hair was dark and shiny," she murmured to the mirror. She had always been aware that he cared deeply for her but she had pretended that it was the concern of an older brother.

Once, he had tried to kiss her. By the next day, and for the next thirty-some years, they pretended that it had never happened. She had ignored his attempt at love because, even though she cared for him, the drive to get away from Mt Pleasant and her father was stronger. She dreamed of leaving and making her own way. And a much younger Iris had believed she couldn't have both—the man and the dream.

Now standing in front of the mirror, she asked herself, "Would it have been so bad? Loving Ethan, getting married and living in Mt Pleasant?" No, that life wasn't for her. Instead she had run toward the life she had visualized for herself, a life of grand experiences instead of simple existence. This she had known about herself and it was still true. She belonged to another world, a world outside of this one. To get back there, she would have to stay in Mt Pleasant for a little while longer.

"Don't cry for me, Mt Pleasant," she sang. She had gotten out the first time and she would do it again, somehow.

Back in her bedroom, she lay on her bed in the dark unable to sleep. Surrendering to her insomnia she reached for her laptop and, scrolling through her emails, she spied one from a former Bank US colleague who was fired on the same day as she. *Could that be the Manhattan mystery caller?* The message was a job offer with a global management firm—clearly entry-level. She replied to the offer with a "thanks but no thanks," suspecting she would regret the decision in the morning.

# Chapter 22

Iris softly hummed The Mamas and The Papas' song "Monday, Monday" as she walked with Heyu up Court Street at sunrise. She was meeting Vinnie Quinn at The Early Riser for coffee, and the way she figured it, he was her ticket out of Mt Pleasant and back to her own life.

The previous week Iris had propositioned him. Lee Properties needed a manager but had no funds to pay for one until rental income started flowing again. Iris offered Vinnie the deed to a house on Eastend Street in exchange for his time and talent.

"Mr. Henry needs help with his buildings. Someone he can trust. Ludie told me you guys were saving to buy a house. What do you think? We can get Jonnie's office to draw up a contract," she had said. "But first I want to know if you agree to the offer in principle?"

As Vinnie slid in opposite her in the back booth, Iris asked, "Well? What advice did your dad have for you?"

"He said you were a smart lady and that I should be careful." Vinnie cupped his hands on the table top.

"Tell him I'm smarter than he thinks he is," Iris joked. "Your dad and I used to say that to each other. Did he tell you that we were friends growing up?"

"*Si`*," Vinnie said.

"What's the verdict? Are you in?" Iris asked.

"*Si`*," Vinnie said again. Hearing the young man's Spanish response, Iris wanted to know Vinnie's story but decided that it would have to wait for another time.

"Your dad tells me that you're taking an online math class through Virginia Tech. Will this extra work interfere with that?" Iris asked.

"No," Vinnie said as he stifled a yawn. "This is a good thing. My boss at the lake says he doesn't have any work for me after today. I'm getting laid off."

"I'm sorry to hear that," Iris said. Not wanting to commiserate with him on the miseries of unemployment, she rushed ahead. "The first thing you'll need to do is visit each building and see if there's anything that could violate town ordinances."

Not that she would admit it to anyone, not even Jonnie, Iris suspected that the New To You drug bust was a set-up to confiscate the property. Kooch Kaluchi, the kind Christian that he was, coveted that land for the greater good and Iris counted on him to do whatever it took to get it.

"I know the building inspector over in Franklin County real good. Maybe I can get him to help out, for a fee," Vinnie volunteered.

"I like how you think." Iris said. "If anybody asks what you're on about, tell them you're representing an interested party who prefers to remain anonymous. And that Henry Lee has given you access to the property. OK?" Iris rapped on the café table and Vinnie nodded.

Leaving Vinnie at The Early Riser, Iris started for home. She craved a hot shower and lathering up thoughts of the Mexican Adonis with her aloe body wash. Yes sir-ree, with a little luck sprinkled over the next week or so, Iris would be back in Richmond, sipping beer on her balcony and watching her own private river theater.

On her way to the kitchen to join Mr. Henry for breakfast, she nearly collided with the house ladder parked in the upstairs hallway. Ludie was washing the dusty, horse-hair plaster walls, chasing all the cobwebs away.

"You're tempting fate on that ladder, don't you think?" Iris looked up at Ludie. "Did Vinnie tell you about our offer?"

145

"Yes, he did!" Ludie's enthusiastic response caused gray water to slosh from her maid's bucket missing Iris by inches.

"We're going over to The Shops this evening to start looking around. Perhaps later on this week the three of us can go over to Eastend Street and look at houses."

"Miss Lee, that is so awesome. Thank you. Thank you so much." Ludie tumbled down the ladder and bear-hugged a surprised Iris. Then she bounced back up on her perch, causing more water from the pail to splash onto the stiff and musty carpet.

With the *The Roanoke Times* spread on the kitchen table, Mr. Henry squinted through a cloud of bacon smoke.

"Looks like Miss Bert burned the whole pack of bacon this morning," Iris said as she gathered up the makings of a bowl of cereal and sat next to him.

Mr. Henry grunted.

"I hired Vinnie Quinn, Stumpy Quinn's grandson, to help out with the properties. He starts tomorrow." She spooned in a mouthful of Cheerios and icy milk.

Mr. Henry stared at her in disbelief.

*Wait for it, Iris. Here it comes.*

"You did what?"

"I figure since Mr. Layman retired, we need a replacement," she said. "You know, somebody to fix the leaky toilets on Eastend Street, paint and mend things. I can't do that stuff."

"But that's what I hired Kaluchi's company for," Mr. Henry protested.

"Can't say that I'm all that impressed with what he's doing for us."

"How much are you going to pay the Quinn boy? I can't afford a man on payroll *and* pay Kaluchi's fees." Mr. Henry glared at her with his sharp eyes. "Bert, I need some more coffee. Beeeerrrrrt!"

146

"I got it, Miss Bert," Iris yelled at the basement stairs. She refilled his cup as she explained, "As you'll recall the last time we talked about this, we discussed our cash flow problem. I'm offering him one of the Eastend houses in exchange for his time," Iris said.

"The boy is going to work for me without pay?" Mr. Henry doubted his daughter's words.

"Yep, I'm having Jonnie draw up a contract. He'll report to you every week, just like Mr. Layman did. Lee Properties will actually save money. From what I could see in Jonnie's reports, Kooch's management fees make up the bulk of our monthly expenses. Give Vinnie a week or two to make sure he's got it in him. Then you can turn Kooch's outfit loose."

*Will he bite? Wait for it. Wait for it.*

"He won't like that," Mr. Henry reasoned. Then he grinned. "You know, missy, that might work. You say the boy starts tomorrow?"

"As I live and breathe," Iris stood and cupped her hands to her mouth, "ladies and gentlemen, come hear the greatest news on earth. Henry Lee actually thinks his daughter has a good idea."

Bert and Heyu popped up from the basement.

"Isn't it great?" Iris said while standing on a kitchen chair.

"Child, what are you doin'? You gonna fall and break your neck!" Bert exclaimed while catching her breath.

Heyu hefted his front paws onto Iris's chair and barked once.

"Mr. Henry thinks I have a good idea," Iris said as she jumped down from the chair.

"Enough with the sarcasm, Iris," Mr. Henry said as the contents of his overturned coffee cup soaked into the Monday editorials.

Before all the stuff-marts came to Fallam County, everybody purchased their groceries and sundries at The Shops and the farmer's exchange. Downtown Mt Pleasant, located west and below the perch of the center of the town, came along later in the 1950s. The retail district consisted of a grove of dress shops, a hardware store, the post office and Dupree's Department Store. The entire town had fallen on hard times. The place was dying, if not already dead.

*Why aren't people doing anything about this?* Maybe Kooch was right, Iris thought as she crested the hill which separated uptown from downtown, something was needed to breathe new life into the place. It was Monday evening and she was taking the long way around to catch up with Vinnie at the New To You second-hand store.

When the feds raided the place, they had bulldozed through the aisles of bric-a-brac, lava lamps and occasional tables. The place was a wreck. Iris posted a For Rent sign on the grimy store window with a byline proclaiming "Under New Management."

"Do you think we could unleash Ludie to do her Tasmanian Devil routine? Clean up this place?" Iris asked.

Vinnie pulled on his soul patch in the way that sent her to the moon. "Ludie and I could clean this up for you," he said. "Can we keep what we want?" he asked in sincerity.

Judging from his response to her questions, Iris suspected that Vinnie was too young to know who the Tasmanian Devil was. Every day this "getting old" business was challenging her at every turn.

"Absolutely! You and the Tasmanian Devil can have it all!" She threw her hands up in the air. "Move it out. Have yard sales. Take it to the dump. But I want any old books or letters." Iris said as she remembered the mysterious Bella Sorin letters.

Iris handed Vinnie the property listings ledger and a ring of keys. "Visit each one of these sites and give me a report by the end of the week on what needs to be done to make them rentable."

"We'll get started tomorrow—"

"Hold up." Iris's phone vibrated in her pocket. "Yeah?" She walked away from Vinnie.

"This is Kooch. I'm at Town Hall. We just finished up our council meeting. You said that you'd drop by."

"I believe we agreed I'd drop by. I don't recall telling you when," she reminded him.

"Yeah, whatever." Under his heavy breathing, Iris heard a room full of voices. "Are you coming by tonight or not?"

"I'm in a meeting. How about tomorrow morning?" she suggested while looking down at her dirty t-shirt and jeans, not her best negotiator outfit. "I'll bring Mr. Henry by 'round eleven." She hung up before he could object to the time.

Mr. Henry was hovering by the front door when she got back to Grove House. "Who was that?" he asked pointing toward the beat-up truck backing out of the driveway.

"Vinnie Quinn," she said. "We're looking at The Shops. Taking inventory of all the work needed to get the place back into shape to rent."

"Oh," he gazed out into the dark yard, following the trucks taillights down the street.

"You OK?" Iris asked. He didn't answer. His reading glasses were propped on his barbered head. Suddenly she feared he had conjured up more bandits in the yard. She dreaded the day she'd have to take the keys to his gun safe. "I got a call from Kooch a few minutes ago."

"What does he want?" Mr. Henry ambled back into his library where he was reading James Lee Burke's latest thriller. He patted all his pockets before he sat down in his Morris chair.

"Looking for these?" Iris pulled his glasses off his head. "He wants to pitch another proposal for The Shops."

149

"I told you and told you. I am not going to sell property to Robert Kaluchi."

"Take it easy." Iris sat in the chair next to him. "I didn't say I was going to sell anything. But we can listen to what he's offering, can't we? He's up to something. Let's try and find out what it is." She unlaced her worn-out sneakers, slipping them off.

"That rascal is out to steal everything I own. That's what he's up to." Mr. Henry was physically shaking with anger or fear, Iris couldn't tell which. "I'll have no part of him," Mr. Henry continued. Iris sensed that something bad had happened between those two and he probably wouldn't tell her what it was even if she asked.

"Go with me tomorrow. You don't need to say anything. Just shake your head when I do. I'll make sure he doesn't steal anything from you or anybody else."

He opened then closed his book, tossing it on top of the stack of newspapers on the ottoman.

"Hey! Look on the bright side. Now that Vinnie's working for us, we can fire Kaluchi tomorrow, if you want to. It'll be worth going just to see the look on his face when we tell him we're terminating his contract, don't you think?" She grinned to try to cheer him up.

For the first time since she was a little girl, Iris took her father's hand in hers. It felt fragile and cold. She had never seen him so confused and lost. He seemed to be sinking into the cracked leather of the chair. Her retreat back to Richmond was going to have to wait. She couldn't abandon him now.

# Chapter 23

Bert stopped at the doorway of Iris's room. "Whoooeeee! You clean up right nice."

Standing sideways in front of her bedroom mirror, Iris admired how well her lucky grey power suit fit. Head to toe and back she was ready for her old adversary. Her favorite pumps got her to her fighting height of five-eight. Ending just below her knees, the pencil skirt accentuated her shapely legs and behind. The white-collared blouse with French-cuffs and seams clung to all the right places. On this day, Iris fluffed her hair and applied a little mascara and lipstick

"Does this skirt make my butt look big?" Iris asked.

"Yeah, it does, but in a good way. You'll get all the heads turnin' today, sweet pea." Bert dodged a tossed towel. "I bet Elizabeth would let you borrow her pearls."

"Good idea."

The two stepped into Elizabeth's room where the lady of the house was dressing herself for the day.

"Elizabeth, the sweater goes over the blouse not under it. Here, let me help." Elizabeth automatically raised her frail arms like a child so Bert could help her out of her fashion faux pas.

"Mom, may I borrow your pearls?" Iris asked as she opened Elizabeth's five-drawer jewelry chest which stood on Queen Anne legs.

"Let me," Elizabeth said. While standing in her underwear, she reached in and lifted out the luminous two-strand necklace. She handed them to her daughter. With her slight, trembling hands, she reached into the chest again then cupped the earrings into Iris' hands. "Happy birthday, daughter." Elizabeth smiled.

"But Elizabeth, it ain't—" Bert's dentures clacked. Iris gently elbowed Bert.

"Thanks, Mom. I'll always treasure them." Iris reached over and hugged her mother.

"Iris!" Mr. Henry called from the foyer. "It's going on eleven o'clock. We're late. And it looks like it's going to rain so you better bring an umbrella."

"Don't forget you got a doctor appointment this afternoon, Mr. Henry," Bert called to him from the top of the stairs.

"We're not late," Iris said as she came down the stairs stuffing her phone into her black leather purse. "We're making sure everybody's there when we arrive."

Mr. Henry was stunned into silence. With his beat-up Fedora in his hand and his jaw on his chest, his eyes followed his daughter down the stairs and over to the front door.

"Let's go see what Mayor Kaluchi has to say for himself," she said.

Scratching his head then pulling the old hat over his floppy ears, Mr. Henry shuffled out the door with the help of his Fallam Community Bank golf umbrella. A cold faint mist and promise of rain greeted them as they walked up Grove, over to Court and into Mt Pleasant's Town Hall.

"Thank y'all for coming out on this chilly day." Kooch extended his hand, doing a double take on the new Iris. Both Iris and Mr. Henry nodded at the same time. Neither offered to shake hands with the mayor.

"Where's the model you invited us to see?" Iris asked, looking around the high-ceilinged first-floor lobby. Echoes from footsteps and conversations magnified its size, and yet somehow it didn't seem as majestic to Iris as it once had.

"It's up in my office," Kooch said as he placed his readers on top of his head. "Since we're still in the planning phase, I didn't want to put it in the lobby just yet." Kooch used his husky paw to wipe his sweaty brow. Leading them back to the elevator, he hiked up his wide pants and re-tucked his wrinkled, starched shirt.

"You mean Louie Pyle and the other council members haven't seen it?" Mr. Henry asked as he followed Iris and the mayor into his second floor office overlooking Court Street and the midday pedestrian traffic.

Ignoring Mr. Henry's question, Kooch said, "You see, Iris, our vision is to make Mt Pleasant the gateway to the Crooked Road." He thrust his arms toward a scale model of a "before" and "after" uptown Mt Pleasant on a green felt covered table underneath the mayor's Wall of Fame. Using a laser pointer, Kooch continued, "See, everybody coming from the north and east will come through Mt Pleasant. We'll get first dibs on tourist revenue. It'll be a boon for the town."

"How are you sure they'll take the Mt Pleasant exit instead of the others?" Iris asked as she surveyed the model.

"Good question. You always were a step ahead of everybody else in school." Kooch cajoled. "We're putting a deal together with the county and the landowners along Route 220 to build roadside signs. They're those new L-E-D kind that you program remotely. You know? Like the welcome signs off the expressway into Atlantic City? We can put messages about shows at the center and stuff like that," he answered confidently.

"And the county approved that?" Iris questioned. The Fallam County Iris knew took ten years to decide to add a stoplight. She wasn't buying what Kooch was pitching.

"Iris, it's been a long time since you've spent any time here," Kooch said. "Things have changed. This is big and it's going to bring in new revenue for the town and the county."

Iris noticed how he avoided her question.

"What's that?" Iris pointed at the "after" version of the model.

"We're proposing to tear down the old movie theater, The Early Riser and The Shops," he said pointing with the laser. "That's where we'll build the Mt Pleasant Culture and

Performing Arts Center. The auditorium will seat two thousand people, it'll have music studios and classrooms, a small folk art museum. This area here, where the Grand Hotel used to be, will be a parking deck and retail space for restaurants and shops. It's gonna be niiiicccce," Kooch boasted.

"You talk like you've already broken ground. Where're the market and revenue projections? The community input? Has anyone done a traffic study? And who's gonna fund this thing?" she asked. "None of this was covered in the plan you left with me."

Mr. Henry spoke up, "I see Louie Pyle every week, and he hasn't mentioned this. When were you going to let Town Council know about this plan?"

"Those are all good questions," Kooch answered. "Let's go into the conference room and I'll walk you through it. Mrs. Byrd," he called to his assistant, "can you bring in the refreshments? What'll y'all have? Juice? Coffee?"

"Nothing for me, thanks," Iris said.

"Not interested." Mr. Henry put his hands in his pockets and appeared to be rearranging his undershorts.

"Y'all have a seat," Kooch prompted as he led them into the adjoining conference room. Mrs. Byrd rolled in a full coffee service complete with pastries and bagels. Kooch unfolded a paper napkin over one knee and placed a sliced bagel on a paper plate, slathering cream cheese over each side of the bagel. Muted sounds of traffic down on Court Street seeped through the office windows. The only other sound was the ripping of paper as Kooch emptied sugar packs into his coffee. Then he said, "Sure y'all don't want anything?"

"No, thank you," Iris said glancing around the room.

Mr. Henry grunted. The veins above his tight shirt collar bulged. He pulled at his tie to loosen it.

"Where were we?" Kooch stuffed his mouth with most of a bagel half.

"You were telling us why you're sneaking behind the backs of Town Council," Mr. Henry accused. "Where are they? Weren't they invited to this meeting?"

"Mr. Henry," Kooch spoke while chewing his bagel. "I can assure you—", he swallowed the bagel and slurped his coffee, "that the council is kept informed on my activities and—"

"Which are?" Iris interrupted.

"They know that we're moving forward with a development plan. I assume, Mr. Henry, that they're not sharing any of this information with the constituency until everything is finalized." Kooch went in for the kill on the other half of the bagel. With puffed cheeks, he sucked cream cheese from his fingers then wiped them on the paper napkin.

"But Mr. Henry is the owner of the property," Iris spoke slowly. "Wouldn't his councilman approach him before spending time and money on architectural models? Aren't you getting the cart before the *ass*?" she asked looking directly at him.

"We've made several offers to Mr. Henry." Kooch ignored Iris's barb. He reached for a pastry. "We can't wait on his decision before we start our planning. Iris, you're in this business. You know how long these things take," he said as he bit into the fruity German Baptist danish.

"Two minutes ago," Iris said "you talked like it was a done deal. Doesn't sound like it has taken you long at all." After a second of silence, she said, "Forgive me, I'm confused. For my sake, could you go over the offers again?"

During another minute of silence Kooch swallowed the pastry in two gulps and went through his finger-licking routine again.

"In September of last year we offered to pay Mr. Henry a pre-recession, market value price for all the lots in question. In return he must pay his tax obligations and the expense to raze the buildings. The lawyers thought it was a fair offer." Kooch placed his hands flat on the table.

"Your logic is creative," Iris said. All she could focus on was the glistening piece of pastry filling on the mayor's right cheek.

"Mr. Henry chose not to exercise this option. So in January of *this* year, being sensitive to his desire not to sell his property, we offered a long-term lease. It calls for Lee Properties to meet tax obligations and to tear down the structures on the property. In turn we will pay a monthly lease fee with options to purchase the land every five years should both parties agree," Kooch said.

"No banker in his right mind would finance a deal like the one you've just described," Mr. Henry spoke with the confidence of a Virginia landlord. To a Fallam County Lee, land titles were a birthright never to be handed over or controlled by someone not related to the family, either by birth or marriage. At this, Kooch turned to Iris and offered an expression of "can you help me out?"

Iris lobbed another question toward Kooch, "Who's 'we'?"

"Pardon me?" The top of Kooch's starched collar was growing darker with sweat.

"You referred to 'we' when talking about the lease and the project. Who is 'we'?" Iris stopped talking and folded her hands in her lap.

"Oh, well, the town, of course, and the development company." Kooch took his readers from atop his head and vigorously polished them with a soggy handkerchief he pulled from his back pocket.

"What's the name of the development company?" Iris turned to her cell phone to search for information about them online.

"Ennie Bay Development. We're working with their 'e-tail' development group." Kooch made air quotation marks with his nubby fingers.

"Can you spell that for me?" Iris asked. Internet retail and property development, something about that combination didn't jive.

"E-n-n-i-e-b-a-y. I know, they sound foreign don't they?" Kooch made his air quotation marks again. "But I talked to the guy, and he sounded American as you or me."

"Did you have them checked out? What does the town attorney say?" Iris asked.

"They are a privately held firm based out of Delaware," Kooch offered, again ignoring the actual question. "They approached us with the idea of developing uptown. Tying it in with the Crooked Road was my idea," Kooch preened. "And they liked it. The town would gain access to a new revenue stream."

"Who are the principals?" Iris asked. This whole story stank like rotting bait on a fishing pier in August.

"They're represented by the Campbell Law Offices in Roanoke," Kooch replied.

"And you've never met the principals?" Iris asked.

"Sure I have. Over the phone," Kooch answered defensively.

"Uh-huh," Iris grunted. "Has the town received anything in writing from this firm?"

"Not yet," Kooch said. "I'm still trying to reach an agreement with your father to secure the land."

"I've seen all I need to see." Iris added, "Mr. Henry, do you have any questions?"

"Like I asked Mr. Kaluchi earlier, does Town Council know about this scheme?" Mr. Henry's head jittered. "You guys give the developers huge tax breaks without getting the OK from the town. Then the taxpayers have to fund the maintenance. I know how that operates. And who will own the property? The development firm or the town?  You never said."

"And, as *I* stated earlier," Kooch answered with strained politeness, "the council is aware of my activities on this and all will be revealed when the plan is approved."

"Send me your info on this Ennie Bay Development." Iris stood. "Specifically the CEO's name and number. Until we see more details, we'll consider other re-development opportunities. Which reminds me," she leaned into the conference table and made eye contact with Kooch. "Lee Properties has made other arrangements for its maintenance. Send us a final bill." She smiled like a Miss USA contestant vying for a crown. "Let's stay in touch." She turned and walked out of the office with Mr. Henry huffing behind.

He called after her, "But Iris. Wait. Can't we discuss this?"

While in the elevator, Mr. Henry leaned against his umbrella and winced, "You probably want Jonnie Bailey to follow up with a service termination letter on that mess you just made in there, although I'm glad you did it. I can't abide a man who eats while trying to conduct business."

"Thanks. I think." Iris frowned with concern. "You OK?"

"I'm fine," he answered but not in his usual gruff manner. The elevator jerked to a stop, causing Mr. Henry to steady his balance by leaning against the wall. He griped at his umbrella. "Like I told you, Iris, there's something rotten in Denmark," he said softly. He grinned at her with that crooked, down-turned mouth of his.

She warmed to his calling her by name and that hopeless smile.

"And we have to figure out what's causing the stink," Iris smiled back. Maybe it wasn't too late. Maybe she and her dad could become friends.

# Chapter 24

Iris stood on the town hall steps scrolling through a thicket of missed calls. One from Jonnie, one from Vinnie, two from unknown local numbers, and there it was again, the mystery Manhattan number. Someone from that number called her at eleven fifty-seven.

"What the double hockey sticks," she mumbled. So if it wasn't the guy with the lame global management job, who was it?

"Can't you leave that infernal thing alone for one minute?" A sallow-looking Mr. Henry pointed at the cell phone then he placed his bony hand over the other one atop his umbrella.

Ignoring him, she dialed the Manhattan number. She crossed her free arm around her waist and stood tapping her foot on the sidewalk.

"Detective Eddie Green, N-Y-P-D. Leave a message," said a Brooklyn accented voice.

"Look I don't know who you are, but this is *not* funny. Stop calling me. Lace! If it's you, you owe me!" Iris's New York ex-coworkers, including Lace, knew that she was an avid fan of the TV series *Law and Order.* Just hearing the show's trademark pizzicato violin notes triggered a desire in her to curl up with her intimate friends Ben & Jerry for a crack TV marathon. One night when Iris and Lace were showing a new recruit a night on the town, they had stumbled onto the TV crew filming a scene and she had confessed that she lusted after the actor who played Detective Ed Green.

She ended the call and turned the ringer up as loud as it would go so that she could give Lace, or whoever, a proper reaming when they called back.

"Let's go over and see what Jonnie wants." Iris stepped off the curb without looking up from her phone. She crossed Court Street raising her hand in acknowledgement to the farm truck that narrowly avoided hitting her. Standing in front of the glass doors of the Bailey Building, Iris glanced around, searching for her father. "Suit yourself," she said as she spied his backside rounding the corner at Court and Grove.

"Did you get my message?" Jonnie asked when Iris entered her office. "Wow, you look great. Want a job? We offer free parking."

"I didn't listen to it. What's up?" Iris sat down in one of the matching chairs facing Jonnie's desk. She grasped the chair arms and said in mock surprise, "Claire found something in the files about Bella Sorin?"

"No, she's still looking. The reason I called is because of this." Jonnie reached for her electronic tablet and, with a light touch of her French-manicured fingers, quickly navigated through a series of windows. "Here it is." She enlarged the Roanoke newspaper's online advertisements and walked around her desk to sit beside Iris. "Claire found this when she was verifying our public notices."

"What is it?" Iris asked, peering down at the tablet. "It looks like a lost and found announcement."

"It is. Look right before the entry for a metal wheelchair. Read it," Jonnie directed.

"Who loses a wheelchair?" Iris asked. Then she read out loud, "'*Medallion. Lost family heirloom. Searching for lost nineteenth century army medallion believed to be stolen from Roanoke family safe. Reward offered. See our website. Horsedaddy dot com.*' So?"

"Claire, my Internet gumshoe, went to the site," Jonnie said as she tapped on the pad. "And this is what she found." She handed the tablet back to Iris. Displayed on the pad was the picture of the medallion Iris had snapped with her cell phone.

"Whoever did this isn't very bright." Iris gave the tablet back to Jonnie. "See along the right side? That's the tips of my fingers. Who would post this and why?"

"And what a coincidence that someone reports their family jewels missing only days after you discover a similar piece in your mother's closet," Jonnie added. "Who has access to the picture?"

"I've only emailed it to two addresses. Either the world's largest auctioneer of antiquities or Cousin Junie is out to heist *my* family jewels," Iris said. "What do we do now?"

"We finished the depositions stating your grandfather gave it to Elizabeth. After interviewing Mr. Henry, the paralegal threatened to quit," Jonnie said.

"But you think it's a good idea for us to do that. Right?" Iris asked.

"It's solid evidence now. But it would be good to find those letters," Jonnie mused. "I'll get Claire to look again tonight. How about lunch? Upstairs? Salad and cold pizza?"

"No thanks. After our little beer-pizza-tequila bash, I'd be happy never to see Chunky's pizza—" Iris was interrupted by Jonnie's office phone.

"Yes, Claire? Send him up." Jonnie hung up. "It's the Sheriff's Department. They have a summons for one of my clients." Iris stood to leave but Jonnie signaled for her to stay.

"Jonnie Bailey?" A young sheriff's deputy occupied the entire doorway. Laden with law enforcement gear on his duty belt, the officer tilted slightly sideways to enter the room.

"I am she," Jonnie volunteered.

"This is for you, ma'am." The officer had his deputy's cap in one hand and a summons in the other. Iris noticed that he had several others tucked in his back pocket.

"You must be new to the department, Deputy Jones," Jonnie read the officer's name tag.

"Yes, ma'am. Today's my first day." He stared past Jonnie and out the window that framed the memorial soldier.

"Nice to meet you. Can you wait while I read this?" Jonnie unfolded the court document then looked up quickly at Iris.

"Iris, your cousin Ben Lee is suing Lee Properties for all its holdings—and the medallion."

"Whaaaaaaat? Ohhh—he is not. Let me see that." Iris scurried around the desk and tried to grab the document from Jonnie.

"Excuse me, ma'am. Are you Iris Hazel Lee?" The young officer pointed his finger at Iris.

"Yeah, it's your lucky day, you just met me." Iris ignored him while squinting to read over Jonnie's shoulder.

"This is for you, ma'am." The officer pulled another summons from his back pocket and handed it to Iris. "You've just been served, ma'am, have a nice day." With a salute he jingled out of the office leaving behind a trace scent of his peppermint chewing tobacco.

"Looks like I've got my own copy," Iris tried to joke. "Not only is he suing Lee Properties and Mr. Henry, but he's suing Mom and me as well." She tossed it onto the coffee table and planted herself, face first, onto the small sofa tucked in a corner.

"Stay calm," Jonnie said, still reading the summons.

"Calm? It's hard to stay calm while standing at the bottom of a septic tank looking up at all the—you know—stuff—coming down." Iris then screamed into the sofa pillow.

"Snap out of it. You know this is frivolous posturing. He's a lawyer. He smells money and thinks he can get tuition for his grandkids," Jonnie assured her. "Come on, kiddo, let's get some lunch. You'll feel better once you've had something to eat."

"Will you represent us?" Iris asked as she pealed herself off the sofa.

"I'm not charging you a nickel for this one. It will be all my pleasure," Jonnie smiled. Iris knew that smile. Jonnie loved a legal brawl where she had home-court advantage.

"So what's it like dating a policeman? Is it true what they say about guys with handcuffs?" Iris asked as she followed Jonnie up the stairs to the third-floor apartment for a leftover lunch.

"I told you. We're just friends."

"That's not what I heard," Iris teased her. "Have you guys, you know?"

"No, I don't know. And if I did, I wouldn't tell anybody about it." Jonnie turned the tables. "What have you heard about Chief Quinn and me?"

"See, I knew it," Iris said. "You two *are* doin' the dirty dance."

"What type of dressing do you want on your salad? Ranch or vinegar and oil?" Jonnie never offered full disclosure on romantic trysts.

"Ms. Bailey?" Claire's voice floated from the apartment intercom. "Mr. Vinnie Quinn is here with his contract."

"Send him up," Jonnie called from the kitchen table.

"Good. I need some sunshine in my day." Iris sat up a little taller and crossed her legs.

"Iris, leave that poor boy alone. Besides he's married and young enough to be—he's too young for you."

"I can look," Iris protested. "Besides, I like him. I want to help him out. Did you know that he's enrolled at Tech? Wait a minute, of course you do. He's the son of the guy you say you're not dating," she heckled.

"Enough with the innuendos about Ethan and me," Jonnie ordered.

"She calls him *E-thannnn.*" Iris teased.

Vinnie's coils of curls preceeded him as he bounced up the stairs. Instead of his dusty Carthartt's, he was wearing a button-down and plain-front chinos which covered the tops of cracked but polished cowboy boots. In his calm voice he said, "Hello.

I've signed the contract." Not sure who to hand it to, Iris or Jonnie, he placed it on the kitchenette table.

"Welcome aboard! Thanks for taking a chance with me, Vinnie," Iris said. "Have you had lunch?"

"Yes, ma'am." Vinnie slipped his hands into his chinos.

"Enough with the ma'ams. It's Iris or boss or Hey You. Wait, you can't call me Hey You, that's my friend's name and it would confuse us both. Call me Iris?" She smiled at him. "Sit down. Would you like something to drink?"

As he sat Vinnie awkwardly looked at Jonnie and said, "I'll have a glass of water."

Without taking her eyes away from Vinnie, Iris ordered, "Jonnie, get Vinnie a glass of water." Iris pushed her stale pizza aside. "Have you started the surveys yet?" And for Jonnie, she explained that Vinnie and a for-hire building consultant planned to inspect Mr. Henry's commercial properties to determine what was needed to keep them from being condemned.

"That's wise," Jonnie said as she started again on her interrupted lunch.

"I started with the movie theater this morning," Vinnie volunteered. "The structure, it has lovely bones, but that's all. The rest of the building—it has to go."

"Did anyone ask you what you were doing?" Iris asked.

"Yes, ma'am, ah, Iris," Vinnie stumbled. "The mayor?"

"Chubby chap? Aviator sun glasses? Cadillac SUV?" Iris asked.

"*Si`*," Vinnie pulled at his soul patch. "He wanted to know what I was doing and did I have the owner's permission to be there." Vinnie look worried.

*Had Kooch threatened him?* Recalling the conversation she had with Mr. Henry the night before, Iris sensed that Vinnie was leaving something out, just like her old man.

"And speaking of our strudel-scarfing mayor," Iris recounted her earlier meeting with Kaluchi. "Did the mayor's office ever give you anything in writing concerning the offer to buy?"

"Nope. We talked about options. He never sent me anything in writing," Jonnie said as she dabbed the corners of her mouth with a linen table napkin and refolded it.

"He's making verbal offers so there's no trail if the deal goes in the wrong direction," Iris said. Then she added, "I don't have any proof, but I suspect he's bullying Mr. Henry into selling."

"That could be difficult to prove." Jonnie stacked the lunch plates. "Focus on your plan."

"I know, I know," Iris said. "I just get this feeling that he's up to something sneaky."

"What do you mean?"

"Kooch said the town has an interested partner in this arts center—Ennie Bay Development. They're using Campbell Law Offices. Know those guys?" Iris asked.

"I know Stan Campbell," Jonnie replied.

"Something just doesn't square with what he said about the company. According to Kooch they claim to be an Internet-based retail development firm. Why would an Internet firm be interested in brick and mortar storefront in Mt Podunk? There's no market here." Iris started chewing on her thumbnail.

"Don't know," Jonnie shrugged.

"Unless they're looking for space for a data farm or tech support. But in the middle of town? That doesn't make any sense." Iris thought out loud. "I mean, if someone wanted to build a data farm around here, why not go over to one of the actual farms on Route 20?"

"Earth to Iris," Jonnie called through cupped hands.

"Sorry, got carried away. Do you mind asking Campbell about their client?"

"I'll ask," Jonnie said. "But right now I have to be in court. You two need to be anywhere?"

"Yikes! I almost forgot. Mr. Henry's going in for a check-up at Dr. Stone's office this afternoon. I'm tagging along over his objections."

"Don't worry about this Bennie thing, Iris," Jonnie assured her, "He's fishing."

"I'll have an estimate for you by next week," Vinnie extended his hand to shake Iris's.

"What a nice guy," Iris sighed as she and Jonnie stood at the top of the stairs watching the young man descend.

Jonnie gave Iris the evil-eye arch, "Why don't you work on finding a man who isn't attached? Speaking of which—have you heard from Manny?"

"No, all I know is he's in a place called Redacted, somewhere in the Middle East," she said.

"Where? Oh, Iris, please," Jonnie laughed. "Seriously, he can't tell you where he is?"

"Either he's hiding a wife and kids somewhere or he really is a secret squirrel," Iris said as she balanced on one foot to slip on her pump.

"Sweetie, you know I'm always here for you if you want to talk about it." Jonnie patted Iris's arm.

"I don't. We're just—what's that saying? Friends with benefits? But I *do* have custody of Heyu; there's that. He's due back in May." Iris locked arms with Jonnie and, together, they walked down the stairs. "I bet you're glad Quinn moved back home. I mean the dating pool in Mt Pleasant has got to be pretty desperate."

"Oh, I won't say that. There's Chunky Brown. He's had a crush on me since the third grade."

"Somehow I don't see you dating a guy whose wardrobe consists of football jerseys and flip-flops," Iris said. "Hey!

There's Donnie Tyler. How old do you think he is? Wait, he's too short for you."

"But he's available." Jonnie's eyes crinkled as she laughed. "I know! How about Louie Pyle. Someone told me at church last week that he and his wife are separating."

"What? Rebound dating? No thanks, been there."

As they continued down the stairs, their laughter ricocheted off the old brick walls.

# Chapter 25

Saying goodbye to Claire at the front desk, Iris noticed a steady drizzle settling on Court Street as pedestrians walked a little faster.

"Do you guys have an umbrella I can use?" Iris asked.

"There's one in the coat closet," Claire said. She disappeared and returned with a small, black umbrella. "It's been in there since forever." She held the dusty, moth-eaten umbrella with two fingers as if it were a dead mouse.

Iris pocketed her cell phone and unfastened the rusty snap on the umbrella's tie. With her purse strap draped across her torso, she backed into the front doors and twirled around into the blowing mist. With one metal rib poking out from the fabric, the sad little brolly contradicted Iris's Wall Street cut, but with only two blocks to go, it would get her home in a reasonably dry state.

A half a block down Court, Iris reached into her pocket to pull out the screaming cell phone. Grove House was calling. "Hello?" She stopped underneath the awnings attached to the law offices next to the Bailey Building. Water from the crooked umbrella dripped down the back of her suit.

"III-RRR-ISSSSS!" Bert wailed. "It's Mr. Henry!   The po-liceman came with these papers. And Mr. Henry read them. And he tore up the papers." She was hyperventilating into the phone.

"Slow down, Bert. What's wrong?" Iris started walking again. The cold rain, now a steady early spring shower, pooled on the sidewalk squares unleveled by the roots of the old maple trees.

"Mr. Henry. He's fell down on the fo-yeah floor," Bert cried. "What'll I do?"

"Hang up the phone. Dial 9-1-1!" Iris stopped again to focus.

"But he can't speak. He's gone all white and I—"

"Bert!" Iris yelled. "He's having a stroke or a heart attack! Disconnect our call then dial 9-1-1! I'll be there in two minutes." Faster than an instant she ran out of her pumps, abandoned the once jilted umbrella and sprinted down the narrow sidewalk. "Son-of-a—Mr. Henry don't do this to me." Anger and fear pulsed through her as she gritted her teeth and bowed her head to keep the rain out of her eyes. She couldn't see where she was going, but she knew her way home.

She raced down the middle of Grove pumping her arms as hard as she could, passing the Wingfield's, old man Frith's, and all the other residents who had died or escaped from the memories of her childhood. "We still need to—you haven't—I haven't—."

Dialing Chief Quinn's personal number, she hot-footed down the sharp-graveled driveway in her stocking feet. Her quick stride was erratic, leapfrogging from one patch of downy moss to another. The smell of wet wool rose from her dripping suit. Her saturated blouse stuck to her chest.

"Iris?"

"Ethan!" She had only called him by his first name once, a long time ago. "My daddy. Having a stroke. Not sure Miss Bert got through to the rescue squad." Her teeth chattered.

"Where are you?" he asked.

"Grove House driveway. Don't hear sirens." She slowed to a quick walk. Her entire body shivered. She tilted her face to the sky and gave herself over to the hard, stinging rain leaching through the canopy of bare tree branches. "Please come as fast as you can, Ethan." Tears of mascara and rain streaked down her pale face as she exhaled a silent scream.

She resumed her monologue to Mr. Henry. This time she was pleading, "Please don't leave me. I'm not ready for you to go. I've things to tell you." Then she steadied herself for what she would find inside her father's house.

"There you are," Jonnie rushed toward Iris. "The nurse at the ICU desk said you were back here. Quinn called and told me what happened. Bought you some clothes. Donnie asked me to give them to you." The hallway clock's hour hand pointed between ten and eleven and Iris was still in her dank business suit. "And Bubba Law sent these," she reached into an oversized canvas tote and pulled out Iris's scuffed-up high heels. "He said that he saw you run out of them when you took off like a blue tick hound chasing a jack rabbit. He brought them over to the office. How are you holding up?"

"I'm tired," was all Iris could think to say as she looked down at her damp running shoes. In all of the commotion at Grove House, she'd managed to get her running shoes onto her cold, bruised feet. Now she was staring out at the fast, vertical rain silhouetted by the hospital's exterior light poles. Sometimes the cold rains of early spring whipped up muddy flash floods, washing away livestock and newly planted fields. Tonight it was collecting into pools in the spongy brown grass of the hospital courtyard.

"Why don't you go home and get some rest? I'm sure they're doing everything they can to make him comfortable."

"I'll stay here tonight. The doctor said that if he makes it through the night, he has a chance. I want to be here when he wakes up." Iris blew out a long breath and pushed her drooping bangs out of her weary eyes. "Thanks for the clothes." She took the canvas tote from Jonnie and ducked into the ladies bathroom.

Following Iris, Jonnie folded her arms and leaned against one of the sinks. Quickly Iris stripped to her underwear, slipped on her jeans and sweatshirt. The search for a scrunchie in the canvas tote was unsuccessful. She raked her fingers through her hair.

"Miss Bert said that he got agitated when he read the summons from Bennie. He started screaming at the deputy to leave. And after," Iris paused as her eyes filled with tears. She looked into the mirror and said with a shaky voice, "Holy mother earth, I look like a drug-crazed raccoon." She splashed cold water on her face and wiped it with a stiff paper towel. Her shoulders started shaking as she leaned against the sink. Propping herself up with her hands, she inhaled deeply and continued, "after the deputy left, Mr. Henry tore up the summons. Then he fell." She paused for another breath. "I sent Bert home to get some rest. The doctor gave her something to help her sleep. They're worried about her blood pressure."

"Who's with Elizabeth?" Jonnie asked.

"Ludie offered to spend the night," Iris replied as she held up her suit jacket for inspection. "I don't think this one's gonna make it." She balled up the jacket and skirt and stuffed them both into the tote. "Miss Bert was so flustered by what happened to Mr. Henry and me yelling at her, she couldn't remember how to dial 911." She felt as if there wasn't any hope left inside of her.

"Why don't you go home and get some sleep," Jonnie tried again. "They'll call you if anything changes."

"I've been leaving Mr. Henry all my life, Jonnie. Just this one night, I'll stay with him." Fresh tears filled her eyes. In her heart she knew that the tears were not for him but for the relationship that neither one of them had tried to make work. In a lifetime, her yearning for her father's love had been shellacked over with too many years of layered resentment. But, on this day, she had made a promise to try to love him and forgive him and to tell him so.

"Iris, let up on yourself," Jonnie said softly. "Mr. Henry can be a difficult man to love."

"How would you know what it's like?" Iris shot back. "You and your perfect Dad and your perfect family." She resented the searing accusation as soon as she'd said it. She saw the hurt in Jonnie's tired, hazel eyes. "I'm sorry. That was uncalled for. Maybe you should go. I'll call you if there's a change."

Exhausted with a mind full of white noise, Iris wandered back to the intensive care unit. The night shift was settled in for its tour, speaking in low whispers. In Mr. Henry's room the overhead lights were turned down with only the swarm of monitors and life support systems illuminating the room, emitting beeps from time to time. The low, rhythmic sound of the respirator kept time for the thrashing rain pounding against the long third-floor window.

Iris gazed out at the sheets of rain parading down Court Street under the bright street lights. Across the street the boarded-up Shops of Mt Pleasant appeared heartbroken. A Mt Pleasant patrol car entered the Shops' parking lot and backed into a space facing the hospital and killed its headlights.

She walked over to Mr. Henry's bed. The indirect monitor lights made his skin appear iridescent and unnatural. Even though monitors assured her that his heart was beating, his face showed no life, no expression of contempt or confusion like it did most days. His face was gone, replaced with the death mask of an old soul whose hours were numbered. Suction tubing pulled at the corner of his lipless mouth and a ventilator forced air into his exhausted lungs. In the high bed his body was cocooned in a white sheet, his arms tucked at his sides.

She cupped one of his hands with both of hers; it felt cold and stiff and unbending. She leaned in and whispered, "I'm sorry your life wasn't what you wanted it to be. I forgive you for not trying to love me the way I needed you to." Then the silent sobs of grief flowed out of her like the rain cascading from the night sky. The pain of true grief was something she had never experienced, and it surprised her that she would mourn his passing.

Slouched in a chair next to the window, she tried to recall the poem to help her fall asleep. *Do not go gentle into that good night. Rage, rage against the dying of the light.*

Outside the rain finally subsided and a fast wind swept the high, spent clouds away. The street lights faded. The patrol car merged in traffic as another Mt Pleasant morning was on its way.

# Chapter 26

Iris watched the ever-changing panorama of the distant Blue Ridge Mountains from the small family waiting room where she, Bert, and Donnie kept vigil for Mr. Henry. The long, constant downpour had rinsed away the dust in the air and left the sky a brilliant blue. A string of pearl gray clouds floated over the mighty firs standing atop the mountains on the far-away range.

Two days had passed since Mr. Henry's stroke. His doctor and the medical technicians had told Iris that it was a miracle he had survived. In their clinical manner, they recited the slim statistical chances of surviving the stroke. Decades of puffing filter-less cigarettes and tipping the flask had taken their toll on the old man's carotid arteries. The nurses and technicians hinted that a doctor would be talking with her soon about end-of-life decisions.

To Iris's surprise an endless stream of people came to visit Mr. Henry. Some wanted to pray with him, while he lay comatose in his bed, and cried when she suggested they pray in the lobby. She assured them the staff was doing all that could be done to keep Mr. Henry on this side of the Jordan.

"Iris, you got to understand that yo' daddy had a hard time sayin' nice things to other people," Donnie said while pacing around the stale-aired room the way a dog circles before it sits. "Mr. Henry cared by doin' things for folks." Donnie stopped with what he was about to say and appeared to change directions. "He was good to a whole lot of people in this county. He wasn't the kind of cat who tooted his own horn."

"What do you mean?" she asked, crossing her arms and pushing her hands inside the sleeves of her sweatshirt.

"People the bank turned down, he'd loan them money. One old fella told me it took him ten years to pay Mr. Henry back and your daddy never charged him a dime of interest." Donnie sucked on his teeth.

"I didn't know—he was so involved in other peoples' lives," Iris said.

"If you couldn't make your rent one month and Mr. Henry thought you'd be good for the next month, he'd let you slide. But I seen him kick people out too!" Donnie chuckled and told Iris about Mr. Henry physically evicting a truant renter on Eastend Street years before she was born. "Yes sir, he had a mean streak in him. And Mr. Henry always knowed how much money was owed Mr. Henry. But it wasn't just about money. Did you know that when the grocery store was still open over at The Shops, he kept an open account?"

"Well, sure. That's how we got groceries," Iris said.

"Naw, sweet pea. He kept another account at the store for folks who couldn't afford to buy groceries. Sometimes people paid him back. Most times they didn't."

"How did you find out about that?" Iris asked as she nudged up against Bert for warmth.

"Oren Smith, the owner, told me. You remember him? He was in Elder Home for a few years 'fo' he died. Big O, he was the only man Mr. Henry could actually beat at poker—and neither one of them could win a poker game if their life depended on it," Donnie tittered.

"I think he wanted to you to think he was lousy," Iris lightly smiled. "He taught me how to play when I was a kid. On Sunday mornings before Mom and me went to church, he would play a hand or two with me." Looking at Bert, she continued, "Remember? Mom would get so mad at him. She said it was un-ladylike to play poker and a sin to boot because we were playing on Sunday." Bert nodded sleepily, her eyes half-closed, her Bible sliding from her hand.

Later, Bert and Donnie stirred from fitful naps as cool corridor air swirled around them.

"Hello. I'm Louie Pyle. You must be Iris."

A weary Iris stood to shake hands with the paunch-bellied man who had entered the overheated waiting room. He removed his Braves ball cap and shook out his salt and pepper mane. His face broke into deep vertical lines as he grinned at her. He pointed toward the ICU entrance and said in a low voice, "Glad I caught y'all. How's he doin' today?"

"No change," Iris said softly.

"Louuuu-I," Donnie exclaimed. "What's up, slick?" Standing, he struggled with his balance and extended his gnarled hand to Louie.

"Donnie Tyler." Louie ignored the man's arthritic hand and gave him a bear hug. "Thought I'd stop by and see if the old man was up for a game of cards."

"Well, you're gonna have to wait 'til he wakes up," Donnie said. "You ever meet Mr. Henry's daughter, Iris?"

"I'd know her anywhere. She's just as pretty as her mama." He winked at Iris with one of his warm, chocolate-brown eyes.

"Howdy, Bert. How y'all gettin' along?" He waved at her with his cap. She murmured something incoherent then heaved herself up off the sofa and stiffly walked out of the room toward the ladies bathroom. "Iris, I'm real sorry to hear about Mr. Henry. My family's praying for him every night."

"Thank you, Mr. Pyle," Iris said as she tried to suppress a yawn. "Excuse me." The days of too little sleep were finally catching up with her. She widened her eyes to force them to stay open and lightly smacked the sides of her face with both hands.

"Iris, can we go somewhere to speak in private?" Louie asked. Iris looked around and noticed the room filling up with visitors.

"Let's take a walk. I could use some fresh air." Iris and Louie exited out onto the hospital's courtyard. She shaded her eyes with one hand from the near noon sun and turned to Louie and asked, "So, what's on your mind?"

He put on his Braves cap and wrap-around sunglasses and looked down at her, reaching for her other hand with his rough mitts. "First off, I want you to know that I think the world of your daddy and I would do anything for him. You let me know if we can do anything for y'all, ya hear?"

Iris felt love and loyalty pouring from his words and his calloused hands. *If he starts crying, I'm not sure I'll be able to hold it together.*

"All's I wanted to tell you, in private, was that your daddy helped me out of a bind once, kept me from going to jail. Guess you could say he saved my life. He's been like a father to me ever since." With that he dropped Iris's hand. Not sure what to do with his own, he stuffed them in the front pockets of his jeans. "So you let me know if there's anything—anything–I can do for y'all or for him."

"Thank you, Mr. Pyle. When he wakes up, I'll let him know you came to see him." Silence a yard thick dropped between them and left her with thoughts of Mr. Henry and his chances of seeing another sunrise.

"Well, I got to get over to the store and make sure they haven't burnt the place down." Louie reached into his back pocket and pulled out his wallet. "Here's my business card. You call me if you need me. Ya hear?" He turned and walked toward the hospital's parking garage.

Iris jogged after him. "Mr. Pyle? Do you know anything about this performing arts center the mayor is pitching?"

After a few seconds, Louie's face lit up.

"Oh! You mean the Kaluchi the-ate-er?" Louie mocked. "Yeah, I heard about that. Is Mr. Henry gonna sell him the property?"

"It's very confusing. Kooch has made all these plans to build this center, but he's not formally put it in front of the town for approval. Has there even been a public hearing?" Iris asked as she realized this was the first time in two days she had thought of anything besides Mr. Henry.

"Sweetheart, you know that's how politicians work. Commit the taxpayers' money, *then* tell them how much they're gonna like it," Louie smiled, exposing a mouth full of veneered teeth. "Serious, Iris, don't worry about it. You focus on gettin' Mr. Henry well. Our new mayor fancies his-self a city-planning genius when all the town really needs is somebody to make sure the garbage is collected and the sewer doesn't get backed up. This thing's gonna happen when Mt Pleasant says it's gonna happen," he assured Iris. "Shoot, it took us ten years just to get the stoplight at Court and Route 20."

"It's just that I'm afraid that this whole property fight with the town, and my cousin," she paused, confused about what to say next, "caused Mr. Henry to have a stroke." The stress and lack of sleep were finally affecting her ability to reason.

"Hey! It don't work like that." Louie took off his sunglasses and stooped with his hands on his knees, his eyes level with hers. "Only the Big Man his-self decides when to call the roll. Don't even think that you or anybody else has anything to do with it. Square?"

She nodded and fished a crumpled tissue out of her pocket.

Later that day she awoke to the noise of someone lowering the window blinds in the waiting room. The daylight savings time sun rested on the tops of the distant mountains. Light leached through the metal blades and cast shadows of long geometric lines across the carpet. Trying to remember where she was, Iris focused on the water-stained ceiling tiles then looked around the waiting room. Bert and Donnie were gone.

Another family rushed the room. Two oversized women wailed as they clung to each other. One of them was missing her front teeth and the other one had tattoo sleeves of flowers and fat-tired motorcycles. The rest of the clan hovered around them, unsure how to comfort unspeakable grief.

"Miss Lee?" The day nurse had her coat, purse and lunch bag draped over her forearm. "Miss Lee, are you awake?" Tangled in a hospital flannel sheet someone had placed over her, Iris rolled off the narrow sofa onto the dirty floor.

"What the…?" she objected.

"Your daddy is awake and breathing on his own. You can't go in there now, the doctor's with him. But I thought I'd tell you before I went off my shift." The nurse extended her free hand to help Iris off the floor. "You don't remember me do you?" she asked.

Ignoring the nurse's question, Iris pushed her hand away and asked, "When can I see him? Is he going to be OK? Can he talk?" Standing on her own, Iris tugged at the bottom rib of her sweatshirt, which had risen up her back. She scratched her head, pulling her greasy hair from her face.

"You'll want to make sure you speak with the doctor after she finishes with your dad," the nurse advised. "Let me ask the night nurse to come and get you before the doctor leaves. My name is Cricket Bowles, by the way." The curly headed woman stood by the ICU door and extended her hand again.

This time Iris accepted it. "Thanks."

Cricket placed her belongings on a waiting room chair and walked back into the ICU.

While Iris waited to speak with Mr. Henry's doctor, the new occupants of the waiting room sobbed on about someone named Sammy. The family seemed to be multiplying by the minute and before the hour was up, the room was packed. The noise of this family's boundless love hypnotized Iris. She watched in amazement the public display of this family's loud

179

grief. Red-eyed men and women hugged and rubbed each other's sizable backs. A baby, juggled from one set of arms to another, cried. The racket increased decibel by decibel while a couple of Goth teenagers hunkered in the corner next to the exit doors, one gnawing at his vanishing fingernails.

"Y'all, I know it's really sad about what happened to Sammy, but you're gonna have to keep it down out here. My patients need peace and quiet," a nurse boomed from the ICU door. Immediately, the room submerged into silent heaving and loud sniffing. Looking at Iris, he said, "The doctor can talk to you now." Iris followed the man to the nurses' station.

Standing with an electronic tablet in her hand, a white-coated doctor looked up at Iris with violet eyes magnified by thick reading glasses. Extending her hand, she said, "Hi, I'm Dr. Bowman. Let's find a place to talk."

Iris wasn't sure if this meant good news or bad, but she followed the petite doctor into an empty patient room.

Using her clunky clogs to lock the wheels of a chest-high rolling table, Dr. Bowman placed her tablet on top of it. "Mr. Lee is a very sick man."

"Tell me something I don't already know. Who are you?" Iris had met more medical types in the past few days than she had in her entire life.

"I'm the head of neurology. I'm based in Roanoke. The medical team here has asked me to consult on your father's condition." Then she asked, "Mr. Lee is your father, correct?"

"Yes," Iris replied. "What's the prognosis?" As always she wanted to get to the bottom line.

"He's breathing on his own and asleep at the moment. He can't move, but that's understandable, considering what he's experienced."

"Can he talk?" Iris asked.

"He's responsive by closing and opening his eyes. Miss Lee, your father's atherosclerosis is in an advanced stage. The team tells me that according to hospital records your father has refused several recommendations for a procedure known as carotid endarterectomy." As she said this, the doctor pressed two fingers to her neck.

"Is that where you go in and remove the plaque from the neck veins?" Iris asked.

"Something like that." The doctor took off her glasses and shoved them in her coat's breast pocket. "We could perform the procedure, but in his current condition, the chances of survival of the procedure are small." The doctor folded her arms.

"In other words, he could die either way. With or without the operation," Iris stated.

Dr. Bowman nodded. "The medication we're giving him will help, but there is the risk that pieces of the plaque can break away and find their way to the brain, blocking blood supply."

"Too little, too late." Iris stuffed her hands into her hoodie pockets and looked out the room's window. The view was the same as the one in the waiting room. By now the sun had disappeared behind the mountains. Its last embers reflected on evening clouds. Above the orange clouds, the sky's color palette spanned from grays and blues to deep purple velvet. A solitaire Venus sparkled. The wailing in the next room began anew.

"Does your father have a medical directive?" Dr. Bowman asked.

"I don't know. He has a will and I have power of attorney," Iris said as she looked back at the doctor.

"They're not the same."

"I've never thought about it. I don't know if he has one," she said.

"How about your mother or other family members? Would they know?" the doctor offered.

"I'm an only child and my mother has—is not able to tell me if he has one. What are his options?" Iris asked.

"Without a medical directive, we're obligated to do whatever it takes to keep your father alive. We'll monitor his recent progress. If his condition improves, we'll consult with him on his options." She stuffed her stethoscope into her coat pocket.

"If he gets worse?" Iris asked.

"As I said, without a medical directive, we'll do whatever we can to keep his heart beating and his lungs breathing until…" her voice trailed off.

"Then let's hope that he gets better," Iris replied.

"I have to warn you, Miss Lee, it's just a matter of time before he has another stroke," the doctor advised.

"I appreciate your candor, Dr. Bowman," and she did.

"He's sleeping now. Go home and get some rest yourself," the doctor said. "I'll leave instructions with the nurses to call if his condition changes." With that, the doctor dismissed Iris by looking down at her tablet.

Iris stepped into Mr. Henry's room, his body still draped in a white hospital sheet. She couldn't see any difference in his face from her visit at noon. His breathing was faint and without rhythm. She discovered herself trying to breathe for him like a kid taking in air and then blowing out while watching a friend blow up a balloon.

Taking his hand, she said, "Louie Pyle says hey. He stopped by to see you. I'm going to Grove House to check on Mom. When I come back, I'll bring the *Journal* with me, and we'll read the stock reports together." She squeezed his hand, hoping for time to stand still then go backward. She wanted to get to know the man who all those people had come to see, the man who gave of his time and heart. She wanted to know and love that man.

# Chapter 27

Soaking off the past few days of grim, sweat, and fear in the bathtub, Iris played messages that had accumulated on her cell phone.

"Iris, this is Sara Ward from down the hall. You need to come to the next—" Iris thumbed the seven key to delete the message.

"Iris?" Quinn asked. "Listen, forgive me for bothering you, but I thought you would want to know. Some meathead from the New York Police Department called me, asking about you. Call me when you get a minute." She skipped this one.

"Iris. Fred Kitter. Sotheby's. The Louvre's ready to play ball. How are you coming along with the provenance? Give me a shout." Message skipped.

"Miss Lee, I can assure you, this is no joke. I *am* Detective Eddie Green of the NYPD and not some character on a TV show. I need to speak with you immediately." Sirens blared and people shouted in the background, and then "What the? Tell him to stick—" Message skipped.

"Iris Lee? My name is Jane Savage. I'm an AP reporter based in Los Angeles. I interviewed your cousin Ben Lee about a story on a rare military medallion that he claims your family stole from his father. I'm calling to get your comments on your cousin's claims." She saved the message so she could replay it for Jonnie.

"Iris, Plinkus Young here. I'm so sorry to hear about Mr. Henry. We've set up the prayer chain for him. Let us know if there is any—" Message deleted.

The rest of the messages were from concerned townspeople. She marveled at how quickly bad news traveled in Mt Pleasant. Iris wondered what the prayer group would say if they knew of Mr. Henry's thoughts about the afterlife. But then from all the Good Samaritan stories she'd heard in these past few days, she wouldn't be surprised if he did have faith. Faith in what, she wasn't sure. Mt Pleasant, maybe?

"Knock, knock. Can I come in?" Jonnie rapped on the bathroom door.

"Door's open." Iris tossed the cell phone onto the bathmat and draped a Road Runner wash cloth over her boobs. Tweety Bird covered her crotch. "Come on in, I'm decent."

"You nut!" Jonnie said while she hovered over the tub. "Where did you find Road Runner and Tweety Bird?"

"Santa Claus put these in my Christmas stocking when I was in junior high," Iris joked. "A Lee never throws anything away." Iris held up Rocky & Bullwinkle, extending her pinkies. Light filtered through the thin flannel.

"Got your message and the answer is 'no,'" Jonnie said as she kicked dirty clothes with her pointed pumps, making a path to the bathroom throne. "Mr. Henry hasn't left a living will or any other type of medical directive with us for himself or your mom. Maybe he's filed it away in his library somewhere."

"Remember when we used to smoke pot in here and blow it out the window," Iris mused. "Think Quinn could get us some?"

"Iris, you're kidding, right?" Jonnie was scrolling through her Blackberry messages.

"Yeah, maybe." Iris rested her head against the rim of the claw-foot tub. The water was getting cold so she gripped the stopper chain with her toes and pulled the plug. "We've got to find his directive." Iris shivered as the tub drain gurgled. She motioned for Jonnie to throw the bathrobe her way. "The neurologist says his carotid artery is blown. I'm afraid he may have made his last trip to Bubba's Barber Shop."

"Oh, Iris, I am so sorry," Jonnie said.

Iris bent at the waist to towel dry her hair with a thread-bare Wonder Woman towel and twist it in a top-knot on her head. "I am too." She tucked her dirty clothes under her arm. "I hope he'll be able to tell us what he wants." Iris led Jonnie down the hallway and into her bedroom. While she dressed, the two traded updates on other matters.

"I've got some good news," Jonnie volunteered. "Claire found your Grandfather Lee's old case files. She found a copy of a letter requesting payment of services to Bella Sorin. And," Jonnie paused for a ta-da, "we found the receipt for the medallion."

"All right, good work, Claire," Iris cheered as Jonnie followed her back to the bathroom. Over the noisy hair dryer, she shouted, "I got a call from Sotheby's. They've heard from the French and they're ready to negotiate. That receipt will help. But it sure would be nice to figure out where Bella Sorin got it."

"I can get her to keep digging. There may be something in the files we found that could lead to her or to the letters. About Ben, I've heard from his attorney. They've submitted an account on why they believe he has rights to Mr. Henry's property. All they've got is an invalid will. Don't worry about them now, Iris," Jonnie said as she took the hairbrush out of Iris's hand and began brushing her hair. "We'll get them out of your hair and soon."

"You've got to listen to this." Iris played the voice mail message from the LA reporter.

"Don't even think about calling her." Jonnie pointed the hairbrush at Iris. "And if she calls back and you answer the call, tell her 'no comment.' You got that? Repeat after me, 'no comment.'" Jonnie yanked on Iris's hair with the brush.

"Ow. OK. No comment. Give me my brush back."

Bert called from the bottom of the kitchen stairs. "Iris, I'm leaving now." Her voice sounded shaky and uncertain.

"Do you want me to give you a ride home?" Iris asked as she stood at the top of the unlit kitchen stairs. "You sound tired."

"Naw, I'm fine. Can you come down here? I got something I need to say to you."

Jonnie followed Iris down the dark stairs toward the light of the kitchen.

"Iris, I'll talk to you tomorrow," Jonnie said. "Miss Bert, sure you don't want a ride home? I can wait outside."

"I'm fine. Thank you, anyway," Bert said.

Jonnie kissed Bert on her tear-stained cheek and waved good-night to Iris.

"What's wrong?" Iris asked.

"Come sit down at the table." Bert's overcoat was buttoned all the way to the top. A red wool beret, stuffed with all her wiry gray locks, framed her round face. Her smooth brown hands gripped a chipped Bank of the Brethren coffee mug.

As Iris pulled out a kitchen chair, its screeches and echoes rattled the silence of the old house. She noticed that Bert's face had aged in the last three days. Her sepia-colored eyes floated in tears.

"I just want you to know that I've decided not to retire and go to Ohio. If I hadn't made such a fuss about quittin' this place, Mr. Henry wouldn't have gotten so upset, and then—" Bert heaved a deep breath and lowered her chin to her chest.

"No, no, no, sweat pea," Iris steadied her voice. "He's sick because he's an old man who smoked unfiltered cigarettes most of his life. For over forty years you did nothing but take *good care* of the old misanthrope." Iris reached across the table and grabbed Bert's hands.

"I don't know what that word means, but I feel like I made things worse by wantin' to leave," Bert cried.

"Not that he would ever admit it, but I think Mr. Henry *is* sad that you're leaving." Iris smiled at Bert and tightened her grip on the older woman's hands. "You were right. It's your time. You're going on your trip and staying as long as you want. When you get back, we'll talk about what to do next. OK?"

"Naw, I just don't want to go no more." Bert raised her eyes to Iris's. "Folks gettin' sick. It just takes the fun out of livin'."

"Yeah, I know. It sucks," Iris replied. Earlier over dinner she'd explained to Bert the doctor's odds on Mr. Henry getting better. "Let's see what the next few days bring."

"I feel so helpless when I see him in that hospital bed, Iris." Her hands tightened on the coffee cup again.

"You know how you can help?" Iris voice cracked as she pried the cup from Bert's hand. "Help me find his personal papers. Do you know where he keeps them?"

"Oh, that's an easy one, sweet pea," Bert struggled with a smile. "He keeps all his important stuff up in his desk in his bedroom. He keeps a spare set of keys to his desk in the bourbon pitcher. It's in the liberry." Bert pushed herself up and away from the kitchen table. Iris followed her into the library.

Nestled on a shelf in the middle of all of Mr. Henry's books perched a pair of dusty, matching decanters on a tarnished silver tray. Iris swiped at the dusty tray with her index finger and said, "We gotta get Ludie in here tomorrow." She lifted the heavy decanter and saw two keys joined by a small satin ribbon inside.

"Come to think of it," Bert said, "Mr. Henry told me to tell you about those keys if anything ever happened to him. I guess it's that time now." She remembered her sadness and folded her hands together over her stomach.

Iris held the decanter by the neck with one hand and rubbed Bert's back with the other. "You sure you don't want a ride home? Or you could spend the night here."

"Naw. I got to get home and feed Trixie." Bert cupped Iris's face and said "I know sometimes, shoot most of the time, you and your daddy don't see eye to eye on things. But in his own way, child, he loves you. He's proud like you was a son. He never showed it 'cause no one ever showed him how."

"He could've tried." Iris bowed her head.

"Something happened to him when you went off to college. He changed. That's about the time he quit drinkin'. I think he was sad 'cause you was gone. Lord knows your mama missed you something ter-ra-ble." Bert fished her keys from her coat pocket but stalled her departure as tears fell down her round cheeks. "I don't know why he never tried to show his love, sweet pea. Don't know." Bert left Iris standing in the library with the keys to Mr. Henry's fate and her future.

Running on only four hours of sleep in three days, Iris poured cold, burnt coffee into a mug. The phone rang and she glanced at the late hour on the wall clock.

"Iris, this is Junie Marks," the jeweler from Links said. "I wanted to call you to let you know that I might've made a mistake. How's Mr. Henry, by the way?" He sounded nervous and tentative.

"He's seen better days," she said. "What do you mean you made a mistake?"

"Well," he paused. "It's about the medallion you brought to me to be appraised."

"What about it?" She thought about the jeweler's box wedged into the safe deposit box.

"Well," he stalled.

"Just tell me," she commanded.

"I sort of told Bennie Lee about it. I thought that, being family and all, it would be ok to tell him that, you know—"

"No, I don't know Mr. Marks. Tell me."

"He got all upset."

"Why don't you start from the beginning?" she said as she massaged her temple.

"As you know Bennie's mama and my wife are, or were, sisters," he began.

*I didn't mean to start with the story of Eve.*

"And my daughter Millie and Bennie are first cousins." He sucked in a noisy breath. "And they keep in touch with one another and Bennie came to town last week. They came by the store to see me. Said he was in town for business and met Millie for lunch in the mall. Did he come by and see you?"

Iris thought of the lawsuit her cousin's lawyers had filed against her father, then answered, "No. We spoke on the phone a few days ago. He was at his home in California, or so I thought."

"That's odd. He told us that he'd been to see you."

"Mr. Marks, why did you tell Bennie about the medallion? You said we could trust you not to talk to anyone about it."

"Well, like I said, I thought that since y'all are family, it would be OK for him to know about it. Because you were interested in learning about its history, I thought he might know something about it. But I've had time to think and I realize I did wrong. And that's why I'm calling you now."

"Did you show him the picture?"

"I did. And when he asked me what my appraisal was, I told him what I told you. And, well, that's when he got mad. As a kid, Bennie was what we used to call 'high strung.' But I swannee, I never saw a grown man act the way he did when I told him how much the thing is worth."

"What do you mean?" Iris asked.

"He was like a kid. Pounding his fists on my glass jewelry case and kicking at it. I thought we were going to have to dial 911—if that glass had broken—but Millie managed to claim him down."

"What did he say?"

"Well, he wanted to know where you got it. And I told him you wouldn't say. Then he started cussin' you and Mr. Henry. Ugly words, Iris. I won't repeat them to a lady, no ma'am. I'm real sorry I brought it up with him. Real sorry."

"Tell me what he said," Iris demanded, gripping the fat phone receiver.

"He said that you, and I'm not gonna use the word he called you, and Mr. Henry stole it from his daddy. The medallion was his and by G-O-D-D-A-M-N-E-D he wanted it back. Then he made me give him a copy of the picture file you sent to me."

"Made you?" Iris tried to keep her voice even. "Made you?"

"He threatened to sue, and his yelling was scaring all the customers in the store. What was I to do? I didn't have a choice."

"We have choices, Mr. Marks. Why didn't you call the police?"

"Iris, he's family." Pause. "I'm calling to tell you to watch out for him. In my opinion, Bennie's running around with a belly full of gasoline and a lit match between his teeth, if you catch my meaning."

"Thanks for the warning." This explained the crazy call from the LA reporter and the online lost and found announcement, Iris thought. *But what was his game?*

"Again, Iris, I'm real sorry—"

"Just don't talk about the medallion to anyone," she interrupted him. "And if he contacts you again, let me know."

"I will. How's Elizabeth holding up?"

"She's not aware of what's happened."

"You know I fell in love with her the first time I laid eyes on her," Mr. Marks reminisced. Iris cringed at the thought of having Junie Marks for a father. In her eyes, compared to him, Mr. Henry was the father for all ages. "That's why I begged my daddy to give her a job when she was first startin' out on her own." Iris remained silent, hoping he'd take the hint and end the call. "But fate intervened and your daddy came in the store one Christmas to buy his mama a present."

"Your store? That's where my parents met?" Iris's interest in the conversation changed.

"I believe so. 'Cause it looked like love at first sight when she helped him pick out the gift. A pearl broach, I believe it was. After that, she wouldn't have a thing to do with me." In this Iris knew that Junie Marks still pined over his unrequited love for Elizabeth Carter.

"I didn't have a snowball's chance in Hades after that. Your daddy was older and more handsome than a bugged-eyed boy like me," Mr. Marks offered. "'Cept my ears won't as big," he chuckled.

Iris grunted.

"Well, I've kept you too long on the telephone. Now I can go to bed with a clean conscience. I'm truly sorry for what I did. You take care now, young lady. And I'll let you know if I hear from Mr. Bennie Lee again." Mr. Marks disconnected the call.

# Chapter 28

Before she went rummaging through her father's room, Iris tiptoed into Elizabeth's suite. Warm light from the bedside lamp showered over the sleeping woman as she sat, propped up by a mountain of pillows. Her reading glasses still on, the gentle woman snored softly. Iris slowly removed Elizabeth's glasses then tugged at the well-worn Bible and placed both on the bedside table. Iris hovered over her mother.

"Mr. Henry is really sick, Mom," she whispered. "I know you've been praying for him, asking God to watch over him. You've been a good wife." She sniffed and wiped her eyes on her T-shirt, turned out the light and walked down the hall with her cold coffee.

For Iris the lesson of respecting other people's privacy and property had been a bitter pill. The lesson had occurred when she was eight years old. Rummaging through Mr. Henry's Army trunk in his bedroom closet, she had been discovered and, with swift justice, spanked. The dismay of disappointing him had hurt worse than the welts on her legs. He must have regretted his behavior as it was the only time he had ever struck her. Iris never entered her father's bedroom again uninvited.

Now the room smelled of geezerhood. A blend of mothball-permeated wool, muscle-ache cream and stale tobacco crowded the dense air. The room was not as large as Elizabeth's but it suited Mr. Henry's Spartan-like preferences. Allen Lee's enormous roll-top desk, which had resided on Court Street during his time as lawyer, crowded the wall opposite Mr. Henry's single bed. Next to the closet door stood a metal gun case.

Placing her coffee atop the desk, Iris sat in the desk chair. In the still silence of the late night, the oak beast squealed, making her jump. As she reached to unlock the desk, she looked over her shoulder. She half expected to see Mr. Henry standing in the doorway. Her trembling hands were cold as icicles. "Get a grip, Iris," she said aloud. "It's just a desk."

After a lifetime spent in offices, Iris judged a person by the desk they kept. Who needed Myers-Briggs? A person who stacked their personal domain with mountains of paper, bobble-head dolls and other tchotchkes was one who wasn't too organized and belonged in a marketing department, not hers.

Mr. Henry's desk's personality was as Iris expected. When she pushed the top up, she was greeted by a flat desk calendar. The last day marked was the day they had taken him to the hospital. Unpaid bills rested in a left cubby hole and envelopes to be mailed waited in a right one.

Using the same key to unlock the drawers on either side, she discovered paid receipts and bank statements on the left and deeds, titles, and insurance policies on the right. Noticing that they were in alphabetical order, Iris went straight to the back for "wills." There it was, as easy as solving Monday's crossword puzzle, the living will of Henry Lewis Lee.

"Advanced Medical Directive," she read aloud. The document revealed that Mr. Henry requested no extraordinary medical procedures to prolong end-of-life care and she was named as the durable medical power of attorney. Clear as Mt Pleasant tap water, he was telling her what he wanted. Now she had to scrape up her courage to carry out his wishes.

Placing the medical directive aside, she paused to shake off the old feeling of snooping in a place she didn't belong. Then she thumbed through the rest of the right drawer's green file folders. One, written in her father's cursive, labeled "Trusts," caught her eye. She looked up and toward the bedroom door; the white noise of silence filled her ears as her heart quickened. She dove in. Inside the folder were statements from various banks and financial firms. Pulling one of the statements from its over-sized envelope, she noticed the account name—"Trust for Elizabeth Carter Lee." Her eyes widened when she saw the amount. She gnawed on her thumbnail. Frantically grabbing another folder, "Trust for Iris Hazel Lee," she peeped inside one of the statements to see the value of the account. Her eyes expanded again. A third trust belonged to Roberta Tyler Swanson. "Great balls of beeswax. This means we can pay the taxes on Tara and then some." She whistled to herself. "So this is where he squirreled it all away." She stopped counting after a few million.

Wired but too tired to continue on, Iris leaned back in the squeaky chair and felt Heyu nudge up against her leg. "Hey, fella. Let's go get some shut-eye."

She dreamed of Mr. Henry and Uncle Ben. They were rocking in creaky old rockers. Their feet were stacked one over the other against a porch column. The two were deep in conversation but she couldn't understand what they were saying.

Iris awoke with a jerk. Outside the sky was a faded indigo with a thin white line on the horizon. She heard the muffled cooing of a mourning dove as she lay in the small, lumpy bed. What was Uncle Ben's wife's name? Sarah? She closed her eyes and tried to replay the dream. Instead her mind strolled down another path.

To her recollection, Ben, Sr. and his family visited Grove House twice a year: the Fourth of July and Christmas Day. After he chased his first brandy or bourbon down with the second one, Uncle Ben would stand and order his wife and son to gather their things. Young Iris sensed that the visits were an obligation or part of a tradition so engrained in Lee family rituals that no one dared to break them. Iris had begged her mother to let her sit with the adults, but her mother always insisted that she be a gracious host to her guest, Cousin Bennie. Bennie resented being a guest as much as she loathed entertaining him.

As an adult, she had suspected that her mother and Aunt Sarah felt obligated, out of some notion of family allegiance, to encourage the two cousins to form a kindred bond. Along with the Christmas and Fourth of July visits, this was manifest by inviting Bennie to spend a week each summer in Mt Pleasant. Iris resented that her guest was exempt from chores whenever they went to the farm to weed the vegetable garden or get up hay. In fact, their camaraderie was about as congenial as the friendship of the gingham dog and the calico cat.

In those growing up years within a four-block radius of Grove Street, there were enough kids to have teams for touch football, softball, and everybody's favorite game, War. As in the schoolyard so it went on Grove Street; the older kids bossed and bullied the littlest ones. Iris was too young to be considered an older kid, and she was ahead of most of the younger ones in school. She took on the role of leader of the younger kids, the misfits and the Eastend Street gang. Whenever Bennie, an outsider from the big city, came around, the older kids kowtowed to him. This infuriated her. The other kids couldn't see him for what he was—a lazy reprobate, a common bully.

One summer night Iris's gang, for the first time in Grove Street kid history, beat Bennie's team at War. She couldn't remember the exact rules of the game, but she and Ernie Bangor, a black kid from Eastend, somehow figured out a way to use pig Latin to communicate with each other. When the other teams discovered her secret weapon, they cheered her ingenuity. That was everyone except Bennie. He accused her of cheating and was enraged at losing to a bunch of babies and blacks. In front of the entire neighborhood, he pulverized Elizabeth's curbside bed of impatiens. Everyone, including Iris, was hypnotized by the sheer violence and madness of the tantrum.

When Mr. Henry asked the next day if she had seen the hooligans who tore up her mother's flowerbed, Iris didn't dare snitch. After his ruling on the Miss America Barbie case, she was convinced Mr. Henry wouldn't believe her if she told him that Bennie had single-handedly massacred all the flowers. Afterwards, she, like every other kid in the neighborhood, feared the wrath of Bennie Lee. Fortunately, the next fall, the despot moved to California with his parents.

Iris lay tangled in sheets and blankets while thinking about her father's brother and her cousin. No one in her family ever told her why they moved to California but she was glad they had; upon their departure, Christmas and Fourth of July celebrations had become fun holidays.

Thinking of Bennie's demeaning tirades about Mt Pleasant and the Grove Street kids chafed her even now, decades later. She couldn't fall back to sleep, so she rolled out of bed pulling the covers with her as she rambled on, "Bennie you were such a snob, and a bully, and a pig. Bennie the Pig."

She stopped. Neurons fired.

A picture of a shop on Main Street with a sign that read "e-tail store" flashed in her mind. Her eyes widened.

"Eureka!" she yelled.

Heyu awoke from a sound sleep, jumped off the bed and hunched down on all fours, prepared for a fight.

She got down on her hands and knees and squared off with Heyu. "Bennie in pig Latin is Ennie Bay. Coincidence? I don't think so." She stretched into child's pose followed by table top, shifting her butt right then left. Heyu yawned and turned to hoist himself back onto the bed. "Suit yourself," she said as she moved to the desk and booted up her laptop. "I'm going to find out what Mr. Ennie Bay is up to."

# Chapter 29

Mr. Henry had survived another dark night.

Before they rolled him from the ICU to a regular room, Iris gripped his shrunken hand and whispered, "Daddy, I'm here with you. Can you hear me?" She felt a weak squeeze. "Everybody is worried about you. Hoping for you to get better."

Iris pictured herself rolling Mr. Henry up the front walkway at Grove House and talking away the hours in front of the fire; him telling her stories about his life in Fallam County before she was born and her bragging on herself about how she paid out healthy severances for her entire team before they fired her. But who was she kidding? That kind of sappy perfect ending only happened in Disney movies.

She squeezed his hand again and said, "Mom and I want you to come home."

As his face crumpled up in pain, his narrow lips spread across his face, making that crooked smile.

At midday the hospital's main lobby hummed with activity.

"I've thought about it, and I think we need to create a surprise of our own on this Bennie thing," Iris said to Jonnie, who had dropped by for a visit.

"What do you have in mind?" Jonnie asked.

"Since the reporter tipped us off and Bennie thinks that he's going to surprise us with his 'woe is me my father was robbed' story—," Iris paused. Watching Kaluchi struggle with the hospital's revolving doors, she lowered her voice and continued, "I vote we have a press conference right here in Mt Pleasant where the alleged crime took place. We tell the world of the miraculous discovery of this wonderful treasure, blah, blah, blah. I've called the Sotheby's rep I met in Richmond. Mr. Darcy. He's agreed to speak about the thing's authenticity."

"You're good—but don't go overboard," Jonnie grinned.

"What's this 'you're good' crap? You're the attorney representing the grief-struck family. You're the one who should conduct the press conference."

"You kill me. Set it up." Jonnie pulled her Blackberry from her purse. "When do you want to do this?"

"This afternoon. I've already called the press. A Roanoke reporter and two TV stations. Maybe one of 'em will show. Claire's corralling the local dudes. If we're lucky, it'll be a slow news day and we'll make the evening news." Iris watched the mayor pour out of the revolving door and lope toward them. "And, if we can, we work into the interview the fact that my father suffered a stroke right after he read that his nephew, a man whose college bills he covered, is suing him for everything he's ever worked for."

"I can't say those things. Those are the kind of things that get us into trouble in court," Jonnie insisted.

"What things get you into trouble in court?" Kooch joined in. "Hey, Iris. Hello, Jonnie."

"Hello Robert," Jonnie greeted Kooch. "We're talking about Mr. Henry's recovery."

"Iris, I wanted to express my sadness about your father's illness. Ruth and the kids and I are praying for him to get better. Do you want to pray now?" The mayor of Mt Pleasant placed one beefy hand over his chest.

"No, I'm good." Iris said.

After an awkward moment, Kooch said, "Now may not be the right time for this, but I wanted you to know that Mexican boy is crawling all over The Shops. Did you know about that?" Kooch hitched his thumb toward the front doors of the hospital and the Shops across the street.

"Really?" Iris asked.

"I'll run him off if you need me to."

"Maybe you should leave law enforcement to Chief Quinn," Iris said.

This flustered the mayor so he changed the subject. "Due to the circumstances and all, I'll hold off on pressuring you on making a decision about the land," Kooch ventured.

"What are you talking about?" Iris asked.

"Our town plan and Lee Properties' contribution. You know, the one I dropped at your house the other day." Nervous sweat glistened at Kooch's temples.

"I've been kind of busy here, Kooch." Iris opened her palms. "Besides, you never sent me the stuff I asked for. What was the name of that company? Ennie Bay Development?"

The memory of the meeting in Kooch's office popped into Iris's mind. She recalled how frail Mr. Henry appeared while they were standing on the street getting ready to cross over to the Bailey offices. At the time, she thought he was just reacting to the mayor's wacked-out proposal.

She snapped. "I want a copy of any architectural drawings you've dreamed up, along with the Ennie Bay proposals."

"I can't just give you that kind of information," Kooch blurted out. "Look, let me go to my appointment with the hospital administrator. I'll see what I can do about this other thing."

Iris leaned toward the fat man. Without the aid of her high-heeled shoes, her eyes stared at an oily stain just below Kooch's Windsor knot. She grabbed the tie and pulled down hard, causing him to angle his face into hers. With gritted teeth, she whispered, "What about this government transparency I keep hearing about, Kooch?"

"Iris, I can't just give you this information." Kooch bleated and tried to backpedal but couldn't budge.

"Ever heard of the Freedom of Information Act? Oh, that's right, you're a lawyer, you know all about it." She yanked on the tie harder. His face glowed turkey red. "I can reference our meeting and request information that the town has on file. Oh, wait a minute, there's nothing officially filed. You weren't gonna tell anybody about it. You were going to bully Mr. Henry into selling his property to your company, not to the town." Iris yanked harder on the tie and jabbed the petrified Kooch in the middle of his shiny forehead with her index finger.

"Iris, stop it," Jonnie demanded in a low, harsh tone. "Everybody's watching." Jonnie tried to pull the tie from Iris's hand, succeeding only in making the noose even tighter around the mayor's neck.

"I'm on to you," Iris taunted. "I know about the CAT Group and Ennie Bay's plans. I'll see that you're kicked out of office for using municipal resources for private gain. I'll see that you're disbarred."

"Jonnie, help me out here. What's she talking about?" Kooch squawked. His breath was coming hard now. "Let go of my tie. You, you, Republican." Iris opened her hand unexpectedly and Kooch fell against a wall and slid down into a squat.

She bent over and hissed into his ear. "Get me a copy of Ennie Bay's proposal, or I call my new best friends at *The Roanoke Times*." Out loud so everyone one could hear, she grabbed Kooch's massive arm and said, "What happened? Are you all right, Kooch? Do we need to get you a wheelchair?"

"You play dirty, Iris," Kooch mumbled as he loosened his tie, pulled it over his wide head, and stuffed it into his suit pocket. "I'll get back to you." He turned and ambled down the hospital corridor.

Iris had gambled and won. Kooch and her cousin were up to something. And, knowing how sneaky and selfish Bennie was, he was probably playing the small town mayor like a beat up tuba. She wasn't sure if she cared if Kooch, the dumb galoot, got caught up in the trap she was setting for her cousin.

Jonnie turned to her and demanded, "What's gotten into you, for heaven's sake?"

"I'm sorry. The strain of dealing with Mr. Henry, I just lost it," she mimicked in Southern feminine helplessness. Then she said, "I should probably get back upstairs and check on Mr. Henry. You'll meet me at Grove House today at four for the interview, right?"

"I'll try. Don't count on me. If you'd given me more time—" Jonnie tried to explain.

Iris wasn't ready to share with Jonnie what she suspected about Kooch and Ennie Bay Development. The crazy dream about Mr. Henry and Uncle Ben in the rocking chairs had jiggled her memory enough to connect Cousin Bennie to Ennie Bay. She reread the proposal the mayor had given her on the day he visited Grove House, this time with the assumption that Cousin Bennie was behind the deal. She had a few ideas about what the two of them were up to but she couldn't prove any of it. She hoped the press conference about the medallion would flush Bennie out into the open. Her intuition told her that Bennie was more interested in lording over her and taking the Lee Legacy prize than owning a bunch of dilapidated buildings in Southwest Virginia.

When Iris returned to Grove House an hour later, the gang was all there: Bert, Ludie, and Vinnie. Even Elizabeth lounged in her sun porch adjacent to the library. The house smelled of wood soap and furniture polish. A tall crystal vase of forsythia blooms graced the foyer table. Ludie had whirled through each room, sucking up cobwebs in her wake. Grove House radiated the promise of new life. Spring and hope seemed imminent.

"Did you get it?" After making a couple of phone calls to the bank, Iris had dispatched Bert earlier that morning to Roanoke to get the medallion from the safe deposit box.

"Yes, ma'am. Once I got used to sitting up so high in your car, I kind of liked driving it," Bert confessed.

201

"Good, we'll get you one just like it before you start out on your vacation. Where is it?" Iris clapped then rubbed her hands together.

"It's in the liberry where you told me to put it," Bert said. "I'm making chicken salad canapés for y'all's guests this afternoon. It feels good to have a busy house, don't it? I'm glad you're home." Bert snapped her fingers for Heyu, and together they took their shared excitement for chicken back to the kitchen.

Iris stuck her head into the library to check on Ludie's progress. The old room actually sparkled. "Ludie, you're a miracle worker!" Iris exclaimed. In the grand front windows every pane twinkled and winked with the afternoon light of early spring.

Once again, Ludie was atop the house ladder, this time wiping down the exposed wooden cross beams. Gloved hands dangling from the top of the ladder, she took pride in saying, "Almost done." She pointed to the wall of books and added, "I dusted every single book in this room. Your daddy must be smart if he read all these."

"Smarter than any of us knew," Iris responded. Mr. Henry's handwriting on the trust file tabs flashed in her mind. "When he gets home, I know he'll appreciate what you've done with this room, Ludie."

"I'm real sorry he got sick Miss Lee, er, Iris." Ludie dipped her rag in the soapy water.

"Wait a minute," Iris stared up at Ludie. "Let me see that rag."

"What. This old thing?" Ludie held up a sad and holey Rocky & Bullwinkle terry cloth. "I found it hanging in the basement. I thought it was for cleaning." A frightened look passed over her sun-wrinkled face. "Oh, my God. Did I do something wrong?"

Iris's loud laugher sounded like crying. Bert and Heyu rushed in from the kitchen and Vinnie ran into the library brandishing a screwdriver. Iris was pointing at the Rocky & Bullwinkle facecloth. She couldn't get her breath she was laughing so hard.

"Sweet pea, what's wrong?" A worried Bert asked.

"I don't know what's wrong with her. I just showed her this dumb old rag and she started doing that." Ludie pointed to Iris. Grinning the smile of the insecure, Elizabeth had joined them from her perch in the sun room.

"Ludie is using Rocky & Bullwinkle to wash the dirt off the ceiling," Iris said between waves of laughter. She rubbed her eyes as they surrounded her.

Bert proclaimed, "Child have you lost your mind?"

Vinnie looked up at Ludie for a translation of her boss' behavior.

"Santa Claus gave Iris the Rocky & Bullwinkle towel set for Christmas," Elizabeth tried to explain to everyone. Elizabeth's pronouncement caused Iris to hold her sides as another round of laughter erupted. Everyone looked on with concern.

"Wooooo. OK, OK. I'll stop. I'll stop," Iris stammered as she fanned her tear-stained face with both hands. But she couldn't stop. Even if she tried to explain to them why she was laughing, they wouldn't think it was funny. Nobody ever understood what made her laugh. But she didn't give a rat's backside. Rocky & Bullwinkle were finally on their way to the rag bag.

# Chapter 30

When the door chimes sounded, Iris checked from Elizabeth's bedroom window for the TV van. To her surprise Chief Quinn's cruiser was parked in the driveway. "What does he want?" she grumbled.

She fished for the pearl broach—the one Mr. Henry bought the day he met Elizabeth at Links Jewelers—in her mother's jewelry chest. She needed to look her best for the photo-op. As she pinned the broach to her blouse, she checked her lipstick and gave her reflection a thumbs-up.

"How do, Mr. Quinn," Bert greeted the chief with a dishtowel in her hand and Heyu at her side. Heyu had his nose in the air as if trying to recall who the man was.

"Miss Bert." He tipped and doffed his hat. His large ears blushed.

"Hi, Quinn, what's up?" Iris hadn't seen him since the day he had rescued her and Mr. Henry. A stranger, as tall as Quinn, stood next to him. "Hello, I'm Iris Lee, and you are?"

"Iris, this here's Detective Eddie Green of the New York Police Department," Quinn said as he batted his Stetson against his leg.

"What's this about, Quinn? I'm expecting company," she looked at her phone, "any minute. You guys are going to have to come back."

"Miss Lee, you've been avoiding my calls and with all due respect, I need to talk to you about an important matter." Detective Green stepped across the threshold into the foyer.

"With all due respect, Detective Green, as you reminded me in your phone message, this is not a TV show. You can't just barge into a person's home. If you want to question me about something, schedule an appointment or contact my lawyer." Iris wasn't sure if she liked this version of Detective Ed Green, although he favored the good looking one on TV.

"Miss Lee, I need ten minutes of your time." Green's smooth brown hands posed in prayer as if asking for forgiveness.

"Come back in an hour and you can have your ten minutes." Iris crowded his space trying to force him back onto the porch. Green refused to budge. She felt the heat of his body, only his folded hands separated them.

"Iris, this gentleman came all the way down here from New York City. You need to talk to him. Your friend's life may be in danger," Quinn said.

Like a three-way tennis match, Bert and Heyu watched the lobs between Iris, Quinn, and Detective Green from a safe distance behind the vase of forsythia.

"Quinn, I've got a truck load of reporters due here any second." Iris exaggerated. Claire had confirmed that only four people indicated they might attend, one of which wasn't a reporter but a student at Ferrum College who wrote a blog on local history.

"What if we waited in the kitchen and talked to you afterward?" Quinn negotiated.

"Why? Just come back later."

Green wasn't going anywhere. "Because you may not be here later now that you know I'm in town looking for you," Green sang with the tone he saved for his slower criminals.

Iris saw the WSLS-TV van pull up in front of the house. "Look, Detective, Lace is off somewhere having a good time without his wife, and she's mad about it. It's happened before. Let's compromise. You hungry?" She motioned for Bert to join the conversation. "Miss Bert take our guest out to the kitchen and fry him up something Southern. By the time you've finished eating, my guests will be gone and you can have all the ten minutes you want."

The turnout for the medallion press conference exceeded Iris's expectations. All four of the reporters, who said they might come, sat on dining room chairs in Mr. Henry's library. Two newspaper reporters from *The Roanoke Times* and the *Fallam County Citizen* jabbered on about a golf tournament while Ms. Trudy Wray, a rising star of the local NBC affiliate, checked her lipstick as her cameraman nervously shook his leg. A Ferrum College student who ran the *Franklin and Fallam Fortunes*, a local public-access history program, noodled on his smartphone.

For dramatic effect, Syke Darcy, the Sotheby's representative she had met in Richmond, sat in Mr. Henry's reading chair tucked in a corner and behind the medallion.

A white marble pedestal, which in real life was a plant stand for Elizabeth's ferns, stood in front of Iris's guests; atop the pedestal was a red damask table napkin masquerading as a shroud for the objet d'art that everyone had come to see.

"Ms. Wray, gentlemen," Iris started. Behind the media, she saw Bert, Quinn, and Detective Green watching from the kitchen door. Heyu silently took his place beside her, standing like a Dutch prince with one front paw turned out.

"Thank you for coming to my father's home. I speak for him and his wife, Elizabeth Carter Lee. I am Iris Lee. I'd like to make a statement, then I'll answer your questions. And please join us afterward for refreshments." Iris patted her stomach and stood taller.

"During times of life's transitions, we find things that were forgotten or thought lost while cleaning out our closets and attics." She paused to a room full of expectant silence and disinterest. "A few days ago we rediscovered an artifact that has been in my family's possession for over a hundred years. The artifact's previous owner is believed to be General Jubal A. Early."

The chair under *The Roanoke Times* reporter creaked.

Iris continued, "As you all know, General Early was a cavalier for The Cause and a favorite son of this region. We believe that this artifact, a military medallion, was crafted in the early 1800s for a member of the Bourbon family."

The Ferrum College student fumbled with his digital recording device. Jonnie slipped into the library and stood against the wall of Mr. Henry's books.

As Iris nodded a welcome to Jonnie, she said, "We have family records and sworn depositions that trace how my grandfather, then my father and mother came into possession of the medallion. What we don't know is how General Early came to own this unique artifact. That's where I am hopeful you can help us. We need to get the word out about this rare jewel so that we may discover how *he* may have come to own it. I'll open for questions and then we'll get a look at it." Iris sipped from a glass of water on the front window sill.

"Miss Lee, Tommy Gunn, *Roanoke Times*," the reporter was scratching his head. "Help me out with the dots. How did it get from General Early, if it was his, to your grandfather?"

"Good question, Tommy. My father's father, Allen Lee, was an attorney and businessman here in Mt Pleasant. General Early, after the war—that's the Civil war—but in Virginia what other war do we mean when we say 'the war'?" Iris paused for the anticipated chuckles. "After the war, General Early was a client of my grandfather."

"So General Early gave the medallion to your grandfather?" Gunn asked.

"Not exactly." Iris saw Jonnie roll her eyes. "This is where it gets interesting, and we really need your help in discovering the history of the artifact," Iris paused then added, "it's a treasure which belongs to the people of the Commonwealth of Virginia or to the people of France for that matter."

*Bring it on Bennie; let's fight it out in public.*

"Are you saying you don't know how your granddaddy came to own it?" The reporter from the *Fallam County Citizen* joined in.

"Pete? Right?" Iris confirmed and he nodded his head. "Pete, my grandfather was contacted in 1893 by a woman named Bella Sorin. She hired him to represent her on some personal matters involving her mother. Our family's personal documents show that Miss Sorin used the medallion as payment for services rendered by my grandfather. My grandfather, in turn, gave it to my parents, Henry and Elizabeth. Are you with me so far?" Pete nodded. "I apologize that this seems so complicated, but most history puzzles are, aren't they?"

"Now. Here's the twist," Iris continued. "Miss Sorin, according to my grandfather, claimed to be General Early's daughter. We have, on record, that my grandfather told my father this. My grandfather said Bella relayed to him that her mother, on her death bed, gave the medallion to her. Her dying wish was for Bella to give the medallion back to the person who gave it to her. And that person was our General Jubal A. Early."

"OK, OK. Like, Bella's dying mom had the medallion because General Early had given it to her, right?" the college student asked.

"According to Bella Sorin, yes," Iris pointed to the young man.

"And, like, she wanted Bella to meet her father. So like, like, she asked Bella to return it to the General," the student was drawing the logic flow through the air with his ink pen.

"Yes," Iris said. "Therefore, we might be able to draw the conclusion that the medallion at one time was in the possession of the general." Iris paused for that to soak in.

"Are there records saying she's his daughter?" Pete asked.

"According to Fallam County's historian there is no mention of Bella Sorin in any of General Early's personal papers. However, that's not surprising. In those times it would have been rare for one, especially someone of prominence, to acknowledge offspring had they been born out of wedlock. And we have no records of the general ever marrying. We can only speculate that Bella Sorin viewed the medallion as currency and used it to pay her legal bill. Maybe the general refused to acknowledge her as his daughter or maybe she wasn't his daughter. We just don't know." Iris paused again.

"The reason we are here this afternoon is to begin the journey of unraveling the mystery of," Iris held up an index finger, "one, did General Early give the medallion to Bella's mother, as she claimed, and two," she held up a second finger, "how did the Civil War general come into the possession of a military medallion crafted for European royalty?"

The room fell silent.

Iris cued Mr. Darcy and went back to her glass of water.

"We know that General Early left Virginia and was in Mexico in 1865," a voice boomed from the corner of the room. The reporters followed the voice to a lounging Mr. Darcy. "A place and time in which the French were supporting a Spanish monarch named Maximilian I. With his war experience, the general could have easily made his military talents available to the French or the Spanish. And we know that General Early wrote his wartime memoirs while in Canada. The Lee records show that Miss Sorin was from Canada. It supports Miss Lee's theories," Mr. Darcy stood up and walked toward the pedestal.

"Who are you?" Pete blurted out.

"My name is Syke Darcy. I'm an historian and artifacts appraiser for Sotheby's."

Iris thought that his bow-tie and tweed suit were all the bonafides this crowd really needed.

"Without putting everyone to sleep with the French lineage from the 1700s, just accept the fact that this piece *was* made for someone in the Bourbon family."

"Can we see it?" This question came from Ms. Wray. She glanced at her watch.

"Terrific segue, Ms. Wray. I know you're on a deadline so let's have a look," Iris said.

Once all eyes were focused on the pedestal, Iris whisked the table napkin away like a Las Vegas magician. The lights beaming from the ceiling track lighting, which Vinnie had just installed, and the sunlight from the newly washed windows shone on a glass bell jar and illuminated the medallion inside. The folded handkerchief with the initials JAE lay underneath the hanging medallion. When Iris nudged the pedestal, the medallion swung from its wire stand. This created a kaleidoscope of light all around Mr. Henry's library and on the faces of the curious. Everyone, including Quinn and Detective Green, crowded around the pedestal and gawked. She signaled to Mr. Darcy to continue with his dissertation.

"As you can see, there is a clasp on either end of the blue and red ribbon." The white-haired gentleman pulled from an inside suit pocket a fountain pen and pointed at the ribbon. "This confirms that the medallion was worn around the neck as was the tradition. With the Lees' permission, we'll take a sample of the ribbon to date it, but it has all the color and character of the French period we were discussing earlier."

"What about that fat red stone in the middle," Ms. Wray asked, "What kind of stone is that?"

"We shall get to the medallion in a moment. First let's explore the linen handkerchief."

"So, like, do you suppose, like, the J A E stands for Jubal Anderson Early?" the student asked.

"The handkerchief is embroidered with the initials J A E. The receipt from Allen Lee's law files includes such an item. In my opinion, Mr. Lee obviously thought this was an important detail," Mr. Darcy said as he sniffed and cleared his throat. Heyu was standing underfoot. "And the embroidery stitching is of a style common to the 1800s."

"It looks old," Pete added to the conversation. "Wonder if it's been used. Could nineteenth-century snot show up in a DNA test?"

Iris and the rest looked at Pete as if he had just farted.

"What?" he asked defensively.

"Let's go on." Mr. Darcy proceeded with his lecture. "As you can see, the medallion is in the shape of a cross, which represents the one true faith, the Holy Roman Church. In the center of the cross is a ruby symbolizing the heart or the love of country. The blue sapphires represent faith and loyalty to France and the white diamonds are the purity of the Virgin Mary."

"Wow, one of those diamonds would make a killer engagement ring." Ms. Wray contributed. "Miss Lee do you plan to keep it in one piece or break it up?"

"Young lady, you are looking at an objet d'art made two hundred years ago, touched and worn by French royalty. No one, I can assure you, is going to 'break it up' as you say and make common engagement rings from these stones," Mr. Darcy scolded Ms. Wray with his scholar's reprimand.

"Just askin'."

"How do you know that it belonged to some fancy French potentate?" Gunn asked.

"Two clues, Mr. Gunn. First, if you look along the gold channeling in which the stones are embedded, you'll see the iconic symbol, or standard, of the French royal family – the fleur-de-lis. See how the symbol repeats over and over?"

The unknowing students nodded in unison.

"Oh, I love that symbol. It's so classy," Ms. Wray added to the academic discussion.

"In English, fleur-de-lis means lily flower or Iris." Darcy smiled at Iris. "The second and perhaps the more important clue, Mr. Gunn, is the jeweler's mark on the back side. And believe me; I've looked at enough of these to know that the jeweler's engraving on this one is authentic." Mr. Darcy cleared his throat again.

"How much do you think it's worth?" the college student asked as the medallion's sparkle continued to hold his attention.

"At this time it's hard to say. But if Ms. Wray had her way and the stones were sold on the open market individually, they could fetch several hundred thousand dollars."

Pete whistled as the rest of the crowd pushed in to get a closer look. Gunn went back to scratching in his notebook. The student took a picture of the medallion with his phone.

"But as a medallion with a history, it's priceless and museum quality. The French government would probably be interested in the piece as my firm has already discussed with Miss Lee." Mr. Darcy signaled to Iris that he was ready to hand things back to her and remove himself from this room of uneducated hacks claiming to represent the fourth estate.

"Thank you for your expertise, Mr. Darcy." Iris was ready for the show to be over too. "Now, are there any more questions?"

"Let me recap to make sure I've got the scoop," Gunn said as he returned a condescending look toward Mr. Darcy. "Miss Lee, you found this object-de-art while spring cleaning. And Sotheby's tells you that it's an authentic nineteenth- century French military medallion. And it was given to your granddaddy by this Canadian woman for payment of legal services. She got it from her mother who you believe got it from the general."

"That's the scoop," Iris said.

"And the big question you want us to ask our readers and viewers is where General Early would have gotten a-holt of something like this?" Gunn asked.

"That's it," Iris walked toward the foyer and said, "Now, if there are no other questions, please join me in the dining room for refreshments?" Iris led the band of scribblers across the foyer and into the dining room for chicken salad canapés and cookies.

# Chapter 31

After the last reporter left with pockets full of Bert's sugar cookies, Iris turned to Quinn. "In a way it's a good thing you showed up when you did. Everybody will think that we have security for this thing."

"I was thinking that way too. How will you secure it?" Quinn dusted cookie crumbs from his hands.

"Mr. Henry's gun safe. Plus, I've rented a safe deposit box at the bank in Roanoke." As she reached for a carrot stick, Iris said, "You know, Quinn, I've been thinking about Mr. Henry's episode of chasing guys away from the house. I bet there really *were* guys and they were looking for that thing." She pointed toward the library, the bell jar emitting a smoldering, blood-colored light.

"What makes you think that?"

"My deranged cousin Bennie Lee is suing Mr. Henry. The short version is that he claims Mr. Henry stole *it* and Lee Properties from his father. If you want details, get Jonnie to fill you in."

"How did he find out about it?" Quinn reached for another cookie.

She relayed the conversation she'd had with Junie Marks the previous evening. "From what Mr. Marks told me, I wouldn't be surprised if Bennie put someone up to breaking into the house to steal it. Sounds like he's the demented one, not Mr. Henry."

"Hmm. We didn't get any other reports of strangers knockin' on doors that day. If you want, I can have a patrol car swing around every now and then."

"I don't think that's necessary." Iris looked up at Quinn. "You were in the patrol car parked in The Shop's parking lot that first night Mr. Henry was in the hospital, weren't you?" Quinn didn't answer. "Thanks," she said.

"Let's go rescue Detective Green before he explodes from Miss Bert's chicken dumplings." Quinn gently placed his hand on the small of her back as they walked to the kitchen.

A blushing Bert had cornered Detective Green at the kitchen table. She was shoveling chicken dumplings and collard greens at him as fast as he could eat them.

"Detective Green," Iris said as she sat across from him. She sampled a fresh cup of coffee. "Fire away. What do you want to know?"

He held up an index finger to signal that he was still chewing. After he swallowed and wiped his goatee with a napkin, he said, "May I have a refill on the coffee, Mrs. Swanson?"

"Why of course, Detective Green," Bert said while she topped off his cup. She then hoisted Elizabeth's dinner tray onto her shoulder and disappeared up the back stairs.

*Will wonders never cease? Miss Bert's flirting with a New York police detective. She actually batted her eyes at him.*

"Nice lady," Detective Green said.

"Yep, she's our jewel. Now, you want to tell me why you're here?" Iris's feet hurt from standing for over two hours in heels; she was out of practice.

"Lace Barbour is a business associate of yours?" Green fished a notepad and pen out of his suit pocket.

"Yeah, so? NYPD sent a detective all the way to Mt Pleasant to find out if I work with Lace Barbour?"

"He's missing. And we have reason to believe he's tied to a financial scam. That's all I can say. It's like the dude disappeared into thin air. No credit card trails, no phone calls home, nada. You're the last client that we have to interview. That we know of."

"So you think *I* know where he is?" Iris pointed to her chest.

Green shrugged. "When was the last time you saw Mr. Barbour?"

"It's been awhile since I've actually *seen* him. Up until a few weeks, I spoke to him on the phone every day or so. He was helping me find a new job." Iris curled then uncurled the end of a crocheted placemat.

"Why did you break off your communication?" Green watched her reactions closely.

"I didn't break if off. He just stopped calling me with job leads. My guess? He's too embarrassed to call me after the Nexdorf screw-up." She sipped her coffee.

"Explain." Green pushed his empty plate aside and leaned over the table.

"He sent me on an interview for a position in which he led me to believe I was the preferred candidate," she said. Quinn sat down beside her.

"And?"

"I talked to him on the phone right after the interview. In fact, I believe that *is* the last time I actually spoke to him. Told him the guttersnipe who interviewed me said they weren't hiring me. Nexdorf paid my air fare to New York to tell me they weren't hiring me? The frame on that picture doesn't seem square to me. What do you think?"

"What day was that, Miss Lee?" Green noted her comment.

"What do I look like, a savant who remembers every minute of every day?" She huffed as she got up for more coffee but noticed her cup was still full. The wound was still fresh. This conversation was forcing her to think about what almost could have been.

"This is very important, Miss Lee. We've hit a dead end," Green stressed.

"Interesting choice of words," Iris said nervously. "Let me get my phone. The date of the call will be on there." As she walked back into the kitchen, she scrolled through her calls. "Here it is: Friday, March fourth."

"That's the day before his family reported him missing." Green toggled his pen between his fingers.

"He invited me out for lunch then dinner that night and to stay with his sister," she added.

"Did you go?"

"Nooooooo. Once again, the last time I talked to him was right after the interview. I was on my way to the airport. I told him what happened and he kept saying he was sorry. I hung up on him. Then he did something *really* stupid," Iris recalled.

"What was that?"

"He texted me and said he would make it up to me." She was remembering the day and how disappointed she had been about not getting the Manhattan corner office of her dreams.

"Miss Lee, why is that out of character?"

"He ended it with a smiley face emoticon like he was talking to his ten-year old," she said as she folded her arms across her chest and leaned back against the butcher's block island.

"So?" Green said. Quinn seemed confused.

"He called the next day but didn't leave a message. And then I started getting calls from this Manhattan number. Oh, wait. Your number. You never left a message," she accused.

"And you never answered your phone," he volleyed back. Quinn cleared his throat.

"You want to arrest me for not answering my phone?" She held out her upturned wrists. Her eyes lit up. "It was you!"

Green looked puzzled.

"You were the guy with the condo's security guard my neighbor saw. Weren't you?"

He ignored her accusation by asking, "Can you think of anything unusual that's happened since your last conversation with Mr. Barbour?"

"Answer my question, detective."

"I couldn't get you on your telephone, so I asked a Richmond police detective to go by your place. At the time we thought he might be with you. We needed to confirm. Now you answer *my* question. Anything unusual happening since you last spoke with Lace?"

"You mean like Lace neglecting to give me a reason why Nexdorf reneged on a very, very lucrative job offer or my nutbag cousin suing my father for a bunch of rundown buildings and causing him to have a stroke and almost die. Those kind of unusual happenings, detective?" She had reached the limits of her patience with this guy.

"Yeah, like those, Miss Lee."

She walked around the butcher's block and leaned against it, facing the two men. "Ok, here's something. I spoke to Marvin Sheppard when I called Lace's office looking for him."

"Marvin Sheppard? When?" Green had picked up the scent again.

"Let's see. It was right after I was banished to Oz here." Iris opened her arms to the room. "I called Lace at his office to give him hell about screwing up the Nexdorf deal and to tell him that I was firing him. By then I'd put two and two together about what happened at the interview. For some reason Tenney ignored his staff's recommendation—that would have been *me*—and hired the lizard that fired me at Bank US."

"Who was the lizard, uh, the guy that fired you at Bank US?" a confused Green asked.

"Sandy Summers. CEO. In '09 he threw me into the snake pit." She looked around the kitchen. "You know, suddenly I feel like smashing something. Talking about it makes me want to spit fire. The other day I saw a report that he was going over to Nexdorf. Lace and Tenney used me. I don't know how, but I was used. Do you think the two instances could be related, Lace's disappearance and Summers's move to Nexdorf?"

"Can't say. But that's an angle I haven't thought of," Green admitted.

"You might want to give someone at the SEC a call," Iris shrugged.

"Hmmm," Green scribbled. "Why?"

"Rumor has it Summers is under investigation." Iris smiled. "Look, Lace has no motivation to get in touch with me. In fact the next time I see the greasy runt, by the end of the conversation, he'll be even shorter." Iris opened the refrigerator, stared at nothing, then slammed it shut. "So you see, Detective Ed Green of the New York Police Department, you've wasted your time and the taxpayers' money coming all the way down here." She leaned against the butcher's block again and crossed one ankle over the other.

"I wouldn't say I've wasted my time. Tell me about your conversation with Mr. Sheppard. How did he sound?"

"Actually sort of odd. It felt like he had rehearsed the conversation. It could have sounded that way because he'd been talking to all of Lace's clients, repeating it over and over. You know what I'm saying?"

"Uh-huh. Go on."

"Then he said something that struck me as odd at the time." Iris recalled the conversation.

"Believe me, Miss Lee, any small detail could lead to something. What did he say?"

"He told me that they were worried because Lace was supposed to come over that night and he didn't. They said that's when they called you guys. Then he said that Lace had mentioned me to them. How he said it stuck in my mind. He said Lace *thought* a lot of me, not he *thinks* a lot of me." Iris spoke slowly as she pulled the conversation from her memory.

"You sure? A 'thought' not a 'think'?" Green asked.

"Yeah, because I remember thinking how queer I was for picking up on it. Does it make any sense?"

"It might. But it's only conjecture not proof." Green folded the notebook and stuffed it and the pen back into his breast pocket. Green smiled for the first time that night. "Quinn, I believe I got what I needed. Can you give me a ride back to the airport?"

Iris and Heyu followed the two crime fighters to the front door.

"Miss Lee, it was, ah, interesting meeting you. Let's stay in touch."

"You've got my number," she replied.

"Then answer your phone when I call." Green offered a high-five to Quinn, but his hand was stranded in midair.

"I'll get with you tomorrow," Quinn whispered to Iris.

Later that night after the medallion was tucked away in Mr. Henry's gun safe and Elizabeth was snoring into dreamland, Iris lay in her lumpy bed. Each time her eyelids tried to end the day, her mind revved up, another sleepless night. Like it did every night, her right foot untangled itself from the bedding and plopped on top of the covers. Too much was unresolved, Lace and Nexdorf, the medallion, Kooch and the skunk Bennie and their scam. And Mr. Henry? Would he live to tell her all that he knew about Allen Lee and Bella? Knowing the probability of his return home was slim and none, she hoped for it anyway. She was ready to change her stripes and talk with him about love and respect and forgiveness. If only he would come home and do the same, she appealed to the ceiling.

Before she finally drifted off to sleep, Iris inhaled deeply and recited her list of things to do for the next day. Buy Miss Bert a new car, tell Jonnie her suspicions about her cousin, get a new mattress for her bed.

# Chapter 32

In the days after the press conference, everyone settled into a routine. In the mornings, Iris and Heyu walked to the hospital to visit Mr. Henry. Bert stayed with him in the afternoons and Donnie came over from Elder Home for the evening watch. The old man's condition wasn't improving.

Iris read *The Wall Street Journal* to him after his breakfast. At times he opened his eyes and, with a knowing look, encouraged her to go to the next story.

Once, she reached for his hand and whispered in his ear, "Mr. Henry, I found the medical directive, and I'll make sure they follow it." He blinked and formed a half smile. As these words were leaving her mouth, Iris realized that she had acknowledged to herself and to him that he may never return to Grove House. Her eyes watered up. His head gave an ever-so-slight nod.

Gently rubbing his beard stubble with the back of her hand, she asked, "Would you like Bubba to come by and give you a shave? I know Nurse Ratchet out there would squeal about it."

Mr. Henry's head nodded again.

Most mornings she prattled on about simple things such as how Vinnie had surprised her with his hidden talent for managing people and getting things done and how Lee Properties was in capable hands. She filled Mr. Henry's room full of empty words trying to keep out the silence she sensed would usher in darkness and death. Oh, how she wanted him to tell her about his life, about his choices. She wanted to hear him recite his regrets and his happiest times. But she knew the time for this was far behind both of them.

Over time, she told herself, her thoughts of him would reveal the things that she needed him to tell her now.

To crowd out the sadness of Mr. Henry's situation, Iris pondered the lack of responses from the features the newspapers had printed about the medallion.

"You need to give it some time," Jonnie told her. "Did Tommy Gunn say if the AP picked it up? If they did, the story could get exposed to lots of other markets."

They were having a Friday mid-day Diet Coke in Jonnie's office.

Iris snapped her fingers, "Hey! I've been meaning to tell you. I've figured out Kaluchi's scam. I don't think he's the brains behind it though. And I know why Bennie is suing Mr. Henry." Iris looked at her phone and jumped up. "Holy, moly! Time flies when you're doing nothing. I've got to get home. Ludie's leaving early today."

"What is it? Don't just say things like that and leave," Jonnie protested.

"Come by the house after work, and we can sort through it. I'll fix dinner," Iris yelled over her shoulder on her way out the door.

"Watching you cook," Jonnie laughed. "I'd pay money for that."

"Iris, you got a phone call." Now it was Ludie calling her to the phone from the bottom of the kitchen steps. Ludie had answered the phone while waiting for Vinnie to pick her up. A Doral, wedged between her fingers and pointed toward the back porch, seemed to confess, "See, I was in the smoking room when the phone rang. Don't put me out."

"Miss Lee, Miss Iris Lee?" a haughty voice asked. "My name is Davis Devine, Ph.D. of American and European history. I'm calling from Atlanta. Mr. Marks from Links Jewelers provided me with your private telephone number. I hope that I am not interrupting your dinner hour." The caller pronounced "hour" in three syllables.

She never trusted men who wore jewelry and here was her proof why. So much for Junie Marks not telling anyone about the medallion.

"Not at all, Mr. Devine. How may I help you?"

"It's a question of how we may help each other, Miss Lee," Devine assured her.

"OK. How can we help each other?" Iris waved good-bye to Ludie and pulled out a chair from the kitchen table and leaned back on its haunches.

"Junie—er—Mr. Marks told us about your, ah, medallion, you called it. The one which you believe may have once been owned by a Confederate general."

"That's correct. We believe that the medallion which my father and mother inherited once belonged to Jubal Early. He must have read the story in the local paper."

"Yes. Yes. And he called and told us about it. Here in Atlanta, we believe that we may have, how should I put this, found the French connection," Devine tittered.

"Who is 'we'?" Iris reached for her cell phone in her back pocket.

"I represent an interested private investor who wishes to remain anonymous," the caller informed her. "For now."

"Uh-huh," she grunted while she searched for his name on her phone's Internet browser. "So how do you think General Early and this medallion are connected?"

"My client collects Civil War artifacts. In fact *his* is probably the largest in the country, private or public. He's particularly interested in artifacts which belonged to General Lee and any of the men who served under him. Men such as your General Early."

"Uh-huh," Iris grunted again. *What a snob.* She scrolled through the Internet sites linked to Davis Devine, Ph.D., an adjunct professor of American history at a small college in Georgia.

"Before we could verify your claim, we'd like to actually see it. Is that possible?"

"That depends. Before you see it, you have to convince me why you think it belonged to General Early," Iris shot back.

"We have evidence that General Early knew men who served under Maximilian I." Devine spoke as if the identity of a long dead crowned head was common knowledge.

"Who was Maximilian?" Iris shouldered the phone receiver.

After an impatient sigh, Devine said, "Let me give you the long version."

Iris shifted to her best shuck and jive. "I think that would be best since I had a real hard time in school."

"Being a Southerner you should know that after the Civil War some Confederates, who had the means, defected to other countries. General Early, shall we say, ventured down to Mexico," Devine sniffed.

Iris felt his voice's condescension ear worming its way to her eyeballs. She crossed her eyes. "That was in the feature," she said.

"But why, Miss Lee? Why did General Early go to Mexico instead of, say, the Western territories?"

"You tell me. You're the professor." Iris scrolled through online shoe websites.

"It's called the War of the French Intervention or the Franco-Mexican War," Devine huffed.

"Yeah, so, what about it?"

"In the 1860s while we Americans were killing each other off, the last of the great European monarchs were fighting over Mexico and, of course, money. Napoleon III, the last French emperor, propped up an Austrian prince named Maximilian I to rule Mexico," Devine paused.

"Are you saying Early knew Maximilian?"

"We have no proof that the two ever met."

"Then where did Early get the medallion?" Iris reached under the table and scratched Heyu's head. A hind paw started thumping on the floor.

"We think it was given to him by Don Carlo Maria Jose Mendez." Devine pronounced the name with an attempt at a Spanish accent.

"Who's he, or she?"

"*He* was a cousin to Napoleon's wife, Eugenie, and the family's black sheep. Always getting into trouble. But that story's for another day."

Iris heard the muffled sound of a hand being placed over the phone's mouth piece.

"Mr. Devine are you still there?"

"Yes, where were we?" Devine cleared his throat.

Talking up, like a college co-ed, Iris said, "Like, ah, the empresses's cousin Carlo?"

"Yes. To appease his wife, the empress, Napoleon made her Spanish cousin a general in the French army. That was a mistake but we won't get into that either. During the French invasion of Mexico, he led his army in the wrong direction, north toward Texas and—"

"Sir, I'd love to sit here and chat with you all night about Mexican history but can you get to the point?" Iris remembered that she had invited Jonnie for dinner. With Bert away on church business, Iris prayed that there was some chicken-whatever leftovers in the refrigerator.

"Oh, sorry. I get carried away sometime. Where was I?"

"Empress Eugenie's cousin was made a general," Iris said.

"Right. The French Cross, which is what your medallion is called, was given to him by the emperor. That much we know. It's on record in the French royal archives. And isn't it the way of the world and history, Miss Lee? The flashier the medal, the smaller the deed the person most likely performed to receive it?

In Don Carlo's case, he just happened to be born into the right family."

"So the screw-up Don Carlo with the fancy bling and Early hooked up and somehow what?" Iris tried to speed up the telling of the story. *Is there any wine in the house?*

"Don Carlo found himself stranded on the Rio Grande surrounded by some unhappy Native Americans and desperados. His letters to Eugenie talk about a band of Confederates rescuing him. Sort of an out of the frying pan and into the fire-type scenario, if you will."

"So what you're saying is Early went from Confederate general to expatriate to kidnapper?"

"No, no, child. According to Don Carlo's letters to his cousin Eugenie, the relationship was a friendly one. Hence the card games. Most historians, including yours truly, never considered General Mendez's letters worthy of serious study. Don Carlo exaggerated about most things. I mean really, the stories."

"I don't understand. What do card games have to do with this?"

"Dear girl, it's quite evident, Early won Carlo's French Cross in a poker game or for what passed as poker in the nineteenth century!" Devine blurted out.

"You want to run that one by me again?" Iris stood and searched through the old cedar kitchen cabinets hoping dinner would magically appear.

"Yes, I can. Don Carlo couldn't pay his gambling debts so he used the medal given to him by his cousin-in-law to pay off Early. And the rest, as they say, is history. The French Cross referenced in the Mendez letters probably belonged to the Bourbon family and the French have been searching for it for years. Actually the joke was on Don Carlo. If you'd studied your French history, Miss Lee, you would know that the Bourbons were destroyed by Napoleon I. So Don Carlo's dear

cousin-in-law had given him a recycled military medal."
Devine tee-heed.

"Are you implying that the medallion that we own is this
French Cross?"

"I won't know until I've looked at it. If it is, it's very old
and very valuable. Make sure you keep it under lock and key,
Miss Lee. Now, may we examine it?" Devine asked as if he
were speaking to one of his first-year students.

"By all means. Hop on the big gray dog and come on up,"
Iris mimicked in her best Southern redneck woman.

"Excuse me?" Devine asked.

"The Greyhound, you know, take the bus?"

"Oh, we never use public transportation. Too many people.
We'll take our Cessna up. When can we visit?"

"Send me your CV and I'll get back to you." Without his
acknowledgement, she hung up the phone.

While Iris prayed for dinner intervention for the benefit of
her guests, the metallic bell in the kitchen phone rattled. She
waited for the re-installed answering machine to pick up. As
she listened to Plinkus Young prattle on about legal action to
obtain the medallion for Mt Pleasant's Historical Society, Iris
fetched a roaming Elizabeth from the sun porch and helped her
sit in the kitchen nook.

"I'm hungry. I want a jelly sandwich," Elizabeth
demanded.

Iris slathered Bert's homemade blackberry jam on a piece
of bread and placed it and a glass of milk before her mom.

Elizabeth clutched Iris's arm and asked, "Where's your
father? He's not in the library."

"He's at the hospital." She gently rubbed her mom's back.
"Eat your sandwich."

"Who's he visiting this time?" Elizabeth asked. "That hussy
Violet Tyler?" She hissed.

Iris couldn't believe her ears. She'd never, ever, heard Elizabeth Carter Lee say a derogatory word about another human being in her entire life. And Violet Tyler, Bert's mom, had been dead for decades. Iris rubbed her forehead with the heel of her hand and pushed her hair away from her face. Explaining Mr. Henry's condition to her mother, for the umpteenth time, was just too sad for her so she redirected the topic of conversation. "Why do you think Violet Tyler is a hussy?"

"I told Henry to stay away from that Jezebel," Elizabeth warned in a guttural whisper.

"I'm sure he took your advice." Iris bit her lower lip to stifle a laugh.

Elizabeth's eyes blinked as if she was resetting her out-of-synch perception of what was real. "Took my advice? About what? " Her voice had found its way back to quiet petulance.

"Eat your sandwich, Ma," Iris said.

# Chapter 33

Heyu tilted his mop-top head then wagged his way to the mudroom and sat by the door.

Just as Iris helped him exit from the back door, Jonnie called from the foyer, "Yoo-hoo. Anybody home?" Balancing a grocery bag on each hip, Jonnie entered the kitchen.

"Here, let me help you with that," Iris said. "What's in there?"

"Iris, how long have we known each other?" Jonnie asked. She started emptying the contents of the bags onto the butcher's block. "Tell me Miss Bert keeps olive oil in her kitchen," Jonnie said with her hands folded in prayer. Elizabeth appeared at Jonnie's side. "Hi, Miss Elizabeth."

"Are you gonna fix dinner?" Iris mentally crossed her fingers. Her eyes widened when she saw the ingredients for Jonnie's famous broccoli rigatoni. *Halleluiah!*

"What do *you* think?" Jonnie motioned Iris aside and handed her a bottle of wine. "Here. Make yourself useful. Open this."

Iris rummaged through Bert's drawer of beat-up biscuit cutters and tin teaspoon measurers. She found a rusty corkscrew in the back of the drawer along with the remnants of the last drawer liner laid down by Bert sometime in the eighties.

"You know, this kitchen has potential. You should renovate," Jonnie said as she hung her jacket over the back of a chair.

"I guess so," Iris said. She wasn't sure what she was going to do with the kitchen or the house for that matter, when her folks no longer needed it. The discovery of Mr. Henry's trusts was a game-changer.

Breaking up the first garlic bulb, Jonnie commenced to prepare the evening meal. Iris retrieved three crystal wine glasses from Elizabeth's china cabinet in the dining room and poured two pinot noir's and one grape juice.

"Mom, why don't you sit and enjoy your wine while we make dinner," Iris said as she guided Elizabeth back to her chair. Her comment produced a giggle from Jonnie.

As the sautéing garlic perfumed the kitchen air, Jonnie said, "Do I have to ask? What are your theories about Robert Kaluchi and Bennie?"

"First, I have to tell you about the phone call I just got." Briefing Jonnie on the conversation with the snooty Atlanta historian, Iris followed Jonnie around as she opened cabinet doors looking for a pot to boil the pasta. Then, Iris propped herself up on Bert's cooking stool and took her first sip of wine.

"Well?" Jonnie laid down the knife she was using to cut up the broccoli and zucchini, tasted her wine and smacked her lips.

"Well, what? Oh! The Kaluchi caper. Remember the day Mr. Henry had his stroke? We had that meeting in the morning with Kaluchi, and he said he was working with a development company."

"Oh shoot! Iris, I was supposed to ask Stan Campbell about them. I'm sorry."

"No worries. I had some, I'll call it divine intervention, the other night." Iris conveyed to Jonnie her dream about Mr. Henry and Uncle Ben and how it lead to her theory of Cousin Bennie and the development company.

"Why do you think our mayor and Bennie Lee are conspiring with each other?" Jonnie asked.

"I wouldn't say they were conspiring. Kooch is not smart enough to break a law. On purpose."

"Spare me the political ramblings, Mr. Henry Jr. Stick to the script," Jonnie said.

"Kooch has set up a not-for-profit called The CAT Foundation. It's not very original. C-A-T are the first letters of the names of his kids."

"There's no law against setting up a non-profit organization. In fact their numbers are on the rise. It's very telling of this country's commitment to helping others," Jonnie said as she poured the entire box of rigatoni into boiling water. This comment caused a braying snort from Iris.

"Yeah, right. It's a sign that people are learning the business of socialism. Can't find a job? No problem. Start a non-profit and beg the federal government to fund you a meager living. Meanwhile, back to Kooch. Go online, Jonnie, and read his mission statement. I challenge you to tell me if you can understand what the hell he's talking about. It reads like a third-grader wrote it. A third-grader probably *did* write it. Isn't Tatum about that age?"

"Iris, your language!" Elizabeth added to the debate.

"Sorry, Mom." Iris poured herself another glass of wine. "This is tasty. Where did you get it?"

Jonnie blushed. "It's from our vineyards. We've set up a B corporation, a type of not-for-profit company which channels all our profits from winemaking to Ferrum College. We employee two people. They wouldn't otherwise have jobs if they didn't work for us," Jonnie defended herself.

"Un-huh. Believe me, you're not doing your employees any favors. I bet they work less than the number hours which qualify them for full-time health benefits. You probably offer no retirement plan to help them accumulate real wealth from which their families could thrive. Am I right?"

Jonnie shrugged.

"Just like Ayn Rand said, we're all a bunch of second-handers."

Iris watched as her mother placed napkins underneath the plates at the kitchen table. "I'm not sure what Kooch is up to, he still hasn't given me anything concrete on his development plan. I met Mr. Pyle at the hospital the other day, and he assures me that it's all a pipe dream."

"So, what was that performance at the hospital with the mayor all about?"

"I need to know if he's in it with Bennie or if he's getting played," Iris said.

"In what?"

"The other night I woke up out of a dead sleep. Ennie Bay Development is the name of the investment company Kooch claims to be working with. He said he was working with their Internet retail group. Remember? I told you about it the day we had lunch with Vinnie?"

"And?" Jonnie surveyed the pine nuts broiling in the oven. "Miss Bert sure does keep a clean oven."

"She's anal about it. Cleans it every week. But, Jonnie, don't you get it?"

"What? Why you should clean your oven every week? Mine's self-cleaning," Jonnie grabbed an oven mitt and placed the roasted nuggets on a free burner.

"No, Ennie Bay. Think about it. It's Bennie in pig Latin! And you can't tell me that's a coincidence."

"I'd do one better and say your imagination is running away with your sanity," Jonnie said.

Iris watched as the chef emptied the pasta into Bert's wooden mixing bowl and stirred in warm olive oil with roasted minced garlic and zucchini. She added the pine nuts, parmesan cheese and steamed broccoli and gently tossed all the ingredients together.

"Dinner is served."

"Shouldn't we wait for your father, Iris?" Elizabeth asked.

"It *is* his company. I just know it," Iris picked up where she'd left off before dinner. "It's registered in Delaware as a privately held company, the owners are not listed. Their website says they buy blocks of old town real estate and convert it for public use. And they do it with federal funds. I'm telling you, these guys bring eminent domain to a whole new level, Jonnie. And if we let Porky Pig have his way, that's what will happen to Mr. Henry's property."

"There's no need for name calling. What's wrong with the mayor's plan? He's working to create a venue for the public to use and enjoy."

"That's not my point!" Iris paused in frustration. "Let me put it this way, and I quote, 'Serving his king was the important business of his life, though he hoped and intended to serve himself at the same time.'"

"Shakespeare?"

"No, Kathleen Winsor, *Forever Amber*. Look, Jonnie, what I'm trying to say is that these two clowns are up to something that will line their personal pockets. And they're stamping the Mt Pleasant town seal on it. But they're doing it *without* the actual consent of the people."

"Let the free market run its course. Isn't that what you've always preached?"

"What they're doing is moving toward the shady side of illegal and it's their non-disclosure mode of operation that chaps me."

"How so?" Jonnie's working legal mind had left the building after her third glass of Vino de Chateau Bailey.

"It's the way they're going about it. Kooch's foundation bullies Mr. Henry into selling his private property to them. CAT Foundation turns around and sells it to Ennie Bay Development for a tidy profit. Then Ennie Bay builds some substandard rat-trap and CAT Foundation, aka, Kooch's management company, moves in and offers to manage the properties. For a fee, of course. Or it could go like this," Iris was getting worked up, "CAT Foundation buys the land, runs the show, hires Ennie Bay to build and dash. But, I don't think Kooch is smart enough for that play. I could be wrong."

"The first scenario could fit because your dad would never sell the property to Bennie or his company." Jonnie said.

"Bingo," Iris said as the cork on the second bottle of Pinot popped.

"So the lawsuit is a ruse to chase Mr. Henry into the waiting arms of a willing buyer—"

"A willing buyer who would give him a fair market, pre-recession price on his run down, torn-up-by-the-Feds property," Iris finished. "I even suspect that Kooch may have played a part in getting the drug dealers planted in The Shops so he could call the Feds in." Iris's anger was stoked. "The feral reprobate—"

"Do you have proof? He could go to jail for that one." Jonnie held out her glass for a refill.

"Kooch is slow when it comes to strategy but he knows the law and he wouldn't say anything with witnesses around. I don't even know if any of this is true. But you've got to admit, old Kooch was pretty nervous when I started asking questions."

"He's always been afraid of you," Jonnie said. "When you started choking him with his own tie—" Jonnie covered her mouth to hide her snickers.

"I'll bet you forty bucks that the next time he sees me coming, he takes his tie off," Iris said as she poured herself another glass of wine.

After Iris tucked Elizabeth into bed for the evening, she joined Jonnie in the kitchen.

"Think I'm going to stay in town tonight. Can I leave my car in your driveway?"

"Sure, Heyu and I will walk you home."

On the eve of spring's full bloom, the street lights exposed the shabby and untended front gardens of Grove House. A string of volunteer daffodils cartwheeled across the yard of dead leaves and fallen tree branches.

"Guess what's on my agenda for tomorrow?" Iris pointed at the shabby yard. "Want to help?"

Jonnie laughed. "Right, I'll rake your leaves if you'll muck my stalls."

"Jonnie, I've been thinking about something. It'll work on so many levels. It's the right thing to do."

"What are you going on about?" The two were locked arm in arm as they came to the end of the driveway and crossed Grove Street. Heyu bought up the rear.

"I believe the medallion, if it's what they say it is, should be returned to its rightful owner."

"Even if the offer from Atlanta is more money? What's the value up to now?" Jonnie asked as a dying winter's breeze caused her bangs to flutter.

"I'm not selling it. I'm giving it back to the King of France."

Jonnie stopped, causing Heyu to bump into her leg. "You're gonna do what?" Her shrill reaction to Iris's news ricocheted off the side of the town library then echoed down the quiet street. "Where were you the week Miss Ruthie covered the French Revolution? France doesn't have a monarch anymore." Jonnie's questions were mixed with confusion and a dash of desperation.

"Yeah, they do. It's called The Louvre. The king, or the Bourbon Family, is a national symbol, of sorts. And all their treasures are housed there. That's where the piece belongs. Didn't you advise me to find a way to generate positive publicity for Lee Properties?"

"But...but...what's this nonsense about giving it away? I'm sure if they really want it back, the French government will pay you for it. Iris, this is crazy talk. Have you forgotten about Lee

Properties' debts?" Jonnie started walking again to catch up with Iris.

"We'll get by. Vinnie's a natural. He's going to be the next Mt Pleasant land baron," she chuckled. "Think about it, Jonnie. It's a KO in the Bennie fight. I win goodwill with an entire country and probably all the French wine I can drink for the rest of my life. And Bennie's lawsuit peters out. I mean, do you think he would actually lunge into a duel with the French government?"

"When did you decide this?"

"Just now. It makes a lot of sense. It feels right, don't you think?"

"No, I don't think. Maybe you need to sleep on it," Jonnie pleaded. "This is madness. You've got to think through this before you act. Please don't discuss this with anyone. And, for God's sake, don't bring it up at the Monday deposition call with Bennie, all right?"

"Look, I just handed you another point to argue with Bennie's lawyer and the judge. You should be happy," Iris said as she calmly turned the corner at Grove and Court.

It always amazed Iris that those around her lacked the ability to see the outline of the big picture and to dare to color it in.

# Chapter 34

A shivering Elizabeth laughed as she watched Heyu chase squirrels in the front yard. After bundling Elizabeth up head-to-toe, Iris had perched her on the front walkway in an old lawn chair that Ludie rescued from the dusty garage, a faded Fallam County High School stadium blanket draped over her lap. The strengthening midmorning sun shone on her pale face.

Iris raked moldy leaves and stacked dead tree branches into piles across the lawn. As she raked, she uncovered the sprouts of unidentified spring flowers, new grass and weeds that managed to survive through the winter. Shoots from nuts, yet uncovered by Heyu's tormentors, dotted the mulched islands surrounding the trees and bushes. The garden missed Elizabeth's nurturing.

The mindless physical effort helped Iris ponder her newly formed idea for the medallion's future. She paused to watch Heyu tree squirrels. How could she get what she needed by giving the family treasure back to its original owners? They, like Jonnie, would probably think she'd lost her mind.

Her phone vibrated in her back pocket. Propping the rickety rake against Elizabeth's cherished chestnut tree, Iris ambled over to the front steps and sat. The phone screen revealed Fred and Betty's home number.

"Hi Iris, Betty's here too. We've got you on speaker phone. I got the email you sent last night at—3:30 a.m. Do you ever sleep, woman?" He laughed.

"Betty! How are you?" Not caring about an answer, Iris jumped right into business. "Fred, do you know this wacky David Devine?"

"Oh, yeah, we've done business with David," Fred said.

"Do you believe his theory? What I described in the email?"

"He knows his history. He's claiming that the medallion belonged to one of the Louies?"

"Yeah, he didn't specify which one. He wanted to come up and see it." Iris attempted to imitate the professor. "We'll come up in the Cessna."

"Let me guess, he told you he's representing someone else?" asked the Sotheby's expert.

"He mentioned something about a client, that he was doing us both a favor," Iris scooted over to a sun-soaked porch column and leaned her back against its warmth.

"Syke Darcy knows him. He says he's a recluse. Lives on a family estate outside of Atlanta. Way too much family money," Fred said.

"I'm guessing this client he mentioned is probably himself, then."

"That would be a good guess," Fred said. "What do you want us to do?"

"I want to get as many opinions as possible. If Devine is a credible source, it'll help in our negotiations with others. What do you think?" She didn't wait for his answer, "At the same time, Fred, let's assume that the thing did belong to the King of France. I'd like to talk with your client and if at all possible, could they come here to Mt Pleasant?" Iris held her breath. The idea of bartering the medallion for philanthropic investments in Mt Pleasant seemed like a good idea the night before.

"Iris, you want the director of The Louvre, the most influential person in the entire art world, to come to Hicksville, Virginia? Are you serious?"

"If he wants his damned necklace, I guess he'll have to," Iris quipped.

"I'm not sure how to pitch this. Can you let me in on your strategy?" Iris heard the exasperation in Fred's voice.

"Just tell him it'll be worth his while." Oftentimes Iris lacked the ability to comprehend the inconvenient burdens she arbitrarily placed on others.

"It's a she," Fred corrected. "Jacqueline Beaumont."

"Oh, well, all the better. I know from personal experience that girls love to travel. Tell her that she's invited to come and try some of *our* wines." Iris wasn't sure how she'd sell that one to Jonnie, but she'd worry about that tomorrow.

"I'll call them back."

"Iris, did you hear the news?" Betty asked.

"What news?"

"They found Lace." Betty cleared her throat.

"Yeah? Where was he? Vegas?"

"No, you really haven't heard, have you?" Betty paused then said, "Honey, he's dead."

"You're kidding."

"No, I'm not. Somebody's Jack Russell found him. He'd been buried in Central Park. It's all over the news up here. They're calling it the Central Park Cemetery Murder."

"Gee, I don't know what to say, Betty." Iris's mind went out of focus as her body stretched out on the cold porch stones. She closed her eyes and heard Lace's peppy voice ramble on about how great New York was and how she was going to love living there.

"I feel sorry for the poor little dog," Betty offered. "The TV station interviewed the detective on the case. Iris, you're not going to believe this but there is actually a Detective Ed Green on the New York police force. You know, like the one on that TV show you like? And he looks just like the actor. "

"You're not kidding me are you?" Iris murmured.

"What's wrong? You sound funny. Were you two close?" After a pause, Betty continued, "I'm sorry if you were. It's a shame. Did I tell you that I hired that guy who was working for

Summers? He's been a gold mine for The Vine. Want to hear the latest?"

"What's the latest Bank US gossip?" Iris realized that she didn't care anymore about the world from which she had been forced to leave. Like Lace, it was gone.

"According to the ex-assistant I hired, Summers was asked to leave—or be fired. You were right all along, Iris. And the ex-assistant is good friends with wife number two. She's filing for divorce. I guess when the money goes so does the trophy wife. Know what else he told me?"

"No, what?" Iris answered.

"She's dating Jack Storm," Betty whispered as if both Storm, the chairman of the board of Bank US and one of the most powerful men on Wall Street, and Summers's soon to be ex-wife were in the next room of her Connecticut cottage.

"That's nice," responded a zombie Iris.

"Iris, are you OK?"

"Yeah. Lace's death, can't believe that munchkin's gone." Fighting to keep back the tears, her vocal cords tightened as she continued in a strained voice. "Listen, I've taken up too much of your Saturday. Thanks for the news. Fred, call me when you have something."

Iris spread her arms, tears streaming from her squinted eyes.

"Iris, what are you doing on the porch floor?" A wobbly Elizabeth hovered over her.

"I'm making snow angels," she said as she flapped her arms up and down. "Want to join me?"

"All right." Elizabeth got down on her hands and knees and rolled over onto her back. Their heads touching, Elizabeth mimicked Iris's arm motions and said, "When we're done, you'll have to help me get up."

"No problem, Mom. I can do that for you."

And the two lay on the porch for a long time, making snow angels on the stone in April.

After lunch Iris, Heyu, Ludie, and Vinnie all piled into Iris's SUV. The afternoon plans included a tour of the Eastend Street rental houses then a Saturday beer at The Early Riser. Holding onto the driver's headrest Ludie hopped up and down in the back seat. From the expression on his face, reflected in the rearview mirror, Vinnie appeared excited too.

*Lace was murdered. Who would do such a thing?* Out of the blue, Iris craved one of Chunky's tequila shots.

"Here we are." Iris pulled up to the first of three houses Vinnie had selected for his bride to tour. "Let's hurry up and pick one."

"Oh, Iris. Thank you so, so much. We really appreciate it." Ludie said as she spilled out of the back seat. Instantly she reached for her cigarettes in the side pocket of her denim jacket and lit up.

For the next hour or so, the troupe toured each shotgun shack. "They're all the same, pick one," Iris murmured not quite loud enough for the others to hear.

Ludie interrupted her own chatter about home decorating to ask, "Iris, what are you going to do with all that money you'll get from selling that medallion thingy?"

"Ludie!" Vinnie scolded. "That's none of our business." He shot Iris a look of apology for his overexcited wife.

"You're right, Ludie, from what I'm hearing, the medallion is worth a lot of money. But we're still trying to find out where it came from."

"Everybody's talking about it," Ludie said.

Waiting on the sidewalk as the couple and Heyu toured house number one a second time, Iris revisited her strategy of a public boxing match with her cousin. If the town saw her as its luckiest lottery winner, her plan could backfire. Town gossip would paint her and Bennie as spoiled rich kids fighting over the family booty. She needed to expedite her new plan of giving it back to the rightful owners before Bennie, or the town, caught up with what she was doing.

# Chapter 35

Monday morning ushered in a cool fog. As the town hurried on its way to work, Iris and Heyu stopped at the busy corner of Court and Main under the memorial solider. Before the noon shoot out with Bennie and his lawyer, Iris wanted to check on Mr. Henry. The day before had been a bumpy ride for him and Bert had proclaimed that he was on his way to The Glory Land.

Iris and Heyu hustled across the intersection. The pair gathered speed as they walked down the hill of West Main Street. Before crossing to enter the hospital, Iris stood in front of The Shops. From the outside appearance, Vinnie's two-man crew was doing a bang-up job of tearing the place apart.

"Heyu, why don't you hang out with Vinnie? I'll be back in a few." Wanting to catch the night shift before they went off duty, Iris hoped for an update on how Mr. Henry fared the early morning hours. As she entered the third floor hallway, she spied Dr. Bowman and Nurse Bowles standing in front of Mr. Henry's room. Seeing the doctor was not a good sign.

"What's his status?" she interrupted the two.

Ignoring Iris, Dr. Bowman continued with her instructions to the nurse. When she finished, the doctor motioned Iris to follow her into the empty patient room next to Mr. Henry's. "Your father had another stroke about fifteen minutes ago," she said.

"Why didn't someone call me?" Iris's voice cracked.

The doctor removed her glasses. She spoke with her eyes and they reprimanded Iris for asking such an inane question. Then she advised, "He's dying."

"How much longer does he have?"

"Two, three days. You should notify the rest of your family," Dr. Bowman said.

The reality of her father's eminent death sank deeper into Iris. For the past few days she had fed on the false hope that maybe he would get better, that maybe his sickness would cause a transformation in his demeanor and that maybe they might have a better understanding of each other. But wishful thinking ranked right up there with fat chances.

"We've done all we can for him." The doctor continued as she made notes on her tablet.

"Can I see him now? Is he lucid?"

"He's asleep right now. We won't know how this latest stroke affected him until he wakes up." The doctor folded the tablet in her arms and waited for the next question.

"You mean *if* he wakes up, don't you?" Iris asked.

The doctor shrugged her shoulders and widened her eyes. "Go sit with your father, Iris. As I've said, we've done all we can." With those words, the doctor left the room.

Before she went to sit with Mr. Henry, Iris called Bert and Donnie to give them the news. Bert cried and Donnie said, "I'll be over directly."

The lawsuit that Robert Benjamin Lee, Jr., filed against Lee Properties was headed toward the discovery phase. Bennie and his lawyer continued to ignore Jonnie's requests for more substantial documentation supporting their claims. She was prepared to hammer Bennie with demands to follow civil procedures or get his lawsuit tossed.

Before the meeting, Jonnie suggested a postponement because of Mr. Henry's condition. Iris objected. She wanted Bennie to know that Mr. Henry was one block from death's door and that Bennie had a hand in putting him there.

"Shall we begin?" Jonnie asked. Iris, Jonnie, and a court reporter were huddled at one end of the second-floor conference room table, the same spot where Iris and Mr. Henry met Chief Quinn. That seemed so long ago.

Sitting in the middle of the conference table, a wide flat-screened monitor displayed Bennie and his lawyer, Ulysses Marshall III, huddled together at a glass table with a background view of a sprawling Orange County suburb.

"We're ready, Ms. Bailey," Marshall signaled. Unlike his client who was dressed in a faded golf shirt, Marshall's appearance was as formal as his name.

"Before we begin," Iris spoke up, "Bennie, I want you to know that Mr. Henry has taken a turn for the worse. The doctor says he's got two days tops." Bennie shrugged his shoulders and clasped his hands, then laid them, palms down, on the table top. "He suffered a stroke after reading the summons— Owww!" Iris's shin felt the jab of a pointed-toe shoe.

"I'm sure Mr. Lee appreciates the update on his uncle's condition, Iris," Jonnie interrupted. "Shall we proceed?"

Bennie snickered. His lawyer flashed a nasty look at his client.

"Ms. Bailey, if this is an inopportune time for your client due to the illness of a family member, may I propose we reschedule this meeting?" Marshall said.

"Mr. Marshall, my client is grateful for your concern. However, let's continue," Jonnie responded. She nodded to the court reporter to begin and expounded on legal instructions for plaintiffs and defendants. Then, she said, "Mr. Marshall, on behalf of my client, I have requested on four separate occasions that your client produce evidence in the form of documentation that supports his claims as they are spelled out in his lawsuit. My first question is does your client possess such documentation?"

Marshall spoke slowly. "Ms. Bailey, my client has informed me that—"

"I have a copy of Allen Lee's will, and it states that my father was to inherit the business, the house *and* the farm," Bennie blurted out.

"Mr. Lee, please allow me to do what you've hired me to do," Marshall spoke quietly while facing Bennie.

"Henry Lee stole that business from my dad as sure as I am sitting here." Bennie's pate blushed bright red through his thinning hair.

"Mr. Marshall, if such a will exists, we ask that your client produce a copy for our review," Jonnie commanded.

"You know it does, Jonnie. Your father administered it, for Christ's sake," Bennie barked back.

"Mr. Marshall, will you explain to your client that it's the plaintiff's obligation to produce proof of claims," Jonnie calmly retorted.

Iris stuffed her hands under her legs. *Don't say a word. Let Jonnie do her job.* She wanted to scream at Bennie, to reach through the monitor's ether and grab him by the neck and shake the living snot out of him.

"This is outrageous, and I'll not stand for this disrespect," Bennie poked the table with an index finger. "The bastard stole my birthright—"

"Mr. Lee—" Marshall attempted to control his client by pushing his arm against Bennie's chest.

"I'm the son of the oldest son. And the oldest male of this generation's Fallam County Lee's." Bennie was standing now and pounding his chest with both fists like a sports celebrity pumped with victory.

Iris, Jonnie, and the court reporter all leaned back in their chairs. Their collective instincts didn't trust the reality that the physical threat was three thousand miles away and couldn't hurt them.

"Are you getting all this?" Jonnie leaned into the stenographer. The reporter nodded. "The video, too?" The reporter nodded again while holding down a fit of nervous giggles.

"I didn't see that coming," Iris whispered out of the corner of her mouth.

"Good Lord." Jonnie lowered her head.

Meanwhile, Bennie's rage was spreading. "It. Is. My. God-given. Birthright." After each word, a spitting Bennie pounded the glossy table. "That Miss Goody Two-shoed Twat has no right. You hear me? No right to steal this from me!" With his back to the monitor, Mr. Marshall was now shielding Bennie's tantrum from the defendants. Evidently someone on the California end finally pressed the mute button.

"Let the record reflect that the plaintiff has muted the microphone," Jonnie stated as calmly as before. All the defendants could see was Marshall's tailored backside. Then the monitor switched to the blue screen of disconnect.

"Sounds like somebody forgot to take their meds this morning," Iris murmured.

Jonnie reached for the conference phone and hit redial. The phone returned a loud fast busy signal. Jonnie motioned to the reporter to keep recording.

"Let's give Mr. Marshall an opportunity to calm his client and to call back into the conference bridge," she said. The three sat, not saying a word. And after a few minutes, Jonnie pronounced, "Let the record reflect that Mr. Marshall and Mr. Lee have left the deposition proceedings without answering questions posed by defending counsel." She signaled the reporter to stop typing and to turn off the video camera.

"What do we do now?" Iris asked after the reporter left.

"We wait for Mr. Marshall to call us back so that we can reschedule the depositions. If the will that leaves everything to Ben Sr., is all he's got, Judge Taliaferro will throw this case out of court. If it even makes it that far. That will was voided by the one your grandfather wrote a year before his death."

"I don't understand. After all this time, out of the blue he decides this company belongs to him." Iris was truly perplexed over her cousin's misogynistic comments. "I could see if he lived here and worked with Mr. Henry. But to believe that he's entitled to something simply because he was born with a penis? That's so seventeenth century. I don't get it."

"Don't try to apply reason to family feuds where money is concerned, Iris," Jonnie said as she gathered her notes and shoved them in a file folder. "You should go back to the hospital."

Iris sat alone in the conference room thinking about what had just happened. She was stumped but also angry at her cousin for causing such disruption and pain in her parents' lives. She suspected the interloper was probably involved in The Shops drug bust, the land grab scam and the aborted theft of the medallion but knew she could never prove any of it. Maybe that's why he dropped his cookies just now; she had thwarted his plans for what he had assumed would be an easy score.

Bennie's outburst reminded Iris of the day he'd pulverized her mother's flowerbed with a baseball bat. She should have seen this coming. "I got to get back to the hospital," she sighed.

"Anybody contact you about your fancy medallion yet?" the *Fallam County Citizen* reporter asked. He was standing in front of Bailey and Bailey waiting to cross Main Street.

"Pete? Right? Thanks for writing the story," Iris said, ignoring his question. "I may have a follow-up press release for you in a couple of days." She crossed the street with him.

"So, what're you going to do with all that money?" Pete called after Iris as she started down Main Street toward the hospital. Pete held The Early Riser's door open as two other patrons entered. The cowbell, attached at the top, banged against the scratched glass door.

"What?" Iris stopped and turned around.

"What're you going to do with all that money you'll get from selling the medallion? You are going to sell it, aren't you?" he shouted.

She answered by shrugging her shoulders. She turned again and started down the hill.

"If it was me," he yelled after her, "I'd quit Mt Pleasant and start at the county line and play golf from here all the way to Key West, Florida, and never look back."

# Chapter 36

Taking a break from the uncomfortable sofas and antiseptic smells of the hospital, Iris and Heyu drove to Eastend Street to watch Vinnie and Ludie launch their renovation revolution. If the work was successful, Iris thought about asking the Community Bank to invest in a low-income housing project. They could rebuild Eastend Street into affordable first homes for couples like Ludie and Vinnie. The profit from the development could go back into Lee Properties to finance the renovation of the commercial properties. She also wanted to talk to the bank president about setting up a fund for a new library. The Bailey House was nice, but it was old. The town deserved some modernization, and the library was the place to start.

What had Kaluchi been doing with his days between the time he punched his time card in the morning and when he clocked out at night? According to Jonnie, Lee Properties was his maintenance management firm's only client. And Mr. Henry had fired him. Maybe town council would give Kaluchi the heave-ho once his term expires. *One could hope.*

While standing on the cracked and crumbling sidewalk, Iris's phone rang.

"Iris, this is Fred Kitter at Sotheby's. Good fortune on The Louvre meeting. They want to talk with you, but instead of them coming to Virginia, they want you to fly to Paris. Our Atlanta friend David Devine has them convinced that it's the French Cross made for Louis XVI, a gift from his wife—"

"Marie Antoinette," Iris finished his sentence. "Me going to Paris—that's not what I asked for, that's not the plan."

At the hospital earlier, Iris had sounded ideas off a comatose Mr. Henry. She dreamed of developing real commerce, not the homogeneous retail big-box trash lined up off the interstate. Her vision for Mt Pleasant centered on the old buildings: convert the old Bailey House to a small hotel and restaurant, restore the movie house to a modern cineplex and auditorium, build condominiums where the Grand Hotel once stood, and rebuild The Shops of Mt Pleasant as retail stores. And get Chunky his own pub, for crying out loud. All it took was money and not the kind that politicians in Richmond and Washington doled out with teaspoons every year. She wanted investors, innovators, and entrepreneurs.

To Iris, the medallion represented the hope and prosperity that restoration brings. The medallion could open global doors for Mt Pleasant. Like the Mystery Date game she played as a kid, she wasn't sure what would be behind the doors, but she wanted to give Mt Pleasant a chance to open them, that was, if the town wanted the opportunity.

"Fred, I'm not selling the medallion to the highest bidder. I'm giving it back to its rightful owner."

"You're what! Iris, are you crazy? If it *is* Louis XVI's, it's worth millions. You sell it, you're set for life. And you want to give it away?"

"The sale price is not enough. I need more. I want to give it back to France. In return, I want them to invest in Mt Pleasant. That's why I want them to come here, you know, to see the place."

"Hmm. That's an interesting idea." Fred said this with the kind of commitment one gives when asked if they want white or brown rice with their steamed vegetables.

"Go back and tell them I want to trade the cross for some French goodwill. We want educational contributions, financial investment offers. I've got a million ideas. I hope they've got millions to fund them."

"What you're telling me is that you want the French to come to Mt Pleasant for a pitch on how they can make scratch by investing in the place?" Fred asked cautiously.

Suddenly Iris pictured Kaluchi and the director of The Louvre conversing over Miss Bert's chicken salad canapés. She shook her head, violently. This idea needed more time in the ragout pot.

"You know what, Fred? You're right." As Iris considered her next move, she watched Ludie grab a rotting roof eave as the ladder the new homeowner had been standing on fell to the ground. "Tell them I'll come to Paris," her voice quickened, "but I want a meeting with the director. Not an assistant or some other lackey who isn't authorized to think for themselves. And their top private contributor. See if you can get them to pay for the trip. And your commission. Oh, and remind them that we have national museums, too." She hung up without saying goodbye or giving Fred a chance to object and rushed to help Ludie.

Iris got the news of Mr. Henry's death while watching Vinnie help Ludie, the screaming banshee, from the backseat of her car at the hospital's emergency room entrance.

"Iris, he suffered another stroke. I'm afraid he's gone," Nurse Bowles reported to her on the phone. "Where are you and what's that noise?"

"What's that? Cricket, I can't hear you." Iris covered her ear to drown out Ludie's piercing squeals and obscenities. But she didn't have to hear Cricket to know what she was saying. There would be only one reason why she was calling.

Before the sun set on Mr. Henry's lifeless bones, the Lee family discovered that he had already made his own final arrangements for the sweet hereafter. A call to Briarwood Funeral Home informed Iris that Mr. Henry had already contracted them to handle "the final disposition," as they called it. He had ordered up one cremation with nothing on the side, no viewing and no eulogy, just like he was asking for a plate of fried eggs with no toast or jam. His ashes were to be buried on the farm at the family cemetery. Iris smiled when the funeral director read from Mr. Henry's instructions. Dead and gone, yet he was still barking orders.

"How am I to have closure if we don't have a proper funeral, Iris?" Bert cried. She insisted that Mr. Henry's final disposition was disrespectful to the people who knew and loved him.

"We'll figure something out." Iris put her arm around Bert's shrinking shoulders.

"Sissy, that was just Mr. Henry's way. You got to respect his wishes." Donnie's haggard face tried to hide his grief for his oldest friend.

It wasn't how quickly the news of her father's death spread to every corner of the county that amazed Iris the most. What stupefied her was the volume of protests on how the old man had denied everyone a bereavement day, a social time to connect with old or lost friends, a peek at their own inevitable future and the curiosity of wondering who would be next. How could he withhold from them the simple pleasure of sharing a few ham biscuits and potato salad, all for the remembrance of him?

The day after his death, to appease Bert and the church ladies, Iris agreed to a memorial service at Mt Pleasant Methodist Church. Out of respect for Mr. Henry's many years of boycotting religious ceremonies, she drew the line at holding the service in the sanctuary and insisted that the gathering take place in the basement fellowship hall of the sprawling church.

The evening before the memorial service, Iris watched as Bert tried to rearrange donated casseroles so she could close the refrigerator door.

Iris said to Bert, "You know how Mom gets whenever we take her away from the house? I don't think she should go to the church tomorrow." Iris recalled Mr. Henry's orders to keep Elizabeth at home. The memory revealed a tenderness in his voice, compassion which she had missed. For the first time since his passing, Iris felt Mr. Henry's presence.

"Iris, it's her husband we're putting in the ground tomorrow. Elizabeth should be with him and in the bosom of her church family," Bert insisted.

"I don't want a repeat of the incident we had at the hospital when we took her to visit Dad. She can be with him right here at Grove House. I'll have Briarwood deliver his ashes here instead of the church."

"I, I can't believe I'm hearing this." Bert cried while staring at Iris as if she were the devil's host. "Did you just hear what you said? The salvation of this man's soul is already in jeopardy for burning his-self up and now you don't want the preacher to consecrate his remains? I pray for you, sweat pea. Every day, I pray for you."

"You do that," Iris snipped. "I'm sorry. I'm just thinking of mom's dignity or what's left of it. Her screaming at the nurse to stop sleeping with her husband is probably all over the county by now."

"But what you gonna say to Plinkus Young and the rest of those fussy hens when Elizabeth don't show up?" Bert grabbed at her elbows.

Iris shrugged and said, "I'll invite Pastor Tim here for a prayer over the ashes. That way you can tell all the busybodies that we had a private service."

"But, Iris—" Bert protested.

"I'm done talking about this." Tired of arguing with Bert on the finer points of Mt Pleasant's funeral etiquettes, she turned and walked out to the back porch to look for Ludie's private cigarette stash. Bert followed her.

"We're having Briarwood's limousine chauffeur us to the church tomorrow," Bert insisted, "then over to the farm's cemetery."

"Fine. Whatever. If riding in the back seat of a funeral car comforts you, we'll do it." Iris was dumbfounded at Bert's resolve to assure that Mr. Henry's send off to the Great Reward was carried out with such celestial precision. She lit one of Ludie's smokes and sucked in a lung full of carcinogens.

"You shouldn't smoke," Bert pointed her finger at Iris. "Look where it got your daddy." Bert's voice cracked, and she left the porch crying.

The next day Iris blinked twice when she saw the older woman enter the kitchen. Dressed completely in black, Bert Swanson was radiant. Crowning her head was an Edwardian style hat with raven feathers and inky silk roses nestled in dark tulle. Her understated dress coat was opened, revealing its companion empire-waist dress. Seeing the transformed woman, Iris now understood why Bert had demanded a memorial service for Mr. Henry. The man had been her employer and benefactor for most of her life. With reverence toward him and her faith, this was Bert's final and most loving act in the caring for Mr. Henry.

"There you are!" Plinkus Young said as the driver opened the back door of the limousine for Iris and Bert. When Iris stepped out of the car, she heard a loud hum of voices coming from the bowels of the church. She was surprised at the sea of cars in the church parking lot and the stream of people crossing Main Street from the church's annex parking deck. "We've taken care of everything, dear. Where's Elizabeth?" a confused Plinkus asked while the plumes on her own church hat vibrated nervously. Bert's eyebrows rose as she pursed her lips and nodded her head toward Iris with an "I told you so" glare.

"She's not feeling herself today," Iris answered solemnly. Elizabeth and Ludie were dancing to the disco song "YMCA" when Iris and Bert had left the house.

"What a shame. Bless her heart. I know she'll miss Henry, and everyone will be disappointed that they couldn't deliver their condolences to her personally." Ignoring Bert, Plinkus grabbed Iris's hand and said, "Iris, you know there's a reason for everything. Mr. Henry's in a better place now, bless his soul." She pulled Iris along. "Now come with me."

After a five minute eulogy for a man he barely knew, Pastor Tim delivered an effusive prayer of thanks for the bountiful sustenance accumulated on tables arranged in the middle of the crowded fellowship hall. The nourishing of the living souls commenced.

Against one wall, a table displayed photographs and mementos of Mr. Henry's life, a 1960s newspaper article about the reopening of The Shops, various photos of Mr. Henry and his poker buddies, one of his family, and a photo of Mr. Henry shaking hands with the Commonwealth's last Republican U.S. senator. Next to the table, a studio photograph of a young Mr. Henry, dressed in his military uniform with the future vibrant in his eyes, perched on a gold easel. Iris and Bert stood beside the photograph receiving condolences from, what Iris figured, every man, woman and child in Fallam County.

"At least he lived a long life," one of the church ladies offered. The comment reminded Iris of the lesson her mother used to impart to her: "If you can't say anything nice about a person, don't say anything at all."

"Your daddy bailed me out of trouble. I was just a kid," offered another mourner as he shook Iris's hand. "If it wasn't for him, I don't know where I would've ended up at. Jail, I guess."

"Mr. Lee got me my first job over at the furniture factory in Franklin County," cried a red-faced woman. "He hoped my mamma and daddy too when they couldn't make rent. God bless his soul."

"He's in a better place now, Iris. You be strong now and help your mamma deal with her grief," said one woman who claimed she knew Mr. Henry before he was married.

The end of the receiving line was nowhere in sight. Iris had no idea that her father knew so many people. When shaking the hand of Pastor Tim, a dizzying sensation came over her. Pining for fresh air, she excused herself from the warm room and wormed her way through the crowd, up the stairs and into the church's vestibule. All the while, she held her breath hoping it would stall the tears. It didn't. They washed over her face. She found refuge on an iron bench under the ancient oak tree that greeted all to live and worship in Mt Pleasant.

"Iris, I'm sorry to disturb you." Donnie Tyler hovered over her, jingling his keys. "I'm headed back over to Elder Home. You gonna be OK?"

She looked up at him and said, "Why didn't I know about this—this—Santa Claus in a car coat?" Tears, snot and spit were everywhere as she tried to control her breathing.

"Sweet pea. That's just the way he was. He didn't need to tell everybody about his good works. He just did them." He sat down next to her and put his hands between his knees.

"He didn't love me," she stammered. "But he loved all those people." She pointed at the church doors. "All those strangers."

"Say what?" Donnie stretched his skinny arm around Iris's shoulders. "Your father worshiped you and your mama. Don't you say words like that. They ain't true."

"But you don't understand, Donnie," she bleated. "He never told me once that he loved me, that he was proud of me—"

"Stop it. Stop it right now. He was proud of you plenty. Why you suppose he went to all those poker games? Damn sure wasn't 'cause he wanted to play poker, know what I'm sayin'?"

She stared at the sprouting chickweed on the ground.

"Sweet pea, he went so he could brag on you. 'Iris got this promotion,' 'Iris running this office.' The man never shut up about you."

"But, he never seemed interested in what—"

"Listen," Donnie interrupted. "Look at me. You know why he let you alone and didn't hang on you like all the other parents did they kids?"

"Why?"

"Your daddy left Mt Pleasant when he was twenty years old with every intention of never coming back. He hated this place. Did 'til the day he died, is my guess. He wanted to live in California. But he stayed here 'cause his parents expected him to. He didn't want that hangin' over you. He wanted you to have what he didn't get to have." Iris looked at Donnie and crinkled her forehead. "Your freedom to do as you want," Donnie said quietly. "Now, you honor your father's memory by doin' just that, ya hear me?" Donnie stiffly patted her back.

"Ok." She heaved in some air and added, "Donnie, I need your advice on something."

"What's 'at?"

"I'm worried about Miss Bert. She's taking it harder than I ever imagined. As much as those two fought and bickered, I'm amazed at the grief that woman has for him." The sound of happy, well-fed mourners returning to the rest of their day floated in the air.

"You really don't know?" Donnie asked

"Don't know what?"

"About Bert?"

"Know what about Bert?"

"Bert is Mr. Henry's niece," Donnie stared at his hands as he rubbed them together. "Actually he is, or *was*, more of a father to her than an uncle."

"Wait a minute. Miss Bert? Miss Bert is my cousin?" Iris asked in disbelief. "But, who? How?"

Donnie put his arm around her shoulder again and chuckled softly. "Mr. Henry or Sissy never said anything to you about this?"

"No, I was the kid, remember? Nobody ever told me anything. What? Does everybody in Mt Pleasant know about this except me?"

"Just about," Donnie laughed. "You see, Roberta, that's her full name, was named for her father, Robert Benjamin Lee. That's all I'm gonna say about it. I'll let Sissy tell you the rest." Donnie stood and loosened his necktie.

"Yoo-hoo, Iris!" Plinkus Young was flapping her arms as she walked toward them.

"Look out, here comes trouble," Donnie said.

"Iris, honey, are you OK? You look terr-ble. It's almost time for you to ride over to the home place cemetery. Do you think Elizabeth is feeling better now? I could tell the driver to stop by your house and pick her up for the burial service."

"Thank you for everything you've done. I think we'll bury Mr. Henry's ashes another day."

"Well, if that's what y'all want, child. But you know the funeral home will charge you for another day?"

"We'll manage," Iris said quietly.

"Listen, while I got you, when can I stop by to talk with you about the Historical Society and the medallion?" Plinkus lowered her voice and added, "To your knowledge, is the Historical Society a benefactor in Mr. Henry's will?"

"Ho-oh!" Donnie interrupted loudly. "That's my cue to leave." He waved goodbye and abandoned Iris to endure the persistence of Mt Pleasant's chief do-gooder.

# Chapter 37

A few days later Heyu led the way up Court Street toward The Early Riser. Iris noticed his matted brindle fur. "Heyu, I wish you had opposable thumbs so you could turn on the bathtub faucets. Take your own bath." He stopped and looked back at her as one eye ticked. Then, he scooted ahead.

Once they were situated at their favorite table under the front window, Iris ordered their usual, coffee and water. She was reading Mr. Henry's day-old *WSJ* when her phone vibrated across the table.

"Hello, Fred from Sotheby's." She answered while a *Journal* headline about Sandy Summers caught her eye.

"Good morning, Iris. Wanted to reach you before the day got too crazy. Can you talk?"

"Yeah," Iris said without much enthusiasm.

At the bar, Chunky cranked up a morning news program on the monitor.

"You got what you asked for," Fred said excitedly. "The French agreed to your terms. Never seen anything like it. They even want to talk to you about planning a publicity campaign on the return of the cross. Isn't it wonderful?"

"Sure." Iris's enthusiasm didn't match Fred's.

"You OK?" Fred asked.

"Fine. What's our next step?" She saw no need to detour into a conversation about Mr. Henry's death. The dizzy feelings were back, along with the tears.

"Meet me at JFK next Tuesday. We're off to Paris!" Fred sounded as excited as a retailer on Black Friday. "Betty's coming with us."

"Send me the itinerary." Iris pulled a napkin from the Goodwrench #3 Car napkin dispenser on the table and wiped her eyes and blew her nose.

"You sure you're OK? You sound like you've got a cold or something," Fred chattered on. "We'll review whatever proposal you have on the flight over. The first meeting is scheduled for the following Thursday. Look for an email from Boomer Travel. Later."

"*Merde!*" Proposals didn't grow on trees. She had to come up with something quick.

"Stinking bankers. They ought to put those guys *under* the jail," Chunky shouted at the TV as a reporter rattled off the latest mortgage loan default statistics.

"Turn it up," Iris yelled.

"In other news in the banking world this morning," the reporter's voice blasted throughout the near-empty cafe, "a New York grand jury is scheduled to convene today to consider charges against top financier Sandy Summers. Summers's career spanned over thirty years at Bank US with a recent move to Nexdorf Financial Services. More on that story later. In London today..."

*Just desserts.*

The old Iris would have immediately rushed at her contacts for the inside story and an angle for landing a job. Staring at her phone she had no idea whom she should call. Lace? He was gone. Tenney? No way was she calling him. Her phone vibrated in her hand. Seeing a New York number, she thought of the real Detective Ed Green and decided she should answer it.

"Hello, this is Iris Lee." She stared out at the stone soldier.

"Iris, Jack Storm. I suppose you heard that we lost Sandy Summers to Nexdorf?"

"I heard."

"You know, I was truly i-rate with him for lettin' you go." Storm's big Texas voice filled her head.

"So why didn't you hire me back?" She surprised herself by talking trash to the most powerful man on Wall Street, a man who could make things happen for her with the snap of his Yalie signet-ringed finger. But she didn't feel like licking boots today, not even Texas-CEO-of –the-world boots.

"That's why I'm calling you now. I want you to be on my team. I need a filly in my stable here in Manhattan. Somebody to tell me that the perfume I smell is really horseshit. And I think you're the person for the job."

"What job?" *Negotiations 101, ask a question then shut your trap.* Mr. Henry's voice rang out to her.

"I'm thinking of restructuring the mortgage lending group. I got two other applicants of the three-legged kind champin' at the bit for this spot. What do ya say, missy?" Storm's heavy breathing violated her ear.

"I need to think about it." A thousand questions swirled in her head. If Summers was indicted, wouldn't she be called to testify at the trial? And if she was employed by the company at which he conducted his alleged illegal deeds, would Storm expect her to protect the interests of the company? By offering her a job, was Storm just trying to cover his own hind parts? And the job, was it a bribe or the real deal?

"Don't think on it too long. I'll give you 'til midnight tonight. How 'bout that?"

"I'll let you know by tomorrow morning," she replied.

"Missy, I'm gonna love havin' you around. We probably won't see eye-to-eye on a lot of things but it'll be fun sparrin' with you. Do you hunt?" He clicked his tongue. The sound turned Iris's stomach. Compared to this king of boors, Sandy Summers was a stand-up guy. Disconnecting the call, she fought the urge to go to the restroom and wash her ear.

As Chunky reached across the table to refill her coffee, Iris pulled his pencil from behind his ear. She scribbled in the margin of the newspaper the reasons why she should even consider working for Jack Storm. She scratched through nearly all of them. Two remained: the money and the privileges it afforded *and* the sheer thrill of boardroom challenges. With his coarse manners and penchant for bimbos, Iris calculated that the good ol' boy had a year before he toppled from his high perch. She could wait him out. Then what? Work for the next tyrant? Or become the tyrant herself? She smiled. What would Mr. Henry tell her? She knew. "Figure it out yourself. I can't do it for you. But whatever you decide, don't go about it half-cocked. When you're in, you're in." Tears filled her eyes.

"Iris, I gotta step out back for a second." Chunky glanced around at the handful of patrons in the café. "Can you keep an eye on the cash register while I help the beer man unload?" He clicked off the TV and a dense silence filled the room.

"Sure, Chunky, go ahead. I'll make sure Billy the Kid doesn't bust in here and take the till." Chunky tilted his head with a puzzled look. Nobody got her jokes.

Just as Chunky opened the back door for the beer truck, the cowbell bounced against the front door. Iris noticed a pert, twenty-something wave to a friend sitting alone in a back booth. With the TV turned off, their voices floated over to Iris's table.

"Hey, Tabitha. You home for spring break?" the friend at the booth asked.

"Heeeyyy. We got in last night about midnight." Tabitha fiddled with her key ring-cell phone holder-stuffed bunny dongle.

"When are you leaving to go back to school?"

"Jeez, I just got here. The first thing you want to know is, like, when I'm leaving?"

Iris smiled at the young women. She thought of the times when Jonnie or other friends or relatives asked her that same question. Over the years she was emphatic that Mt Pleasant was where she was born and not where she lived. Did she want to change that? Was Mt Pleasant home or was it a place where she came to visit from time to time?

Chunky signaled to Iris with two thumbs-up as she stood to leave. "No wranglers today, hoss," she called to him.

"Huh?"

"All clear of bandits here in the front."

"What?" Chunky scrunched his face.

Iris waved Chunky off while holding the scratched glass door for her friend. She asked, "Heyu, what's it going to be? New York or Paris?"

Heyu raised one eyebrow then the other.

"Paris it is. You don't mind staying with Cousin Bert for a few days, do you?"

Standing at the curb of Main and Court in uptown Mt Pleasant, Heyu looked both ways before crossing, then led the way home to Grove House.

# Book Club Discussion

## *Self-empowerment*

The primary theme of the story is a common one. Like Dorothy of *The Wizard of Oz*, Iris realizes she had the power within herself all along to solve her problems and to figure out what she really wants.

How did the author convey her discoveries?
Discuss times when sudden insights helped you take control of your life.

## *Southern Tendencies*

While no fictional mule was harmed in the writing of this story, there *are* attributes, aside from the actual location, which make this a "Southern" novel, including strong connections with family and community (home), hope for social justice and fair play, and absolute faith in a higher power.

Discuss the southern-ness of the story. How does it convey a sense of place and time? Does Iris finally reconnect with her hometown community?

What does Iris's desire to give the medallion back to the French people say about her character and sense of fair play?

Explore the differences in Iris's and Miss Bert's perception of God?
What impact, if any, will the postmodern age (the Internet, immigration, and globalization) have on Southern literature and its pastoral roots?

*Embracing change*

We've all experienced drastic disruptions in our lives and are judged on how we react to these upheavals.

How did Iris adapt, then cope with, the loss of her identity, the loss of her father, and the loss of physical looks (aging)?

*Family relationships*

Family love makes us who we are. As Miss Bert told Iris "[Mr. Henry] he never had nobody show him how to love."

Could Iris's choice of not having a family of her own be a reflection of the sterile and unloving parenting Mr. Henry doled out?

Even though Virginians suffered plenty during the Jim Crow era, not every household with an African-American housekeeper endured extreme indignities the likes of those suffered by the characters in the novel *The Help*.

Discuss Miss Bert's role in the dysfunctional dynamics of the Lee household.

Why was the identity of Bert's father never revealed to Iris?

Was Jonnie's judgment of Iris and the way she handled her relationship with her father fair?

## Role Models

Growing up in the second half of the 20th century, boys played with GI Joe and girls had Barbie and her friends.
Discuss how these characters impacted the Boomers and Generation Xers' view of the world.

Who is Barbara Carson (nee Roberts), the woman who Kooch references when inviting Iris for brunch after church?

Discuss how family members impacted Iris's life. (Bert, Elizabeth, Mr. Henry, Bennie)

## Living with uncertainty

The story is told from Iris's point of view so the reader never learns of Mr. Henry's motives in not sharing family history. The story ends with lots of open ended questions. Is Iris successful in giving the medallion back to France? And, does she parlay the gift into opportunities for the town? Was Iris a pawn in a corporate scandal which ended in murder? Will Iris ever move back to Mt Pleasant and embrace her origins? Will she ever know the truth about her grandfather and Bella Sorin and the rift between her father and her uncle?

Like Iris, we all live in a world of uncertainty and ambiguity. Discuss the author's decision to keep the story open-ended.

## About the author

After graduating from the University of Richmond in Virginia, Ms. Gay worked as waitress, data entry clerk, and sales rep before becoming a product developer in the telecommunications industry.

Growing up in southwestern Virginia among farmers and factory workers and later working in the corporate world, she was exposed to the ideas of strong work ethic and individual accountability.

Her stories and essays champion self-reliance, independent thinking, and encouraging others to learn how to help themselves.

Ms. Gay can be reached at author@melissapowellgay.com

Made in the USA
Lexington, KY
29 August 2018